LONDON
BELONGS
TO US

LONDON BELONGS TO US

sarra manning

HOT
KEY
BOOKS

First published in Great Britain in 2016 by
HOT KEY BOOKS
80–81 Wimpole St, London W1G 9RE
www.hotkeybooks.com

This is a work of fiction. Names, places, events and incidents are either the
products of the author's imagination or used fictitiously. Any resemblance
to actual persons, living or dead, or actual events is purely coincidental.

A CIP catalogue record for this book is available from the British Library.

ISBN: 978-1-4714-0461-0
also available as an ebook

This book is typeset in 10.5 Berling LT Std using Atomik ePublisher

Printed and bound by Clays Ltd, St Ives Plc

Hot Key Books is an imprint of Bonnier Publishing Fiction,
a Bonnier Publishing company
www.bonnierpublishing.co.uk

Dedicated to absent friends: Jacqui Johnson, Jacqui Rice, Karen Auerbach, Peter Knight, Adam Lowe and Rupert Jones – companions on so many adventures through London during my own wild teen years.

In people's eyes, in the swing, tramp, and trudge; in the bellow and the uproar; the carriages, motor cars, omnibuses, vans, sandwich men shuffling and swinging; brass bands; barrel organs; in the triumph and the jingle and the strange high singing of some aeroplane overhead was what she loved; life; London.

Mrs Dalloway, Virginia Woolf

LONDON

A city of eight million people. Eight million lives. Eight million stories.

This is just one of them.

Dear Sunny,

The important thing is to remember that you'll be fine staying on your own in the house for a week. Absolutely fine.

If you do get scared then Emmeline or one of your other (female) friends can stay. But no boys overnight. Please do not abuse our trust in you by using this as an opportunity to have Mark over and then making a decision that you may well regret for the rest of your life. Of course, legally you're old enough to have sex with whomever you want, but do you really want to lose your virginity to a boy who walks around with his pants on show? Also, seventeen is not old enough to vote or buy alcohol or fireworks, so is it really old enough to have sex? Think on!

Mark is a very nice boy, I'm not saying he isn't, but there's something about him that I just can't warm to. Call it mother's intuition. But my mother's intuition

2

also knows that YOU'RE SENSIBLE ENOUGH TO DO THE RIGHT THING!!!!!!!

Don't forget that the hot water comes on at six every morning. It will be the boiler making that funny thudding noise and not someone breaking in to burgle us. (Though do remember to lock up like Terry showed you. Including all the windows and the back door.)

If you do think there's an intruder in the house, or there's a freak storm and a tree comes through one of the windows, call Max from the upstairs flat. But only if it is an absolute emergency, because you know how stroppy he got when we left you overnight at Easter and you thought we had a poltergeist.

If you really can't handle being on your own then you can go to Uncle Dee and Yolly. There is a chance that your father might get back from Edinburgh early, so you could stay with him like you were meant to, but as your father constantly puts his career ahead of his family obligations, don't hold your breath.

Please don't bring meat products into the house. Even if I'm not there, you know how I feel about eating meat, Sunny, and it would wound me. On some cosmic level, even though I'll be on a campsite in the South of France, I will know and I'll be very disappointed in you.

3

There is special (and very expensive) wet food for Gretchen Weiner instead of her usual Whiskas. If she starts rubbing her bottom on the carpet again and making that awful mewling sound, you'll have to take her to the vets to have her anal glands expressed. Again. The best way to get her into her carrier is to wear the really long washing-up gloves, throw a towel over her and say a prayer.

No parties. You may have a small gathering of a few friends, but don't put an invite up on Facebook. I don't want to come home to find that five hundred teenagers high on ketamine have razed the building to the ground. I'm sure the insurance won't cover it.

We did a big shop before we left but there's thirty quid in the fake jam jar in the tin cupboard for milk and perishables. I want receipts!

So, to recap: Emmeline can stay. Mark can't. No meat. Boiler clicks at six. Keep an eye on Gretchen Weiner's bottom.

PLEASE DON'T HAVE SEX WITH THAT BOY (IF YOU DO – AND THIS IN NO WAY CONDONES YOU HAVING SEX WITH THAT BOY – PLEASE USE CONDOMS).

We've left you a box of Calippos in the freezer.

See you in a week. You'll be fine. We believe in you!

Lots and lots and lots and lots of love,

Mum and Terry xxx

PS: Dan says thanks for agreeing to feed his lizards. He's left a detailed list of instructions on what to do, but you're not to snoop while you're in his room. I did tell him that you have better things to do with your time than rifling round in his pants drawer.

SATURDAY NIGHT CHECK-LIST

Purse ✓
Oystercard ✓
Topshop sunnies ✓
Cherry lip balm ✓
Mascara ✓
Hair-band ✓
Hand cream ✓
Ordinary plasters ✓
Blister plasters ✓
Tampons ✓
Bottle of water ✓
Phone charger ✓
Mum's Jo Malone Blackberry & Bay perfume ✓
    (REMEMBER TO PUT IT BACK IN HER
    BEDROOM BEFORE SHE NOTICES IT'S GONE.)
Chewy ✓
Tissues ✓

Check yourself before you wreck yourself.

8.00 p.m.

CRYSTAL PALACE

Crystal Palace is one of the highest points in London and takes its name from the Crystal Palace, originally built in Hyde Park in 1851 to house the Great Exhibition. It was moved to a site on Penge Common in 1854, to become the magnificent centre of a Victorian pleasure ground, which featured a maze, thirty-three life-sized dinosaur replicas and so many fountains that two water towers had to be built to keep them flowing.

Alas, Crystal Palace burned down in 1936, but the park remains and is now home to the National Sports Centre.

Famous people who have lived in the Crystal Palace hood include Sherlock Holmes author Sir Arthur Conan Doyle, and Francis Pettit Smith, one of the inventors of the screw propeller.

It's taken us over two hours and we had to get a proper train from Victoria, *not even the Overground*, but Emmeline and I finally arrive at Crystal Palace Park. Well, it calls itself a park but basically it's a massive hill. Maybe even a small mountain.

We walk upwards, ever upwards, panting as the incline increases. The handles of the clanking carrier bags from the offy cut stripes into our wrists, the condensation from the ice-cold bottles brushing against our bare legs. The backs of our necks glisten too because it's still steamy hot – even as the sun starts to ever so slightly droop in a pale-blue sky streaked pink and orange.

We have no idea where we're going.

'The thing about South London, right, is that it wasn't designed to be colonised. Otherwise it wouldn't be so bloody hard to get here,' Emmeline pants.

'True,' I agree. 'But isn't that a bit South Londonist?'

'I don't think South Londonism is a thing, Sun. It's not like racism, is it? Or homophobia. You can choose not to live in South London. Jesus, if this hill gets any steeper, we're going to need crampons.'

'Can't talk any more. I need to conserve my oxygen.'

We trudge on. Emmeline holds her phone out in front of her, like she's divining for water. 'We follow the path round the Lower Lake like we're doing, although there's two other lakes and I'm not sure which one is lower than the others and – oh, look! Dinosaurs!'

'What?' I look up from sending another text to Mark to see dinosaurs right in front of me. Not, like, *actual* dinosaurs. They're made of fibreglass or something and are arranged in candid action poses around the edge of a small lake. 'Oh God, that's some deep *Jurassic Park* shit.'

Emmeline shakes her head. Even though she's slathered in factor fifty, her face is bright red. 'Maybe I've judged South London too harshly.'

'You judge everything too harshly. It's what you do.'

'Yeah, I know. I like to play to my strengths.' Emmeline's attention is fixed on the rocky crag, separated from us by a rail and the small lake, where the dinosaurs are frolicking. I know exactly what Emmeline's thinking before she even says, 'So, there has to be a way that we can get into the dinosaur enclosure and take some pictures, right? You, me, riding on a whateverasaurus. Post them on Instagram. We'd get even more likes than that picture of me pretending to deep throat a Cumberland sausage at your barbecue.'

'You have to take that picture down before my mum sees evidence that there was a meat product in her back garden.' I peer at the water. There's an empty Coke can floating forlornly against the far bank. 'I would happily wade into that lake except it doesn't look very clean and I don't want legionnaires' disease.'

'You can't get legionnaires' disease from paddling. Come on, take off your trainers. We're wearing shorts. How deep can the water be, anyway?' Emmeline is already toeing off her sneakers. 'If we do get some horrible disease and you have to have your legs amputated, I'll visit you every day. Pimp out your wheelchair. Let you have the TV remote.'

'Well, in that case, how can I refuse?' It's not that hard, for once. 'No, I think I'll pass.'

'You have no sense of adventure . . .'

I hear the chirp of my phone. Perfectly timed to save me from Emmeline's attempts to talk me round, which usually end with me doing something that results in detention/grounding/injury. One time, when we were on a school trip to the Globe theatre to see *As You Like It* and Emmeline forced me to join her in her one-woman moshpit, I scored the hat-trick.

When I retrieve my phone from the depths of my bag, Mark's face is flashing up on my screen. 'I got sunshine on a cloudy day,' he sings when I answer. 'Babe, have you made it to Crystal Palace yet?'

'Yeah, it took *ages*! Not even on the Overground but a proper train.'

'Let it go, Sunny,' says Emmeline who, thank God, is putting her Converse back on as she's obviously given up on walking with dinosaurs. 'Least you could do after making me stay round yours this week.'

'You like staying around mine.' Emmeline's mum works nights and Emmeline's older sister, Mary (Emmeline's mum is really into women's issues so she named her daughters after Mary Wollstonecraft, eighteenth-century feminist, and Emmeline Pankhurst, leader of the Suffragettes – Emmeline feels that she got the rough end of that deal), commandeers the lounge with her revolting boyfriend. They always end up horizontal on the sofa snogging wetly, so coming over to mine isn't exactly a hardship.

'Sunny! Stop talking to Em and start talking to me, your boyfriend. Remember me?'

I smile. 'I'm hardly likely to forget you.'

'Good, I'm glad to hear that. So, you're only going to stay an hour, aren't you? Then you're coming back to civilisation, like we agreed.' It's not often that Mark acts like he's pining for me. I wish it happened more. 'Can't believe you had to trek to Crystal Palace tonight of all nights.'

'Yeah, but Em and I have an arrangement. She protected me from intruders all week and so this evening, I act as her wingman.'

'I could have protected you from intruders,' Mark points out. He makes a funny noise: half choke, half giggle. 'Could have done other things too. A whole week of doing other things.'

'But I wasn't sure that I wanted to do other things . . .' I glance over at Emmeline, who never has a problem with shamelessly listening to other people's phone calls – or my phone calls specifically – but she's frowning at Google Maps on her phone, bottom lip caught between her teeth, her fringe sticking to her forehead in damp, blond clumps.

'But you are sure now?' Mark's voice goes up, squeaky high, at the end of the sentence, like he's nervous. 'I mean, you want to?'

'Yeah, I s'pose. I mean, *you* still want to, right?'

'Well, only if you want to.' Mark sounds like he'd be cool with it if I said no, but freaking out a bit doesn't seem like a good enough reason to say no. 'But I'm totally up for it. Figuratively. Not literally. Yeah, actually I'm literally up for it, or I will be. You know what I mean.'

It makes me feel better that Mark, who's always so sure of himself, so clear of purpose, so straight-forward, is freaking out a bit too. 'I'd be offended if you weren't literally up for it.'

'Oh, I will be. I promise.' I hope that sex becomes less terrifying once you've done it because never before has one word had the power to strike this much terror in my heart – not even words like 'retakes' or 'gusset' or 'cauliflower'. 'So, I'm

11

going to buy some, y'know, condoms and I was wondering if you had any, like, preferences?'

Preferences? 'You what?'

'Ribbed or coloured – maybe not coloured 'cause that would be weird. Or if you're allergic to latex you can get these special non-latex ones.' Mark spits out the words. 'You're not allergic, are you?'

'I don't think so. Maybe just get the ones that don't let out any sperm.' I'm amazed that I manage to say it in a calm voice, but then I giggle because this is such a surreal conversation and also proves that my mum's so-called special mother's intuition is obviously broken.

Mark *is* lovely and he's being all informed and responsible about us not catching any revolting diseases of the genitals or me getting pregnant. In short, he's being a god among boyfriends.

'OK,' Mark says. 'I'll get those ones. Shall we meet in the Lock Tavern at eleven?'

'Yeah, I'll see you then. And you'll help me varnish the shed and finish clearing up any traces of meat left from the barbecue tomorrow morning?' I think I might even be more freaked out about Mum-proofing the house before she gets back from France than I am about the sex.

'It depends. If you're a crap shag then I'm going to make my excuses and leave.'

'Don't say that! It might be crap. It probably will be crap. It's the first time. Don't be putting pressure on me to –'

'Sunny! Sunny! It was a joke. I was joking. I have to leave pretty early in the morning because I'm having Sunday lunch at my grandmother's in Godalming, but we love each other, right?'

12

'Well, yeah . . .'

'Then it will all be good. I'll see you later, babes.'

I have so many feelings. All the feelings. All at once. I can't even start sifting and sorting through them, mainly because Emmeline shoves her phone right up in my face and orders me to 'Smile!' – so now my feelings consist mostly of being startled. 'Don't do that!'

'I wanted to take one last picture of you in your virgin state,' she says and shows me her phone screen where I'm gurning in shiny-faced confusion. 'I can't believe you're going to have sex. With Mark!'

'Who else would I be having sex with?'

She jerks her head. 'Come on. We'd better get going if you've got an urgent appointment with Mark's penis later.' Emmeline stomps off without waiting for me. She's very good at stomping. Much prefers it to walking. 'I can't believe you didn't tell me,' she says when I catch up with her.

'I only decided for definite this morning and I thought that you might be a little . . . y'know . . .'

'I just think, Sunny, you're not ready for it,' Emmeline says, like she's so much older and wiser than me, when she's only two months older than me and she had to retake her Maths GCSE. 'No one we hang out with has had sex yet and you're not really – and I don't mean this in a horrible way – a trailblazer, are you?'

She really doesn't mean it in a horrible way. I *am* risk averse. I was the last of our crowd to do boyfriend jeans, neon nail polish or white-water rafting when we went on an Outward Bound trip with school and even then, as soon as I got into the raft, I went full-on panic attack and burst into tears and decided that I could live my life quite happily without the possibility that I might die horribly and painfully by being dashed on the rocks. Even so, it wasn't as if I was jumping on the sex bandwagon before anyone else. 'Alex has had sex and the boys have had sex.'

'The boys don't count,' Emmeline says immediately. 'Because they're all liars. Like, what a coincidence that they've all claimed to have sex with girls we've never met. "Oh, you wouldn't know her. See, I met her at my cousin's house." "Yeah, she goes to a school on the other side of London." Bullshit! They're all virgins, and Alex got really drunk at Glasto, had sex with a random in a leaky campervan and do I need to remind you who she'd gone to Glasto with?'

I sigh. 'Her mum and dad. And yes, I also remember that she had to ask them to stop at a chemist on the way home so she could get the morning-after pill.'

Emmeline shoots me a prim look. 'She said that losing her virginity was the worst experience of her life.'

'Yeah but . . . but it's completely different because Mark isn't a random. We've been seeing each other for eight months and we love each other.'

'Love!' Emmeline really struggles with sentiment. 'Anyway, how much do we even know about him? He just rocks up out of the blue to do his A levels with his posh voice and his posh floppy hair and he'll only go out with you every other weekend, which is deeply, deeply suspicious.'

I don't say anything for a bit because the path is now so steep it's pretty much vertical and all I can do is puff. Then it levels out a bit and I can defend Mark. 'His parents divorced

14

and he had to leave boarding school and move to the other side of London. There's nothing sinister about that. You should feel sorry for him.'

'Look, I'm not saying that he's evil or anything. I'm just saying that he gets my spider sense tingling,' Emmeline insists. 'I'm an excellent judge of character. You know I am.'

'I think you're being a little harsh.' I have to steel myself to say that much, because now Emmeline is flaring her nostrils like an angry little bull. 'He's always been really nice to you. What about when you got locked out and he shinned up the side of your house to get in the bathroom window? Or when you spent your lunch money on a lottery ticket . . .'

'It was a quadruple rollover!'

'Quadruple whatever. You'd have starved if Mark hadn't bought you a sandwich and –'

'Shut up!' That's really, really harsh, even for Emmeline, especially as she also grabs a handful of my T-shirt. 'Shut up and look at that!'

We're at the crest of the hill now and I follow the direction of Emmeline's pointed finger and there's London. The whole of London. Not the London we're used to when we're high up on Primrose Hill or at Ally Pally. We've only ever seen the London skyline from the north before and now it's the wrong way round. The other way round.

There's the Gherkin. The funny building that looks like a cheese grater. The Shard and far, far over to our left is the dome of St Paul's Cathedral. In between are churches and high-rise blocks of flats. Cranes and scaffolding. It doesn't matter what side I see the skyline from; it always feels like home. It's London.

15

As we stand there, Emmeline slings her arm around my neck. It's too hot and sticky for arms slung around necks, but no matter how much we argue, being with Emmeline feels like home too. 'I love this place,' she suddenly says. 'When I see it like this, all big and impressive, I think of how small my life is in comparison, but I'm still a part of it, right, Sun?'

'Maybe it's because I'm a Londoner that I love London town,' I sing in a trembly, ridiculous Cockney accent.

Emmeline unslings her arm and gives me a gentle shove. 'Don't do that. It's horrible,' she says with a shudder. 'You sound like Dick Van Dyke.'

'Gawd bless ya, Mary Poppins!' we both shout as we have done so many times before, and just like that we're over our argument. They always blow up out of nowhere and then melt away because of a shared look, a joke, some tiny remark that reminds us of how our friendship is old and deep and can withstand anything – even Emmeline's bossiness and my inability to form an opinion and stick with it.

Emmeline tucks her arm through mine, we start walking again and she asks quietly, 'Are you scared?'

I'm scared of so many things. Sometimes at night I can't sleep as I catalogue all the things that scare me, and I have a new sub-list of scares solely dedicated to what I'll be doing with Mark in a few hours.

I'm scared that it will hurt.

I'm scared that it will be awful and then I won't even want to kiss Mark and that will be the end of us.

I'm scared that it will be really good and I'll want to do it all the time and everyone will think I'm a total slut.

I'm scared that I'll do something wrong. Oh God, there are so many things that I could do wrong. When I think about sex, of what goes where and for how long, it just seems ridiculously, needlessly complicated.

I'm scared that when I get naked, Mark will look at all the bits of me from boobs to knobbly knees to the faint silvering of stretchmarks on my hips to *there* (and no one has ever looked at my *there* before) and be so repulsed that he *literally* won't be able to get it up.

I'm scared that I'm already hot and sweaty and that I'll be even hotter and sweatier if I don't have a shower first.

I'm scared that Mark might think it would be sexy to shower together and I might be ready for sex but I am not ready to get in the shower with him.

'Terrified,' I say in answer to Emmeline's question. 'But then I'm scared of everything, aren't I?'

Emmeline nods. 'Except, weirdly, you're the one person I know who isn't scared of spiders.'

That immediately makes me feel better. I can handle spiders. If I ever found myself airlifted into the jungle on some awful reality show, I might have a screaming fit about having to walk across a frayed rope bridge or swim alligator-infested rivers, but I could happily deal with creepy crawlies. 'Yeah, well there's that.'

'Maybe you should just picture Mark as a gigantic spider and then you won't be so nervous,' Emmeline says. 'Lots of furry legs scurrying all over you. Urgh! I'm scaring myself.'

'Please don't picture my boyfriend as an outsized arachnid . . .'

'Em! Emmy! Over here!'

On the grassy slope below us is a sprawling group of people, girls mostly, and one girl in particular, Charlie, who's waving to get Emmeline's attention.

Emmeline licks her lips and frantically finger-combs her fringe, which has gone clumpy in the heat. 'Do I look all right?' she asks anxiously. 'Do my legs look unbelievably chunky in these shorts?'

'No! You look great.' I'm already teetering down the slope, while Emmeline just stands there. 'Get a move on! I've only got an hour!'

TEN MINUTES LATER

Another thing I'm scared of are Emmeline's new friends. But I don't think that's a me thing. I think that's a normal thing when you're an old friend hanging out with the new friends that Emmeline's made since she joined the London Roller Derby Recreational League, where she's kind of like a roller derby girl in training.

I didn't think it was possible for Emmeline to be even more shouty or competitive than she already was (I will never play Monopoly with her ever again after the time she hurled the board across the room when I built hotels on Bond Street, Regent Street, Oxford Street and Park Lane), but then she discovered roller derby. Now she straps on a pair of skates and scores points for being shouty and competitive at anyone who dares to get in her way.

Emmeline wanted me to sign up too but I couldn't take the risk that I might fall over and break some essential body part that couldn't be mended. Mostly, though, it was because of the helmet. What it would do to my hair doesn't even bear thinking about.

Still, Emmeline's roller derby friends are really nice when they're not maiming each other, and I'm not the only brown person present, which tends to happen quite a lot when I dare to leave the racially diverse London Borough of Haringey (the People's Republic of Haringey, my dad sneeringly calls it), so even though I'm on a clock, I lean back on my elbows and try to enjoy myself.

We're at a birthday picnic for one of the girls on the London Roller Derby B team. Emmeline and I made cheese straws and rock cakes this afternoon, which we only slightly burned. They're now arranged in all their slightly blackened glory on a paper plate, next to quiches and salads, sausage rolls, veggie sausage rolls, vegan sausage rolls, some very limp sandwiches and a bewildering number of home-made cakes all laid out on a tartan rug and wilting in the heat.

Emmeline chats to her friends and I let their words float over my head like the tiny dark wisps of cloud in the deepening blue sky above me. I take an occasional sip from one of the bottles of lager we bought, though I don't really like the taste – but Emmeline said that if we turned up with bottles of Bacardi Breezer it would create the wrong impression.

Another group of girls arrives with two sandy-coloured pugs. The pugs, Fred and Ginger, try to make a sneak foray on the sausage rolls. Then they see me looking at them and plod over, trails of drool hanging from their mouths, press against me on either side and promptly roll over, displaying two portly bellies that I guess I'm meant to rub.

Even two pugs who I haven't been formally introduced to think I'm a soft touch.

'Hey, Sunny. You all right?' Charlie sits down next to me with a sagging paper plate heaped with food. This means she's also sitting much nearer to Emmeline. 'Did they ask for your passport as you crossed the border into South London?'

Charlie's really nice. She's super nice. Emmeline thinks so anyway, but for all her badassery Emmeline is rubbish at making a move on someone that she's had a crush on for months. It's why I'm here – to be Emmeline's wingman.

Wingwoman.

Whatever. It turns out I'm not that good at talking Emmeline up, then gradually including her in the conversation. All I can do is launch into a detailed and very boring account of our journey from Crouch End. '. . . and then we changed at Highbury and Islington, even though I told Ems that we should have got the bus to Dalston Junction and just got the Overground all the way, but she said her way was quicker *so then* we changed again at Victoria and we were still on the train for ages before we got to Penge West.' I snag a delicate goat's cheese and tomato tartlet that looks like it's come from a fancy deli rather than a roller girl's kitchen and shove the whole thing in my gob so I can't talk any more. Best decision I've made all day.

'You have to try one of these, Ems,' I mumble around the savoury taste explosion that's happening in my mouth.

It's the cue she's been desperately waiting for. Emmeline shuffles over on her knees. 'What's up?' she says. 'Oh, hey, Charlie . . .'

'Hey, Ems.'

They look at each other, then both look away like they'd never ended up snogging at the party after a roller derby bout in Cardiff.

'Those blueberry tarts look amazing,' I mumble and Charlie grins at me gratefully.

'Yeah, Chloe said that she only invited *them* because she knew they'd turn up with awesome pastries.'

I stretch out my legs. When I get up I know I'll have a fetching grass pattern embedded in the backs of my thighs. 'Who makes awesome pastries?'

'Those French boys, the Godards.'

Immediately I sit up. 'They're here! Really?'

I look around wildly and on the far edge of the raggedy circle of people gathered by the food are two pale, skinny boys, side by side. It might be hot, but they're wearing black suits, skinny cut to match their skinny bodies, and shades. Their dark hair is almost as big as mine.

Emmeline forgets that she's being shy. 'Oh my God! It's them!' She clutches my hand. 'I thought they were an urban myth!'

The Godards. French boys. First there was just one of them. For the longest time we'd see him pootling about North London on his moped, then suddenly, about a year ago, there were two of them. Like Godard v.01 had had himself cloned. Nobody knows if they're twins or best mates or boyfriend and boyfriend. There's even a rumour going round that they're not even French. Everyone has an opinion on them. There's even a Tumblr, FuckYeah!TheGodards where people can post sightings and pictures of them.

The only person I know who actually knows them is, surprisingly, my mum. They run a coffee bar out of an ancient Citroën van and pitch up two days a week in Spitalfields where she has her antiques shop.

'Lovely boys,' she always says. 'Lovely coffee. Lovely patisserie. Such lovely manners.'

Once, she'd even got one of them to write a stroppy email in French to an antiques dealer in Toulouse who'd sold her a bedroom set riddled with woodworm.

'Apparently, they're not actually gay,' Charlie says. 'I saw them in a club once and they were both trying to get with the same girl.'

'Not that there's anything wrong with being gay,' I say, because I'm meant to be wingwoman-ing. 'Nothing wrong at all.'

'Yes, thanks for that, Sunny.' Emmeline manages to stretch out her leg and kick me and I can't see what the point is of me being her wingwoman if she's not going to make a move – instead she's stealing sly little looks at Charlie and then, when she's not looking, Charlie is making googly eyes right back at her.

I have to leave in twenty minutes. I haven't got time for this.

'Go and talk to her. Properly. Go on!' I hiss.

'I can't just suddenly start talking to her.'

'Yes, you can. It's what people do when they like other people. Do you want me to make myself scarce? I could go and get some more tartlets.' I'm not just offering out of the goodness of my heart. I want to get a closer look at the Godards. 'I could give Charlie one of our rock cakes. One of the ones that isn't mostly charcoal. To showcase your mad baking skills.'

22

'Don't you dare,' Emmeline growls. 'I can handle it myself.'

'By handling it, you mean not actually doing anything?'

'I could kick you again. Would that count as doing something?'

It's too hot and I'm too comfy to tell Emmeline that it really doesn't. 'So, Charlie, Em needs to replace the wheels on her skates. Where do you get yours from?'

It turns out that those are the magic words to get Emmeline and Charlie talking and I'm quite content to sit there and spend some of my Saturday night eating tartlets and stroking fat pug bellies.

Then my phone beeps and, just like that, I'm not content any more.

It will be Mark telling me my hour's up. The fear is back. It's bitter and chases away the sweetness of the pastry and the salty taste of goat's cheese. I pick up my phone and I'm relieved and only a tiny bit disappointed that it's a text from Martha.

Emmeline and I secretly call her OMG!Martha because the first words out of her mouth are always 'Oh my God, you'll never believe what I just found out!' She's Crouch End's answer to TMZ.

I have to give Martha her due, though – her sources are usually impeccable. 'Incoming from Martha,' I tell Emmeline. 'There's a picture attachment, this should be good.'

'Oh, let me see!' I hold my phone up so Emmeline has a perfect view of my screen and . . . then we both say, 'Oh my God!'

I shut my eyes. I can't look. I can't *not* look. I open them again and all I can see is the photo of a boy who looks like

Mark, my Mark, with his mouth attached to the mouth of a girl who isn't me. One of his hands rests on her arse, most of which is displayed in all its pert glory by her short shorts.

OMG! Mark is with this girl in Lock Tavern. Have u broken up? :(Hugs M xxx

'Why would she even think that? She knows we're not broken up. She was at my barbecue two days ago when I was with Mark. Very much together. Anyway, that doesn't even look like Mark.' I sit up and squint at the screen. 'It's not him.'

'Well . . . that does look like the red friendship bracelet you gave him, and that does kind of look like the blue check shirt that you nicked from Terry that Mark then borrowed off you and never gave back,' Emmeline points out.

'Loads of people have red friendship bracelets and blue check shirts. Loads.'

My phone beeps again. It's OMG!Martha again.

Here's another pic. Thought u should see it. :(Luv u M xxx

It's the same shiny-haired girl kissing a boy who can only be Mark. It's taken from a slightly different angle so there's no mistaking his floppy blond hair or the mole on his jawline that I've kissed so many times I've lost count. I even recognise his navy-blue pants because he wears his jeans slung so low that seeing Mark's pants before we've even had sex was inevitable.

The pain is sudden and overwhelming. Like stubbing your toe or trapping your finger in a door. Before I even know it, tears smart and run down my face. I hunch over and take deep breaths. Emmeline lets her hand rest on my back.

There has to be a perfectly reasonable explanation as to why Mark is sucking serious face, with a hint of tongue, with another girl, but I can't come up with one.

'What shall I do?' I ask Emmeline. 'Should I call him?'

'Maybe you shouldn't call him. Not while you're so upset,' Emmeline says, but I've already stabbed at the call button.

There's a static buzz and then it rolls right over to voicemail and I hear Mark's voice, his stupid voice. 'Yo! You know what to do.' I open my mouth and take a big, choked breath, but before I can say anything Emmeline snatches the phone away from me.

'No. You don't leave a message. He shouldn't get off that easy. Kissing another girl and then getting dumped by voicemail. He deserves worse than that and you, you deserve much better!'

'But it might be an innocent kiss. OK, it doesn't look like one, but it might be,' I protest.

Then I burst into tears.

There's a pain in my chest and I'm clammy and cold and I'm crying in front of a bunch of people I don't know that well.

'Sunny, please don't.' Emmeline's not much of a hugger so she punches me gently on the arm instead. 'I hate it when you cry. And anyway, it'll ruin your make-up.'

It takes a huge effort but I come to a shuddering halt. I haven't even taken off my sunglasses and when I swipe a finger under each eye, they're smeared black with my mascara.

'Bad news, Sunny?' Charlie's watching us with an uncomfortable expression; she's an unwilling witness to my

25

sudden plunge into despair. 'Do you want a tissue? Shall I go and get some napkins?'

'Boyfriend stuff,' I mutter. 'Got tissues in my bag, but thanks.'

'Ex-boyfriend stuff,' Emmeline says firmly. 'Emphasis on the ex. There's no coming back from this. That is proper evidence on your phone. Those pictures could be used in court as proof that Mark is no good. I knew it! I just didn't know that he was a cheater too.'

'Cheaters are the worst,' Charlie agrees, like I want to hear what she thinks about my boyfriend. I really don't.

'My boyfriend cheated on me once; I didn't let him cheat on me twice. Kicked his arse right to the kerb,' says one of the girls who are sitting behind us.

'An arse kicking is the only language a cheater understands.'

'Why do they think they'll get away with it when they always get found out?'

'Yeah, you have to have a zero-tolerance policy when it comes to cheaters.'

It's a Greek chorus of roller derby girls all chiming in with their two cents on bad boyfriends they have known and how you have to show them no mercy.

I can't think. Can't sort out the jumble of emotions that are all clamouring for my attention. Can't do anything but stare down at the pictures on my phone.

Then it beeps again and I turn it off and shove it back in my bag. I'm not emotionally equipped to deal with any more concern trolling from OMG!Martha. 'I have to go now.' I struggle to my feet. I was right, the grass has embedded in my thighs, but that's the least of it. 'I have stuff to do.'

26

I have no idea what this stuff might be. Mostly crying into Gretchen Weiner's stinky fur, and periodically trying to screw up the courage to phone Mark and ask him what the hell's going on. Then again, I don't have the guts to phone Mark because I have a horrible, sick feeling that he's gone from nought to not loving me in the thirty minutes since we last spoke. I don't understand how or why, though. I don't understand any of it.

'Yeah, that's the spirit! You go and hunt him down and you tell him exactly what a wanker he is.' Charlie punches me on the arm with a lot more force than Emmeline. It hurts. These roller girls never know their own strength.

'Are you really going to do that?' Emmeline asks doubtfully. 'You're going home to mope, aren't you?' She starts gathering up her things. 'OK, all right, I'll come with you. There will be no moping on my watch.'

'I'll be fine,' I say quickly, because even though I appreciate the offer, Emmeline has hotfooted it all the way to Crystal Palace to hang out with her roller derby friends and, more importantly, make major romantic inroads with Charlie. I didn't want to piss on her romance chips, as it were.

'You're not fine,' Emmeline insists. 'Who would be? Tell you what, when we get back to yours, we'll grab hold of all the stuff Mark has left there and we'll burn it. That'll make you feel better.'

It really wouldn't and there'd already been one unfortunate incident involving naked flames this week; I couldn't handle another.

'Please, Em. I can't deal with your tough love approach right now. I need ice cream and my special sadness blanket.'

27

Emmeline shudders at the mention of my special (and really ratty and kind of smelly) sadness blanket. 'I can dial down the tough love.'

Her face is open, guileless. She's straight up. She means it. If I want her to hoof it all the way back across London so we can go to mine, shut all the windows, black out the summer heat and eat ice cream because that's what you do in these situations then she will. I know that to be true even though I'm uncertain of so many other things. And Emmeline will say, 'I never liked him anyway.' She'll say that a lot. She'll even say, 'That girl . . . she looked like a right skank,' though Emmeline's mum is always going on about how we shouldn't slut shame other girls – even if they do really deserve it.

Emmeline will do that because she's my best friend, but she can't help the tiny glance in Charlie's direction. It's hopeful, so hopeful – then her hope turns into regret.

This best friend thing goes both ways.

'Oh no,' I say. 'I really will be fine. I promise I won't mope too much. I just need to sort my head out, maybe speak to Mark. Anyway I have to clean up the flat before Mum and Terry get back and if the mopes get the better of me I can call Alex or Martha or Archie. I might call them anyway. They helped make the mess.'

Then I lift my chin up and manage to smile. It's a three-out-of-ten smile, at best.

'Are you sure?' Emmeline asks.

'So sure. And if I change my mind then I can meet up with you in town later, if you're still going clubbing.'

A collection of tarts and cakes are wrapped in napkins to sustain me for the long journey. Someone gives me not just idiot-proof but Sunny-proof directions out of the park and instructions not to go to Penge West this time but Crystal Palace station and change to the Northern line when I reach Clapham.

'I should get going then. Sorry to bail,' I say, with a limp little wave to match my three-out-of-ten smile.

As soon as I'm over the hill and out of sight, I take out my phone and I call Mark.

He answers on the first ring. 'Babe,' he says, instead of answering with a song about sunshine, like he usually does. 'Just about to call you. It's not what you think, not even a little bit.'

REASONS WHY I THOUGHT MARK WAS THE HEIR TO MY HEART

1. Every time we speak on the phone, he greets me with a song that has my name in it. On the greyest day, he'll sing, 'Don't blame it on the sunshine, don't blame it on the moonlight.' It always chases the shadows away.
2. And for my birthday, he made a Sunshine playlist on Spotify and got everyone to add songs to it.
3. He's the first boy I ever kissed and now I can't imagine kissing any other boy.
4. He always calls out his mum when she's being borderline racist. Which happens a lot. ('So, Sunny, is that short for something African?' 'Your dad's a barrister? Really? How absolutely extraordinary.' 'I expect you're quite good at dancing, aren't you? I always think that your people have a natural sense of rhythm.') One time he even threatened to report her to the Race and Equality Council.

5. Whenever he goes into Crouch End without me at lunchtime, he always buys me a Belgian bun from Greggs.
6. The day before we first hooked up, in English he read aloud from T. S. Eliot's *The Waste Land* and looked at me the entire time and made me feel things that I've never felt before.
7. Not to be shallow or anything, but Mark's a DJ. People have actually paid him to provide audio entertainment. Well, Archie's dad slipped him fifty quid when he DJed at Archie's birthday party, and he got paid in lager the time that he replaced the DJ at Alex's parents' silver anniversary party because the guy had played 'Hi Ho Silver Lining' on a loop.
8. He always holds my hand when he walks me home from school. Always.
9. He spent most of today, the hottest day of the year so far, helping me repaint the shed. Though Emmeline said that if he and Archie hadn't set fire to the broom and then tried to baton twirl it, the shed would never have got scorch marks. (Note to self: buy new broom before Mum gets back.)
10. I never imagined that he would ever suck face with some skank in short shorts behind my back.

CLAPHAM

Before the railway arrived in 1863, Clapham was all green fields and famed for its lavender crops. Its most noted feature, the two hundred and twenty acre Clapham Common, used to be a favourite hangout of highwaymen in the late seventeenth century when noted diarist Samuel Pepys lived there.

Clapham was part of Surrey until the creation of the County of London in 1898. Clapham Junction station (one of the busiest in Europe) was originally called Battersea Junction, but was changed to Clapham because it sounded posher. Residents of Battersea are still quite sore about this.

Famous Claphamites include Brian Dowling, winner of the second series of Big Brother, Brighton Rock *author Graham Greene, and sisters Anna and Ellen Pigeon, who in 1873 became the first female mountaineers to traverse the Matterhorn.*

At the sound of Mark's voice, I realise that I'm angry. Furious. Quite mad with rage.

My dad always tells me not to be angry. 'Don't be the angry black girl,' he says. 'That's what people expect.'

When he was my age and living in Ladbroke Grove in the 1980s, he'd constantly get stopped by the police simply for walking down the street. Or sitting in the back of a friend's car. Or hanging out on a street corner. Stopped and searched. Called the n-word by those same policemen. He says that getting angry was what they wanted so he never did.

Instead it made him determined to work hard, and now he's a lawyer who fights on the side of justice and good, though he still gets stopped occasionally because the police think that if you're a black man and you have an expensive motor then obviously you're a drug dealer. Which is ridiculous. Like any self-respecting drug dealer would be seen dead driving a Volvo.

What with Dad insisting that people see the colour of my skin first and Mum telling me that it isn't what I am but what I do that's important, it's no surprise that I'm so easily confused. It also isn't any wonder that they split up before I turned three.

Anyway, right now I am mad and it's glorious. 'I don't even want to talk to you,' I tell Mark and I absolutely mean it.

Mark talks to me anyway. He says, 'It was me being kissed, not me kissing her, I swear.'

And I say, 'Yeah, your tongue really looked like an innocent bystander. Try again.'

By now I'm getting on the train at Crystal Palace station and Mark says, 'A bunch of my old Chelsea friends just turned up at The Lock Tavern and they have a different vibe to us. It's all kissy-kissy and "darling" this and "darling" that.'

These are the Chelsea friends that I've never met who Mark spends alternate weekends with so he can kiss girls who aren't me, safe in the knowledge that there's no way that I will ever find out about them. Until now, that is.

'Whatever,' I snap. 'No wonder you never wanted me to meet them. Too worried that I'd bump into your, like, *every-other-weekend girlfriend*, I'll bet!'

'I didn't want you to meet them because they're arseholes,' he says. 'And I turn into an arsehole when I'm around them and then you won't love me any more.'

All the time we speak, my phone is beeping like it's possessed. I think OMG!Martha has shared the happy news and the 'U OK hun?' texts are gathering pace, which is just more petrol flung on the bonfire of my fury.

'I had to find out from OMG!Martha. You've totally shamed me.'

Then Mark goes on a massive rant about Martha, like this is all her fault, when it's hardly her fault at all. 'This is so like her,' he says. 'Sticking her nose into stuff that's nothing to do with her. She's such a shit-stirrer. You know that she's jealous of us, always hanging around when we just want to be alone together. Always causing drama too. Like when she tweeted that clip of Archie trying to skate off the low wall by the science block and he got a detention.'

'She didn't do that on purpose,' I say, though without much heat because now I'm remembering the time I got grounded because Martha tweeted a picture of me on the rope swing on the Parkland Walk and my mum saw it and knew that I'd skived off the revision session I promised I'd go to. 'Someone should take her phone away from her.'

'She's kind of a hater. Anyway, where are you now?' Mark asks, and it's too soon to change the subject when we haven't even begun to get to the heart of the subject, but then I realise it's my stop.

I jump up. 'I'm at Peckham Rye. I have to change onto the Overground now to take me to Clapham.'

'Peckham? Isn't that where *Only Fools and Horses* was set?' Mark asks. 'Would it make you feel better if I let you call me a plonker? Or I could sing the theme tune?'

It's harder and harder to stay furious with Mark. Especially as now I'm furious with Martha too and about how complicated it is to get out of South London. It's as if once they've got you south of the river, they're determined to never let you leave.

Mark must sense that I'm wavering. 'I love you,' he says. 'You're about the only good thing that's happened to me since my parents split. I'm not going to do anything to screw that up. Come on, Sun, you know I would never willingly kiss another girl. Especially not tonight of all nights . . . but we don't even have to do it tonight. We'll do whatever you want. I'll help you clean up and you can make me watch *Mean Girls* for the fiftieth time – just get here soon, Sunny. Where are you now?'

'I'm one stop away from Clapham High Street,' I say. 'Then I have to change on to the tube so I have to go in a minute.'

'But you believe me, right? She was kissing me, I wasn't kissing her, and my hand kind of gripped her arse in shock. It sounds so shady, I know, but it's the truth.'

I'd forgotten about the arse gripping and it did sound really shady, but then there'd been the time on the way home from a night out that I'd lost my balance when I was moving down the bus and it had gone over a speed bump and I'd fallen face down in Archie's lap. Of course, Archie had gone bright red and everyone else, even complete strangers, had laughed at me. And now that I came to think about it, it had been Martha who'd made it even worse. 'I never knew you felt *that* way about Archie,' she'd cackled as if I wasn't embarrassed enough.

And what had Mark done? He'd pulled me out of Archie's lap, seen that my eyes were getting ready to unleash the tears of utter mortification and he'd kissed my cheek and said quietly, 'Accidents happen, Sun. Don't sweat it.'

So now I decided that I wasn't going to sweat this . . . *accident.*

'OK, well then I guess we're cool. I'll see you in a bit then, yeah?'

'I can come and meet you at the station. Are you getting out at Camden or Chalk Farm?'

I'm just about to tell Mark that only a tourist would get out at Camden Town station on a Saturday night, but he says, 'Wait a sec.' I can hear someone shouting to him in the background. I think it might be a girl, but it doesn't necessarily mean it's *that* girl.

'Babes, I have to go. Text me. I'll see you soon. Love you.'

Then he's gone and I'm not angry any more. Honestly, I'm really not angry. Mostly I feel like a bottle of Coke that's been shaken up. I fizzed for a little while but now I'm flat as I walk the short distance to Clapham North so I can get on a tube train. Dear, dear old Northern line. I'll never diss it again. Not after the journey I've had to get this far.

But when I get to the station, the railings are pulled across the entrance to the tube and locked tight. Then I see a notice about planned engineering works, and apparently it's impossible to take a tube train from the south to the north of a major global city on the August bank holiday weekend. Like we're in the bloody Dark Ages or something.

It gets worse. Because written on the notice and then repeated by the surly man in Transport for London livery taking passenger queries and general abuse are the three worst words in the English language. The very worst words.

RAIL REPLACEMENT BUS.

No! No! No! NO!!!!

Oh God, why have you forsaken me?

Right on cue, the rail replacement bus rocks up. A bunch of miserable people stare out of the windows as more miserable-looking people queue to get on.

Is this to be my fate? To spend *hours* of my life travelling from Clapham in deepest South London to Camden in the North on a rail replacement bus that stops at every tube station en route? I'll be lucky to get to Camden in time for breakfast. I can't even cab it. I would never have enough money for how much that would cost.

I look around for divine inspiration. That, or a handy teleportation device.

I've been to Clapham once before, with my stepdad, Terry, and my half-bro (and full-time pain in the arse), Dan, to give a quote on a house clearance. The house belonged to a lady who'd lived there all her life and now had to pack up and move into one room in a care home. Terry reckoned that the place hadn't been decorated since the 1940s. It was like walking round a museum except you could touch stuff, though you kind of didn't want to because it was someone's home. Where their whole life had happened to them.

She sat there, Mrs Sayer, on one of her green velvet bucket chairs and twisted her pale, veiny, liver-spotted hands together. 'I don't know what to do. What to take,' she said. 'How do I choose what things mean the most to me?' Then her narrow, bony shoulders slumped. 'What does it matter anyway? They're just things.'

Terry had said he'd make some tea and he'd asked me to sit with her. Each uncomfortable minute punctuated by the ticking of her funny old clock sitting on the mantelpiece. I never know the right things to say and I'd looked around her living room; the sepia-tinted photos of weddings and babies and a man in uniform. A fragile blue vase, sunlight shafting through the delicate glass. A china windmill with 'A present from Margate' painted on it.

'I'd take the things that made me happy when I looked at them,' I said at last. 'The ones that make you think of all the good things that have happened.'

She'd looked at me like she didn't quite know what I was doing on her sofa. Then she smiled. 'That sounds like an excellent idea.'

Terry had gone into her loft to get some suitcases down for her and then he'd given her a quote to clear the house, which had made Mum shout at him when we got back because she said they'd be bankrupt within a year if he kept quoting so close to the resale price.

After we'd left Mrs Sayer, we went to a greasy spoon and had double bacon, double sausage, beans and chips, then we'd driven all the way back to Crouch End crunching on extra-strong mints so Mum wouldn't smell dead animal on our breath.

That was what Clapham meant to me. Now from my lonely perch at the bus stop outside Clapham North station, I can see a solicitor's office and a beauty salon, a couple of convenience shops and a church. On the corner is a pub painted primrose yellow with people spilling out of its courtyard onto the street; smoking and drinking and chattering. I could be anywhere in London but it's not my London; the London that I desperately need to get back to.

But God's plan for me is the rail replacement bus that apparently runs every five minutes, because another one is trundling towards me.

Suddenly I hear the hoot of a horn. Two hoots. Then there's a cacophony of non-stop hooting and I look past the bus stop to see two boys on mopeds pulling into the side of the road. Two boys in sharp, skinny suits, who I'm betting would have huge volume-defying mops of hair if said hair wasn't currently obscured by their helmets. They still have their shades on and the scooters are the ones that have an Italian name that always makes me think of chocolate. Vespas. They're on Vespas. Like Audrey Hepburn and Gregory Peck in *Roman Holiday* or all those mods heading down to Brighton to fight rockers in *Quadrophenia*, which Terry always makes us watch when it's his turn to choose a film.

It's the French boys. The Godards. I don't know what they're doing in Clapham or why they're tooting their horns like it's a new national pastime, but they are.

Whatever. Not my problem.

I join the people queuing to get on the rail replacement bus.

'Sunshine! Hey! Sunshine! C'mere!'

Only one person calls me Sunshine, even though it's the name on my birth certificate, and that's my mum. She only calls me that when I'm in unholy amounts of trouble. But one of the Godards (how does anyone tell them apart?) has taken off his helmet and is calling out my full name and waving at me.

I mooch over unwillingly. I can't think why two mysterious French boys would want anything to do with me.

'Hey,' I say when I'm within speaking distance. 'What's up?'

'Ah, I was just about to ask you the same thing,' the unidentified Godard says. He doesn't sound at all French. He sounds as if he was born and bred in North London like me. The other Godard hasn't even taken off his helmet but sits on his scooter like he's desperate to dive back into the traffic. 'Your friends remembered the Northern line was closed, but you'd already gone and you weren't answering your phone.'

I look at my phone. I have so many unread texts, voicemails and missed calls that it looks like the phone of someone who's really popular. 'They're running rail replacement buses.'

'That sucks,' he mutters, this boy whose name I don't know, who might not even be French. 'I went on a rail replacement bus once. Someone was sick over my shoes. It was very traumatic.'

I stare down at his feet. His skinny legs end in a pair of black, pointy-toe boots. Then I look up because he's holding out his hand like he wants me to shake it.

'We haven't met, I know, but your mother, *la belle Hélène*, talks about you all the time. I'm Vic.'

'Sunny. Everyone calls me Sunny.' We shake hands. He has a firm handshake and for a second it feels as if he's holding my hand, and that's nice, but maybe it's because I'm still overcome by flatness and I could really do with a bit of hand-holding.

When Vic lets go of my hand, it's a tiny loss. Then he jerks his head and says something in French to his maybe twin, maybe doppelgänger boyfriend. I catch the word '*allez*'. And I also make out the word 'wanker' in the torrent of French that I don't understand because I took Spanish as my language option for GCSE.

Then the other one gets off his scooter and steps towards me and I want to step back because Vic is in a white shirt and he seems light and friendly, but this other guy is wearing a black shirt, which exactly matches the expression on his face.

'Sunny, this is Jean-Luc. He'll pretend he doesn't understand a word of English. He'll also pretend to be a gigantic wanker. Not true in either case. He's just a normal-sized wanker.'

Even though he's wearing shades, I'm sure Jean-Luc is rolling his eyes. I hold out my hand but he ignores it and simply says, '*Enchanté*,' like he's the absolute opposite of *enchanté*.

In ordinary circumstances I'd be stammering and blushing the way I did when there were cute boys present and I was trying to act cool, but these are extraordinary circumstances. My heart isn't quite whole and Mark is the only one who can make it complete again, so I just stand there and I fold my arms and I decide that stroppy French boys are too much to deal with tonight.

'It was nice of you to come and find me to tell me about the Northern line. Thanks.' I mutter. 'I'll get back on the Overground or take the bus or something.'

As soon as I say it, yet another rail replacement bus arrives. If possible, the people on it look even more miserable than the people on the first two buses. Like it isn't really stopping off at all the stations on the Northern line but going straight to the very bowels of hell.

Both Vic and Jean-Luc are still there. What with the helmets and the shades and the maybe being French, I wonder if they've ever thought about forming a Daft Punk tribute band and then I feel the giggles bubbling up and have to turn away.

'Thanks again.' I wave a feeble hand and I would join the reluctant queue waiting to get on the bus, but the Godards are now blocking my way.

'You're going back to North London?' Vic asks.

'Yeah, Camden. Well, Chalk Farm but . . .'

'It will take you hours and someone may throw up on your shoes, or worse!' Vic shudders theatrically. Then he takes off his helmet. Immediately his hand is in his hair to tug and pull at it so it regains its former volume. Only then does he speak. 'It's too much.'

I don't know if he's talking about the transport situation or his hair, but Jean-Luc nods and takes hold of my arm. He has impossibly long fingers. Of course he has. 'And you're suffering from, er, the romantic disappointment.'

42

'Suffering from . . . ? Oh God, does everyone know that my boyfriend has . . . has . . . has disappointed me romantically? Anyway, he hasn't. We sorted it out. It was just a misunderstanding. I'm going to meet him now.'

They both stand there and share an amused look, like they're well used to the delusions of young women who have been romantically disappointed. Then Vic turns to look at me – a comprehensive up and down, then a decisive nod as if I passed his inspection. 'We know all about your boyfriend,' he says with a smirk.

I put my hands on my hips. 'Oh yeah?' I'm not normally so challenging. I don't know what's got into me, but his smirk is *infuriating*. 'How come?'

'Your mother,' Vic says and my heart sinks. 'In fact, I was going to come over and say hello at the picnic because I recognised you from *la belle Hélène*'s photo that she has on her desk in the shop . . .'

'And always she's showing us yet more photos of you on her phone and your *petit frère*, Daniel, and even *le chat* with the ridiculous name –' Jean-Luc adds.

I had to stop him right there. 'Gretchen Weiner isn't a ridiculous name for a cat! She's got loads of poufy fur like she hides all her secrets in it and sometimes when you're trying to shift her off an armchair she gives you this "You can't sit with us" look, which I suppose doesn't really mean anything unless you've seen *Mean Girls*.'

It's obvious that neither of them have seen that cinematic masterpiece because Jean-Luc shakes his head and makes a tiny scoffing sound. I hope it's hot and sweaty inside his helmet and

43

that he gets heatstroke for dissing my cat. '"Oh, my Sunshine, she's so pretty if only she'd smile more,"' he says in this weird, high-pitched voice. '"And now she's going out with this boy who walks about with his underpants showing and there's something very untrustworthy about his face. I do worry about her."'

'I bet my mum doesn't say anything like that.' Except I know that she does. I can *hear* her saying it. She was also fond of saying that she should have called me Storm Cloud rather than Sunshine. But to say it to the Godards who I don't even know . . . I make a mental note to kill her when she gets back from camping.

'She worries about you,' Vic says. 'Like a good *maman* should. And it's only right we help you get home safely.'

'But I'm not going home.'

'Your friend Emmeline said that you were,' Jean-Luc says. He's definitely the bad cop. 'That your boyfriend was *un cochon total* and you needed to mope and eat ice cream.'

I make a note to kill Emmeline too. 'She's wrong. I'm not going home and I'm absolutely not moping.' It doesn't sound very convincing out loud, and for some reason the thought of Emmeline absolutely determined not to give Mark the benefit of the doubt makes my eyes prickle as if more tears are amassing in my tears ducts like coffee dripping through a filter. I swallow and try again. 'Mark and I are fine. Just fine. He doesn't make a habit of going around and kissing other girls. The girl he was photographed with was kissing *him* and he was an unwilling participant. Very unwilling.'

I'm not wearing shades because the light has almost died and also I'm not a total poseur, so maybe they can see the one tear that clings to my lashes and then ever so slowly trickles down my cheek.

None of us says anything. I'm too scared to open my mouth in case I do something stupid like sob.

Jean-Luc is the first to turn away but he's only opening up the little pannier thingy on the back of his scooter. He pulls out a helmet, looks at it doubtfully, then looks at my hair.

'You may need to, er, squash down your hair so this fits, *non*?' He thrusts the helmet at me. 'Come on! *Allez!*'

'You're going to give me a lift to Camden on the back of that?'

'Much quicker than the bus,' Vic adds. 'You don't have to go with him. I'll give you a lift. *La belle Hélène* will know you're in safe hands with me.'

La belle Hélène would have ninety-nine fits if she knew I was so much as thinking of careering around London on the back of a two-wheeled motor vehicle – even if one of her lovely French boys is steering. In fact, I'm sure she'd rather I got pregnant or committed murder or failed my AS levels than got on the back of one of their Vespas, especially as odds are that one of them will take a corner too fast or get cut up by an HGV and the emergency services would have to scoop up the bits of my body left scattered across the road.

'No, it's OK. I can get the bus,' I say as yet *another* rail replacement bus turns up. 'But thanks. I'll tell Mum you said hi.'

I shove the helmet back to Jean-Luc – with some force because he responds with a pained 'ooof', then I hurry over to the bus stop so I can ask the driver how long before we get to Camden.

45

'Buggered if I know,' he says helpfully. 'How long's a piece of string? Took me two hours on the last run.'

Vic and Jean-Luc are still there. I walk back to them. Jean-Luc hands me the helmet.

'I'm not dressed for riding on the back of a moped,' I explain. 'I don't want the paramedics to have to pick lumps of tarmac out of my legs.'

The three of us stare down at my legs. I'm not wearing bootie shorts, unlike other people I could mention. I'm not exposing bottom cheeks, not in the slightest. My shorts come down past the annoying fleshy bit of my inner thigh. They're cuffed. They're respectable and weather-appropriate, but now I do this weird, awkward, embarrassed thing where I twist my legs together until I nearly fall over. 'Stop looking at them,' I want to whine, but I don't. Instead I have to confront the uncomfortable truth of the situation: my options are severely limited if I want to get to Camden sometime before Christmas. There's nothing else for it – I'm going to have to do the unthinkable and come to a decision right here, right now, no dithering.

Maybe just a little bit of dithering. 'Which of you is the safest driver? Like, if there was a gun to your heads and you had to choose.'

'*C'est moi!*'

'Me, of course.'

'Gun to your heads!'

Jean-Luc holds up his hand. '*Un moment!*'

The two of them have a quiet, intense conversation in French.

Then it gets louder. They step up to each other, chests out like strutting pigeons. They're saying French stuff like '*zut alors!*' and '*mon dieu!*' and even '*incroyable!*' that I didn't think French people ever said in real life.

I get my bottle of water out of my bag. It's lukewarm and I decide that I have time to get another bottle from one of the shops across the road. But then there's a triumphant '*tant pis!*' and it looks as if Jean-Luc and Vic have stopped jostling each other and talking comedy French and Jean-Luc has declared himself the winner.

Vic humphs in disgust. 'At least I don't ride like a little old lady,' he sneers. He's definitely the nicer of the two of them, but there's a restlessness to him that's unnerving. He's not slouching like Jean-Luc but in motion, snapping his fingers to get me moving as he climbs onto his scooter. And once I'm on the back of Jean-Luc's moped, my heart racing in the same way it does when I'm waiting for a roller-coaster to fire up, Vic has already taken off with a roar of his engine. Immediately he starts weaving past yet another rail replacement bus, then darts through the cars waiting at the traffic lights and I'd much rather be with Jean-Luc, because he really does drive like a little old lady.

THINGS MY MOTHER HAS STRONGLY ADVISED ME AGAINST DOING

1. Getting on the back of someone's motorbike. Never. Not even if I have a crash helmet and a full set of leathers and they promise not to go above twenty miles per hour.
2. Putting anything in my vagina that I wouldn't put in my mouth. This came up while I was helping to make a Thai curry. Mum always likes to combine cooking with a little mother/daughter sex chat. 'So, I can put garlic or chillies or ginger up there, then? If it's all the same, then I think I won't.' 'I was talking as a general rule of thumb.' 'Thumbs are allowed too, are they? Why, though? Why would you want to . . .' 'Oh, just use your common sense, Sunny!'
3. Which leads to: getting pregnant before I'm thirty/ in a stable, committed relationship/able to support myself financially (all applicable).
4. Eating cheese after 8 p.m. Gives you nightmares, apparently.

5. Going out without a hat when it's cold outside. 'I don't care if it messes up your hair – everyone knows you lose seventy per cent of your body heat through your head.'
6. Forming an emotional attachment to any of my dad's girlfriends, as none of them stick around for that long.
7. Informing Childline or the Department of Works and Pensions that she only gives me fifteen per cent commission on the bureaus, chests, bookcases and, once, a ginormous wardrobe, that I sand down, paint, distress, varnish and generally upcycle for her to then sell at a gigantic mark-up. 'It's not below minimum wage, Sunny. Not when you factor in that I've fed you, provided a roof over your head and all manner of other sundries for the last seventeen years.'
8. Having a weave. (She was right about that one.)
9. Believing that Food and Nutrition would be an easy GCSE. (Also right.)
10. Watching *The Exorcist*, even though Dan, who's six years younger than me, said it wasn't *that* scary. (Also right – had nightmares for weeks.)
11. Going out with M . . .

Really, what does my mother know anyway?

9.55 p.m.

CAMDEN

Camden Town, named after Charles Pratt, First Earl Camden, became an important but unfashionable location full of undesirables and ne'er-do-wells when the Regent's Canal was built through the area in 1816.

Camden's famous markets started in 1973 and are an essential stop for anyone requiring bootleg concert DVDs, T-shirts with totally not funny witty slogans or a steampunk starter wardrobe.

Home to the Britpop scene of the mid-nineteen-nineties, many celebrities have lived on Camden's hallowed streets from Charles Dickens and poet Dylan Thomas to Noel Gallagher, Gwyneth Paltrow and him out of Coldplay, and the late Amy Winehouse.

Being on the back of a moped, even if it's being ridden very carefully, is still scary. Maybe the scariest thing that has ever happened to me.

I squeal every time Jean-Luc brakes or takes a turn and my arms tighten round his waist so hard that he grunts. Ordinarily, it would be mortifying to be intimately pressed up against a boy who I've only known for ten minutes (or even a boy that I'd known for much longer than that), but mortification is no match for feeling small and vulnerable like I have a target on my back. If a car or lorry gets too close, the slipstream could be enough to knock us into the traffic on the other side of the road and we'd crumple up like paper dolls. But with more blood and gore.

Then after about five minutes, it's not scary so much as thrilling. The hot, sticky evening now has a breeze that brushes against my legs and makes my stripy tee billow. The hot gush of car exhausts feels almost tropical and for a while we ride alongside a guy delivering pizzas on his own moped who grins at me like I'm a two-wheeling kindred spirit, then gives me a thumbs-up before he turns off.

The best bit is when we cross over the Thames at Waterloo Bridge. Not just because crossing over from south to north always makes me feel as if I've come home, but because seeing the city backlit against the darkened skies, the old and the gleaming new all nestled together, never fails to stir my heart.

It feels as if something else is stirring too. I was so worried about being maimed in a road traffic accident that I didn't give much thought to Jean-Luc, other than to use him as something to cling onto for dear life. Literally. Not even figuratively.

But now that riding through London on the back of a moped is my new favourite thing, I take stock. In my stocktaking I notice that my legs grip Jean-Luc's hips and thighs, my arms around his waist, and as I mimic the movement of the moped, I lean into him, my face pressed against his back.

He smells amazing. Sweet like a cake that's just come out of the oven, but sharp too, like limes. There's also a perfume-y synthetic base note that I just can't place.

Every now and again, when we stop at traffic lights, Jean-Luc turns around and says, 'Ça va?'

The fact that I'm no longer shrieking and clutching him in a vice-like grip should have made it clear that I'm totally ça va, but each time he asks, I shout, 'I'm cool!'

We get to Camden in twenty-three minutes. Take that, rail replacement bus! We drive through Regent's Park and I crane my neck to see if I can see any giraffes as we pass London Zoo, but they must all be asleep. Then we catch up with Vic, who's waiting for us at the top of Parkway.

The traffic is thicker now. We crawl up Camden High Street, slowing as drunk girls in tiny skirts and teetering heels stumble into the road. Beered-up lads shout at us – one reaches out to grab my arm. Jean-Luc has to veer wildly around him, then he shouts at him in French and takes a hand off the handlebars to gesture wildly.

'It's all right. I'm all right. Keep your eyes on the road!'

There's not much road left once we reach the little bridge over the canal. Maybe one hundred metres more and The Lock Tavern is on our right.

Vic turns into Harmood Street, we follow, pull into the kerb and when Jean-Luc switches off the engine I wish he hadn't. That we'd just carry on until we ran out of road. Go to Brighton. Whitstable. The seaside. To sit on the beach and gaze at the inky outline of the water, let the breeze roll in from the sea and ruffle your hair, taste the salt when you lick your lips.

But that would be a stupid thing to do when Mark is sitting a few metres away, waiting for me.

I take off the helmet and shake my hair free of the hair-band I'd tied it back with. It had been very hot under the helmet. I tip my head upside down and zhoosh my fingers through my hair, but it's not back to its previous levels of immenseness.

'You want some of this?'

Vic and Jean-Luc have removed their helmets too and out of their panniers they both produce a familiar gold can. It's the smell I couldn't place. Elnett hairspray. My grandmother bathes in the stuff, my mum swears by it when she's coaxing her fine blond hair into a beehive and I never turn down a product that will embiggen my Afro a little bit more.

I spray it on my hands, then plunge them into my hair and work it through. Vic and Jean-Luc primp too, tugging at their helmet-flattened tufts until their hair is vertical again.

'Your hair.' Vic looks at me thoughtfully. 'It's so . . . *big*. Is it natural?'

I nod and wait for him to ruin everything by asking if he can touch it. People want to do that all the time. It's so rude. Like, I'm a dog happy to have its head stroked.

But Vic doesn't, and Jean-Luc squats down to look at his reflection in the wing mirror of his moped and pouts. Both of them are really quite . . . I don't even know what they are. Odd. Singular, except there's two of them.

By the time I've reapplied my mascara and lipgloss, they're smoothing down their lapels, shades still on. 'OK, so this is my stop,' I say. I don't know why I feel like I'm about to walk naked into battle. It's Mark and we love each other and everything is all right. 'Thanks so much for the lift. I'd still be in Clapham if I'd got that bus.'

'Do you want us to come with you?' Vic asks. 'In case there's trouble.'

'Why would there be trouble?' I frown. 'I told you, it was just a misunderstanding. Honestly, I'll be fine.'

I look down the street towards the pub. As usual, there's a crowd of people gathered outside, even though there are notices up protesting that it's a residential area and that everyone needs to pipe the hell down. Inside, on the roof terrace where we always hang out, will be Mark. Is he on his own? Or are his Chelsea friends, the arseholes, still there? Is *that* girl still there? Is she still all up on him with the kissing and arse-gripping?

Each thought is worse than the last. And with the last thought, I take a step back. Then another one. And another one. I hate confrontations.

So, I can just keep taking steps backwards until I'm at the other end of the street and then I can get a bus and go home and stick to the original plan. There's not much to cry about any more, I don't think, but I can still eat so much ice cream that it's a toss up as to whether I get brain freeze or throw up first.

'*Pourquoi t'es encore là, toi?*' Jean-Luc exclaims. He's taken his shades off, they both have, because it's dark now and it turns

54

out that they're not such poseurs that they'll wear sunglasses when there isn't a glimmer of sun left in the sky. Jean-Luc's very scowly without his shades, though that might be because he is scowling at me. I suppose there are some girls who like the dark, brooding thing, but I'm not one of them. 'Off you go! *Allez!*'

'We talked about this,' Vic gently reminds him. He turns to me. 'Sorry. He's only been in London a year. I keep telling him that he can't be as rude to people here as he was in Paris.'

'I was rude?' Jean-Luc asks me. He sounds baffled at the very idea.

'Well, maybe a little bit,' I say with an apologetic grimace. 'It's OK. I don't mind.'

'*Alors! C'est quoi, le problème?*'

Vic cuffs Jean-Luc on the shoulder. 'In English!'

Jean-Luc shrugs him off with an angry twitch. '*Je ne veux pas parler Anglais!*'

'You can speak English perfectly well, you just choose not to.'

'Whatever! Is that English enough for you?'

I thought me and Dan argued a lot, mainly about how he's an annoying git who needs to keep his snotty little nose out of my business, but Vic and Jean-Luc take arguing to a whole other level. 'OK, right, well I'm going now,' I say, though they're too busy glaring at each other to pay much attention to me. 'So, thanks for everything and, um, I'll see you around, I suppose.'

'Say hello to *la belle Hélène*!' Vic calls out and I wriggle my fingers in acknowledgement and then head up, shoulders straight, forward march.

I fight my way through the crowd on the pavement to even get into the pub, then I walk sideways like a crab through the bar. Stomach sucked in, leaning backwards, then forwards, hunting for tiny pockets of space to open up.

'Sorry, sorry, sorry, excuse me, sorry,' I murmur like a mantra until I reach the stairs. There's a bottleneck at the door to the terrace and it takes me a long time to squeeze through, like ketchup slowly oozing out of a gunked-up bottle. The terrace is heaving with people. I have to do the same crab-like shuffle until I see a red beanie in the distance and I hone in on it like it's the mothership.

It's not the mothership, it's Archie. He's with George and Alex (of Glasto-devirginising-fame) Hassan and Martha. I wave, catch George's eye, and he must say something because they all turn round and as soon as I reach them Martha throws her arms around me.

'You OK, hon?' She thrusts me away so she can stare deep into my eyes. I'm not sure what my eyes are saying to her, but she decides I need another hug. 'Don't worry. Everything's going to be fine.'

'Please, Martha, your watch strap is digging into me.' I wriggle until she lets me go. 'Anyway, everything *is* all right. I spoke to Mark. It's all cool.' I look around. 'Where is he? Has he gone to the bar?'

'He's gone,' Alex says. 'Left about ten minutes ago with his posh Chelsea friends.'

That didn't mean that things weren't all right. I'd said I was going to text Mark when I approached North London, but that had been a little difficult on the back of a moped.

'He's probably texted me.' I reach into my bag and grope for the chunky shape of my phone. 'So, what are his posh Chelsea friends like, then?'

Alex rolls her eyes. 'Posh. Really posh. The word posh doesn't really do them justice, does it?'

The others shake their heads and make general sounds of agreement. 'One of the dudes was wearing a pink polo shirt with a popped collar, two of them were called Giles and none of them knew how to use their indoor voices. *So* posh.'

'Yeah, and one of the girls kept jawing on about her holiday in Cap Ferret.' Martha widens her eyes. 'On a yacht!'

'Ferret? That doesn't sound very glamorous.' I'm determined not to get side-tracked. 'Mark said they were arseholes. So was this the girl who –'

'Bloody inbreds, the lot of them.' George stamps one of his great big feet in disgust. 'I'll tell you what, come the revolution, I will personally escort the whole lot of them to the gallows.'

'Not the firing squad, then?' Hassan asks with a sly smile.

'Nah! Waste of good bullets, mate.'

There's no point in paying any attention to George. He spends all Saturday outside Waitrose harassing people to buy copies of the *Socialist Worker* newspaper. I've muted him on Twitter because he won't stop tweeting links to Change.org petitions to end global slavery and protest against the military regimes in countries I've never even heard of. I mean, after a hard day at school, I just want to click on links to pictures of cats looking grumpy. I told Martha that it was a pity I couldn't mute George when he's in our Sociology class ranting on about privilege.

Then of course Martha told George, who told Emmeline that I had the political conscience of a goldfish and I said to Emmeline that someone should start a Change.org petition to ban George from Change.org, and then he tore into me about it at a party and I had to go into the bathroom to cry, but whatever, I'm totally over it.

'So, Mark explained what happened with that girl,' I say very casually like it's not a big deal, because it really isn't a big deal, as I unlock my phone and wade through all the unread messages. 'Um, Martha, did you text those pictures to, like, well, everyone? That's kind of not cool.'

I cringe a bit because it's the most confrontational thing that I've ever said to someone who isn't Emmeline or immediate family. Of course, Martha instantly draws her shoulders back and opens her mouth in a gasp of indignation. 'Oh my God,' she breathes. 'Don't shoot the messenger.'

There are texts from friends who are still on holiday and one from a girl that I only met once at a Duckie gig, but nothing from Mark. I send him a quick text – '@ the Lock. Where r u? Sunny xxx' – as I explain to Martha and the group at large, 'Look, that girl kissed Mark. Because that's what they do in Chelsea. And his hand wasn't meant to be on her arse. I ended up touching quite a few arses when I was fighting my way through the bar, and what about when I was on the bus that time and I slipped and landed in Archie's lap? Sometimes stuff happens!'

Alex and Martha synchronise their eye rolls, then Alex mutters, 'Yeah, it really looked like their mouths just landed on each other.'

Archie nods earnestly. 'We saw a different side to Mark tonight. To be honest with you, Sun, he was acting like a bit of a dick.'

I'm not that girl – the girl who blindly goes along with everything that her boyfriend says and does, because she can't bear to be boyfriendless. A sad girl. I'm really not her. I've been boyfriendless for all but the last nine, nearly ten, months of my life and I was fine with it. But the evidence against Mark is hardly overwhelming.

'Everyone acts like a bit of a dick sometimes,' I say, and then no one says anything because all of them are looking at me like I've just come back from taking all my clothes off and doing a streak of the roof terrace. An 'are you really that stupid?' kind of look.

I'm really not *that* stupid. But maybe I'm a bit too trusting, a bit too much of a people pleaser, a bit too sensitive, and that's why I can feel the angry, hurt prickle behind my eyes again and I'm almost grateful to George for being the first one to break the silence. 'Well, this isn't at all awkward, is it?' he booms out, and then Archie reaches for something on the seat behind and hands me a broom.

'There you go,' he says proudly, like he's bestowing a great honour on me and not a grey plastic broom with blue bristles. 'Went to Sainsbury's on the way here.'

'Wow, thanks! That's kind of random.'

'Because we set yours on fire on Thursday night,' Archie reminds me. 'When Mark and I were trying to do flaming baton twirling.' That was proof right there that everybody, including Archie, acted like a bit of a dick sometimes. 'Did you get the scorch marks off of the shed?'

'Had to repaint the whole thing in the end. Still got to slap on the weatherproof varnish before my mum gets back.' And remove all evidence of meat eating and alcohol drinking and clean the house from top to bottom. The sheer weight of my to-do list hangs heavy. Saturday nights are meant to be more fun than that, I'm sure of it.

'You all right, Sun? Well, apart from the obvious?' Hassan asks. 'Do you want a drink?'

'Yeah, but, no. I should go and find Mark or go home. I still haven't cleaned up from the barbecue.' I cringe again. 'Sorry to be such a buzzkill.'

'No, you're all right.' Alex strokes my arm. 'If I don't sleep through my alarm tomorrow, I could come over and help you tidy up.'

'Oh, you don't have to do that,' I say automatically, though actually it would be lovely if she did do that. 'But if you *didn't* sleep through your alarm . . .'

'I'll call you,' she says and then she looks pointedly at Archie who mumbles something about how maybe he might be able to come over. Maybe. Then Martha says that she'll come too. Hassan says that he totally would but he has to go to mosque. It's weird how he always has to go to mosque when someone asks him to do something that he doesn't want to do.

'Well, I'm not coming,' George says. 'I don't help people who mute me on Twitter.'

Whatever. He really needs to get over it.

TEN MINUTES LATER

Like he has a sixth sense about these things, Mark calls me as soon as I've fought my way back out of The Lock Tavern.

I'm annoyed that he bailed on me but relieved that he's called me so I don't have to wage a great internal debate about whether it would be really clingy if I called him when he hadn't replied to my earlier text.

'Where *are* you?' It comes out as a sad, little whine.

'Ain't no sunshine when you've gone,' Mark sings. He sounds happy to hear from me, whiny or not. 'You still at The Lock then, Sun?'

'Outside.' For one moment I'm sure all my suspicions about the supposedly innocent kiss and arse-groping are about to come pouring out. That my doubt and the pain that was still lurking at the edges would transform into vicious, stabby words like poisoned darts. But, no. Turns out I'm still not done with the whining. 'Why did you leave without me?'

'Oh, babe! *Babe!*' he says. 'My friends were being twats and I needed to get them out of there. We're at The Edinboro Castle but now they really want to go to Shoreditch.'

'But you don't have to go with them, do you?' I ask.

'Well, no, of course I don't. I mean, except not going with them would turn into a whole *thing* that I really don't want to deal with.'

'Oh,' I say. 'Right.' It's frustrating how impossible I find it to speak my truth.

'Don't be like that, babes. Hang on!' He says something to a disembodied voice in the background. 'Look, why don't you come here and meet everybody?'

'I don't know. Is that girl –'

'It's just we have a car coming in five minutes. We're on the guest list to some club but we have to get there before eleven.

61

Look, babe, I'm desperate to see you. I bet if you run, you can make it. Come on, Sunny! Run like the wind. See you in five!'

He hasn't even hung up and I'm running. Like it's a matter of life and death that I get to The Edinboro Castle before Mark's cab. I run faster than I ever have before. I run like the survival of the planet depends on it.

The pavements are so crowded that I run on the road, arms clamped against my chest so my boobs don't bounce, my bag banging against my hip, clutching the broom.

I hate running.

But it clears the mind and then I have this moment of, like, clarity. I don't see the cars rushing towards me or people swerving away so I don't barrel into them; instead, I see the pattern so very clearly.

Mark says jump and I jump.

Marks says run and I run.

Mark kissed another girl. Or was kissed by her – but even so his priority should be making things right. Chasing me. Not the other way round.

I stop running. What the hell am I doing?

'Hey, little sister! Where you going in such a hurry? You want a lift?' A rickshaw has pulled up alongside me. The guy pedalling it, shaven-headed, tanned and tatted, flashes me a toothy grin.

Taking a lift from a stranger with tats was another thing *la belle Hélène* would expressly forbid me to do, but what *la belle Hélène* doesn't know won't kill her.

Everything will sort itself out once I catch up with Mark. It has to. I leap onto the seat. 'I need to be at The Edinboro Castle, like, five minutes ago!'

He looks over his shoulder at me. Grins again. '*Nila problemo!*'

I never thought much about rickshaws before apart from the times I've been almost mown down by one when I'm in town. Then I haven't liked them very much. Never thought I'd be seen dead in one either because they were just for tourists or what Emmeline sneeringly calls 'the bridge and tunnel crowd', but now I'm sitting in one.

. . . sitting and also clinging desperately onto one of the poles that holds up the canvas hood as the driver starts pedalling full pelt.

He cuts straight across Camden High Street to bomb down Jamestown Road and I wish he'd pay attention to where he's going but he's too busy looking round at me as he talks. His name is Jason and he's from Australia, Brisbane. He calls it Brisneyland. He was meant to be staying in London for a week before heading to Amsterdam to meet up with friends, but he's run out of cash.

'Everything in London is so expensive,' he says. 'Went to this place in Covent Garden. Five quid for a pint! Anyway, what's your name? Why have you got a broom with you?'

'Sunnneeeeeeeeeeeeeee!' Jason speeds up to get us through the lights before they change to red and as we bounce over a pothole, my arse lifts up off the seat. When I land, every bone in my body feels the impact. 'Left! Go left here!'

Jason goes left pretty much on one wheel and sets off a cacophony of drivers pressing down on their horns to let us know that we're a menace and shouldn't be on the roads. I don't care. I can see The Edinboro Castle coming up on the right. But I can't see Mark.

Jason does an illegal U-ey right into the path of a black cab, which brakes sharply so the driver can lean out the window and shout, 'You want locking up, mate. You're a bloody danger to society, you are.'

We come to a gentle halt outside the pub. It takes a little while for my legs to stop shaking and even once I'm back on solid ground, they're still a bit wobbly. 'How much do I owe you?' I ask Jason.

What was the going rate for being cycled a few hundred metres at breakneck speed?

Jason shook his head. 'We're cool. It's on the house.'

'Aw no, that makes me feel bad when you're trying to save up to get to Amsterdam.' I open my bag, even though I know I don't have that much cash on me.

'It's OK. I used to be a boy scout. I like to do one good turn every day. Pay it forward, right?' Jason rests his elbows on his handlebars. He really is kind of cute if you were the sort of girl who went for surfer types.

I am the sort of girl who only goes for very unreliable types.

I glance down at my open bag, see some napkin parcels and pull them out. 'I have baked goods.' I unfold the napkins. 'The rock cakes are more rock than cakes and everything else is kinda smooshed, but you need to keep up your energy levels if you're going to pedal that hard.'

I watch Jason pedal off into the night, one hand raised in salute, then I pull out my phone.

I could go into The Edinboro Castle and worm my way through yet another sticky mass of people who don't want to let me pass, but for the first time tonight I'm certain of one thing: Mark isn't here. He's already left. Otherwise he'd be outside waiting for me.

Oh God! Was this his way of dumping me without actually going to the bother of dumping me?

Why would he do that? He said that he loved me. And God knows, I love him. A few hours ago, he was going to be the boy that I gave it up for, and I wasn't giving it up lightly.

My phone beeps. Text incoming:

Babe! Sorry I missed u. Where u at? Come to Shoreditch. M xxxxx

Where in Shoreditch?

Babe! No love?

U didn't wait for me so no love. Where in Shoreditch?

As I hit send, someone shouts, 'Sunny!'

Mark's come back for me! My heart thuds excitedly, even if the rest of me is doubtful and suspicious. Yup, my heart thinks it would be absolutely dandy to see Mark, but when I turn round it's not Mark. It's a boy in a sharp suit on a moped pulling into the kerb, followed by another boy on a moped.

Jean-Luc pins me with a look as black as his shirt before unleashing a volley of French. I don't get all the little words but I make out an '*imbécile*' and '*une fille stupide*'.

'I'm not an imbecile or a stupid girl,' I say. 'You . . . *you're* stupid.'

Jean-Luc snorts. '*Je vais tout dire à ta maman . . .*'

'Tell my mum about what?'

'Sunny! We saw you in that flimsy rickshaw taking a corner on one wheel. What were you thinking?' Vic clasps a hand to his chest, like the memory of it still causes him great pain. 'We tried to catch up with you but neither of us would ever do an illegal U-turn so we got caught up in the one-way system.'

'I'm sure it wasn't an illegal U-turn. I just needed to get here really quickly because Mark was here and he was about to leave.'

Jean-Luc makes another huffy sound. 'Have you, then?' He draws a finger across his throat and hisses. 'You dumped him, *non?*'

'*Non!* He'd already left. Not that I was planning to dump him. Though, I did think . . . it's all very, very complicated.' The doubt and the uncertainty has returned along with a cold, icy fear that makes me shiver and tastes like rust at the back of my throat. But if I could see Mark, everything would be all right. He'd roll his eyes a little because I was being really clingy, but then he'd take my hand. 'Babe,' he'd say, 'I'm so glad you're here.'

Well, he might not say exactly that, but he'd say something similar that would put my mind at ease. Or maybe he wouldn't. Maybe the very worst thing in the world would happen and he'd dump me for reasons I couldn't even begin to understand, but at least then I'd know. At least *then* I could go home and weep and rage and take to my bed and become a shadow of my former self and not be stuck in this awful limbo.

How to explain that to the Godards, who are still looking as if they were about to grass me up to *la belle Hélène?*

'Look, I did what I had to do. Anybody who's ever been in love would do exactly the same thing,' I add, then wish I hadn't because it sounds really ridiculous. 'What's important is that Mark's on his way to Shoreditch and that's where I need to be.'

'But, Sunny, that's still no reason to let that madman on a rickshaw risk your life and limb,' Vic protests. 'Also, where did you get that broom from and – hey! What are you doing?'

Pulling out his spare helmet was what I was doing. 'You ride like a madman too!' I glance down at my phone. 10.43 p.m. 'Can you get me to Shoreditch before eleven?'

'No, he can't,' Jean-Luc states firmly.

'I think you'll find I can!'

'But you're not going to!'

Vic obligingly helps me onto his moped, hand in the crook of my elbow, fingers lingering longer than necessary when I was sworn off boys and we were on a clock. 'You're not the boss of me,' he tells Jean-Luc.

'Or the boss of me either,' I add.

After tonight, I will be a slave to no man, I vow, as Jean-Luc mutters something in French, then sighs and starts his engine too. After tonight, only I will be the boss of me, but first I need to make sure that me and Mark are cool.

'You'd better hang on tight,' Vic tells me. 'I'm taking no prisoners.'

WHAT THE HELL AM I DOING WITH MY SATURDAY NIGHT?

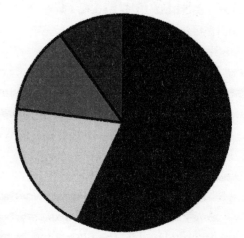

 57% Finding Mark

20% Risking life and limb on a moped driven by unknown Frenchmen

 13% Worrying about my shorts riding up my thighs

 10% Broom management

10.57 p.m.

SHOREDITCH

The parish of Shoreditch in London's East End has been in existence since before Ye Olde Medieval Times and was known as Soers Ditch or Sewer Ditch, as it was once pretty much a glorified bog.

The first playhouse in England, The Theatre, was built in Shoreditch in 1576 but the po-faced Powers That Be did not approve of the shady behaviour of the theatrical folk, nor the taverns, gaming halls and brothels that littered the narrow streets.

The area was taken over by mostly French silk weavers in the seventeenth century, but by Victorian times the theatrical folk had moved back in.

These days, Shoreditch is full of media, arty and creative types being all media and arty and creative in converted factories and warehouses. Famous residents have included William

Shakespeare, responsible for many an English GCSE meltdown, shouty artists Tracey Emin and Damien Hirst, and Barbara Windsor, late of the Queen Vic, Walford.

I scream all the way to Shoreditch. Not out of terror. Not any more. Just from the sheer, giddy, heart-skipping exhilaration of going really fast. Probably not that fast, but when you're on the back of a moped, just you and the open road, it feels fast enough to break the sound barrier. It also feels bloody fantastic.

It's late Saturday night, bank holiday weekend, so there isn't that much traffic. All the better for Vic to bomb along the Euston Road and zip down tiny side streets while I hold onto his waist like it's the last lifebelt on the *Titanic*, the broom tucked tight under my arm.

Vic doesn't mind the screaming or the holding or that the broom keeps poking him in the head; he roars with laughter and jerks the scooter this way and that and I scream even more, which just makes him laugh even harder.

By the time he pulls into the side of Shoreditch High Street, we're both a bit hysterical. 'Jean-Luc is probably still in Camden. He has no sense of danger.'

I don't know Jean-Luc well enough to pass comment. 'I hope he's not really going to tell my mum what I've been up to. Normally I have a midnight curfew at the weekend.'

'Oh please! Nothing exciting in life ever happens before midnight.' Vic turns his head and grins roguishly. That pain in my heart is still niggling and Vic is so far out of my league that I'm languishing in the third division. But despite all that, he's very pretty and it's such a pity that for most of the evening his face has been obscured by either his shades or his helmet or both. 'Where to next?'

Who knew? There were a lot of clubs in Shoreditch. Lots of cool people milling about; the girls wearing cut-off dungarees or weird sack-like cocoon dresses, the boys also wearing cut-off dungarees with pork pie hats and dodgy beards. It's an older, hipper, way more up-itself vibe than I'm used to.

I take out my phone as Jean-Luc appears in the distance with a forlorn toot on his horn. 'Oh God, he's going to be mad. His shoulders look mad,' Vic says, but I can't spare a look for Jean-Luc's shoulders when I see that I have a text from Mark.

Babe. @ Shoreditch Working Men's Club. We got in, but massive queue. Ring me when u get here. Luv u xxx

I call Mark but his phone goes straight to voicemail and I hang up because I know that if I leave a message it will just be more whining.

'I can't get hold of Mark but there's probably no signal in the club,' I say to Vic and I show him Mark's text. 'What do I do now? We're never going to get in if the queue is that big.'

'Don't worry. I can get into any club. I laugh in the face of massive queues. I go, "Ha ha HA!" and then they unclip the rope and they let me walk in,' Vic says loftily as Jean-Luc comes to a halt beside us.

This isn't as comforting as Vic seems to think it should be. 'You're not drunk, are you? Or have you taken too much hay fever medication?'

71

'No, he always talks like that,' Jean-Luc says. He has to squeeze his words out of the tight thin line that used to be his mouth. 'Like, how do you say in English? A gigantic wanker.'

'You're so cruel,' Vic says to him and I wonder what their deal is. Up close, they're not identical like I first thought. They both have wild, dark hair and pale skin, but Vic's eyes are a lighter blue and he's altogether more twinkly. Maybe because he smiles so much, whereas Jean-Luc's eyes are the dark blue of school uniforms and storm-tossed seas and he absolutely doesn't twinkle. Mostly, he glowers. 'I don't know what I've done to deserve such cruelty.'

They are definitely related. 'Are you two brothers, then?'

It's my turn to get the glower. 'No. *Quelle horreur!* Cousins,' Jean-Luc says shortly. 'Not gay either, despite what people say. But yes, French. Or at least *I'm* French.'

'Hey, I'm French too!' Vic protests as he starts up his moped again.

'*À piene!* You left France when you were eight. You support Arsenal. Back home we call you *le rosbif*!' Jean-Luc grins a Vic-like grin and shoots off.

'I'll roast beef him,' Vic grumbles as he pulls away, and when he catches up with Jean-Luc he gives him the finger so the scooter lurches wildly and I have to dig him in the ribs.

'Please! Roast beef him later.'

The Shoreditch Working Men's Club is two minutes away and down a grimy alley hidden between a bookies and a kebab shop. I don't think many working men hang out there any more, if the queue that snakes back down the alley and past the bookies is anything to go by. Although I do spot two girls in boiler suits and a boy wearing a Maccy D uniform, but I think it's meant to be ironic.

I don't really understand irony.

And Vic doesn't understand the concept of queuing. 'No time for this. Errant boyfriends to be found and all that.' He grabs my hand and marches us to the front, Jean-Luc trailing behind and muttering about the British and how we love to queue.

I would have much preferred to wait in line instead of pushing in and having everyone stare at us with eyes like razor blades. 'Um, I can probably take it from here,' I say, even though I probably can't. 'Honestly, I'll be fine.'

'*Ce n'est rien*,' Jean-Luc murmurs and he actually smiles at me. It looks odd, like his face isn't made for smiling. The angular lines of his face and his sulky lips are built for brooding, glaring and scowling. 'I could not look at your mother ever again if you were found dead in a skip.'

'Well, I suppose there's that,' I say and then walk smack into Vic's back because he's come to a sudden stop.

'Oh shit!' he says. 'Change of plan. Let's go! Away. Far away from here.'

He backs up, almost trampling me in the process, and suddenly an ear-piercing voice chimes out, 'Not so fast, French boy! You get your lanky arse over here, right now!'

I look past Vic to see a Valkyrie of a girl on the door, flanked by two bouncers with rippling muscles and earpieces. She's a Marvel superhero in a tight leopard-print dress. She has long red hair, sculpted and surprised eyebrows under a short fringe and a look of utter fury on her beautiful face as she points a red-tipped finger at Vic.

'Me?' Vic points at himself. 'You want to talk to me?'

'Don't make me come and get you!' I have visions of her stomping over to us in her spike heels, bashing Vic over the head with her clipboard, then seizing a handful of his hair and dragging him back to her doorstep eyrie.

The huge queue of scenesters, club kids and fashion victims perk up no end. Everyone's looking at Vic as he unwillingly stumbles towards the door as if he has no control over his own feet. It wouldn't surprise me if this girl has put a hex on him.

Jean-Luc and I follow behind. Jean-Luc's smiling again. A slightly evil, gleeful smile as if he already knows the punchline. 'What's so funny?' I ask him.

He shakes his head. 'You'll see.'

What I see is the girl leaning forward to snap her fingers in Vic's face. He holds up his hands in surrender. 'Now, Audrey, *chérie, ma belle, mon amour, ma petite fleur*, I can explain,' he says, his accent suddenly very French as if he just stepped off the Eurostar that morning. 'This is all a terrible misunderstanding.'

'Don't try and French-talk your way out of this,' she snaps. 'Someone told me that you're not even French. Like, you support Arsenal!'

'I am French!' Vic again looks horrified at the suggestion that he isn't. 'For God's sake! You can support Arsenal and still be French.'

'Whatever!' The girl whips her head back to quell the small group of people trying to reason with the bouncers and gain admittance while her attention is elsewhere. 'Don't even think about it! Get back in line or I'll ban you for life. I never forget a face.'

74

She makes being a badass into an art form. I totally want to be her when I grow up.

She turns back to Vic. 'And I never forget a no-good bastard who doesn't call, doesn't text . . .'

'Oh chérie, I lost your number . . .'

'I put my number in your phone. You watched me do it.' She puts her hands on her hips. With her skyscraper heels and the step she's on, she's perfectly positioned to stare down at Vic like he's some particularly disgusting form of mouth-breathing pond life.

'I lost my phone!'

'And I must have lost my mind to let you charm my pants off with those little chocolate tarts you whipped up and the way you kept saying stuff in French. You *murmured* in French. That shouldn't be allowed.'

'I can't be blamed for speaking in my mother tongue.' Vic lowers his eyes and places his hands in the prayer position as if he's on the side of the angels. The effect is quite devastating. '*Je suis vraiment désolé.*'

'Oh my God! You're doing it again! You just can't help yourself, can you, Jean-Luc? Stop saying words with your stupid sexy French accent.'

There's a strange hissing sound from where Jean-Luc stands next to me. '*Incroyable!*' he suddenly explodes. 'You've been using my name? Again? *Ça va pas la tête?*'

Vic cowers away from the double-pronged attack. 'Of course I'm not crazy!' He turns back to Audrey. 'Don't listen to him. He doesn't understand much English. He hardly knows what he's saying.'

'I know how to say gigantic wanker!'

'My God, just what kind of evil are you? You didn't even give me your real name?' Audrey holds up her clipboard. I think she might bash Vic over the head with it for real. To be honest, he kind of does deserve it but we're running out of time.

'Um, he's no good. He has all sorts of emotional problems,' I squeak, and suddenly I have Audrey and the whole queue's attention. I have never been more aware of just how much my shorts keep riding up my thighs. 'We're getting him help. Medication, therapy, that sort of thing.'

'If that doesn't work, we plan to lock him up for a long time,' Jean-Luc adds. 'A very, very long time.'

Vic spreads his hands wide. 'Obviously I'm not to be trusted around beautiful women. My common sense, it just disappears, and –'

'*Mon dieu!* Not another word!' Jean-Luc steps forward, but he doesn't try to do anything smarmy like smile winsomely at Audrey or take her hand, though chances are she'd smack him if he did. 'I'm Jean-Luc. This . . . this imbecile is my cousin, Vic. Let's pretend he doesn't even exist. And this is . . .' He ushers me forward.

'I'm Sunny and I'm trying to find my boyfriend . . .' I start to say but the door opens to let out some sweaty-looking clubbers and the queue surges forward. Audrey holds up her clipboard, like a shield.

'Order! Order!' she shouts. She has a very Khaleesi vibe about her. It wouldn't surprise me to see three pet dragons circling above us. Audrey scans the hopeful, expectant faces lifted towards her. 'You, you, you. No, not you, no beards. And definitely you in the green. Love your frock, darling.'

The four chosen ones scurry quickly through the door as if they expect Audrey to change her mind at the last moment. Then she beckons me with one imperious finger. I trudge forward. It feels like a summons from my great-grandma who always used to make me come close enough that she could examine my hair or my clothes or my complexion and then give them a yay or a nay. Usually a nay. 'Sunny, right?' Audrey confirms. 'Missing boyfriend, so you're not . . . with either of them?'

Jean-Luc and Vic are nose to nose and arguing in French again. 'No! They're just helping me find him. They're friends with my mum.' How pathetic! To talk about parents to someone as awesome as Audrey. She'd probably arrived on earth after hitching a ride on a shooting star.

'Urgh! I would never let my mum choose my friends. She'd want me to hang out with born-again Christians who are really into singing madrigals.' Audrey tosses a couple of stray red curls over her shoulder. 'What are you doing with that broom?'

I look at the broom still clutched in my hand. It's not even a cool, old-skool wooden broom. 'Oh well, I had this barbecue and some of my friends got drunk and set our broom on fire so one of them bought me a new one. Well, see, my mum's coming back from her holiday tomorrow and she'll be all like, "What happened to the broom?" so, y'know, new broom.'

Audrey shakes her head like she doesn't even have words for how dull my story and my life are. 'Now, about this boyfriend.'

I try to keep it brief. Stick to the point. Because, Vic notwithstanding, I can't believe that Audrey is the kind of girl who would ever let a boy even *think* about kissing another girl. Not that Mark thought much about it. According to him, it just happened all sudden-like.

I don't keep it brief. It all comes streaming out in a messy gush of words and I end up showing her Mark's latest text as I try to explain that: 'I thought we were cool, that it was all sorted out, but now every time we make an arrangement, he goes off with his friends and I don't even know if *that* girl is still hanging around. He's being elusive. Why would he be elusive if he had nothing to hide?'

'Darling, I hate to break it to you but he sounds like a dick,' Audrey tells me kindly. 'And he said he was inside? In *my* club?'

I nod and show Audrey a photo of Mark. Not *the* photos. I can't bear to look at them again. 'Do you recognise him? He must have got into the club about half an hour ago. Said he was on the guest list, but the list closes after eleven.'

Audrey perfectly arches one already perfectly arched eyebrow. 'Firstly, I'm in charge of the guest list and I don't put random people on it. Secondly, what would be the point of a guest list that closes at eleven? Nothing fun ever happens before one in the morning at the earliest. And thirdly, does he always wear his jeans like that?'

'Like what?'

'Like some sad R&B singer from ten years ago,' comes Audrey's crushing reply. 'So everyone can see his pants. I would *never* let him into my club. Never.'

'What if he'd pulled his jeans up so you couldn't see his pants?'

'I never forget a face. Honestly, Scotland Yard should use my services. Oh, sweetie, cheer up!' I can feel my face drooping, smile turning upside down. 'London's tiny. It is. You'll find him. Though I'm not sure why you'd want to.'

When she puts it like that, neither do I. Mark should have been waiting for me, with chocolates and a bunch of over-priced flowers bought from a garage. He shouldn't expect me to run myself ragged trying to catch up with him.

'He is being a bit of a dick, isn't he?' I'm not even admitting it to Audrey but to myself. I feel my heart, shoulders and smile sink.

Audrey sighs. 'I hope, really hope, you are going to make his sorry arse beg for forgiveness.' She peers at my face. 'No. Maybe you're not there yet.' She sighs again and pulls out her phone, which has been nestling in her cleavage all this time. 'Text me that photo, then I'll send it out to every door girl I know. I'll text you back with any leads.'

'That's so kind of you. If there's anything I can do to . . .'

'Well, if you're hanging out with Mr 'I'm Going to Murmur Things in French', maybe you could slip some laxatives into his drink when he's not looking. Or push him into the path of a bus. Something like that. I'm not fussy.'

'Oh, why are we waiting? Why are we waiting? Why are we waiting?'

The queue is getting impatient.

'I'd better get on. The natives are restless.' Audrey put her hands on her hips. 'I can't let anyone else in until people come out! It's against health and safety.'

The crowd jeers its disapproval. Audrey claps her hands to shut them up. 'I can also ban the whole lot of you for life. I have that power! Don't make me wield it,' she shouts as I head back to Vic and Jean-Luc who have stopped arguing and jostling but have turned their backs on each other.

'I refuse to speak to him,' Jean-Luc announces. 'Not until he apologises for his deplorable behaviour.' It's like he learned to speak English with the help of a textbook written in Victorian times.

All three of us are at a dead end. Mark's trail has gone cold. He's lied about where he is and what he's doing and I haven't even started processing this new hurt and Jean-Luc says that he's almost out of petrol.

'Let's go back to ours,' Vic says.

'Maybe I should just go home.' The urge to eat ice cream and cry on Gretchen Weiner is back, stronger than ever. 'Yeah, I should really go home.'

'No, you come to our unit,' Jean-Luc says in a firm voice, steering me to his scooter with an even firmer hand. 'Then I shall drive you home in the van.'

It occurs to me that I know hardly anything about Vic or Jean-Luc. Yes, they are charming and French but they could be charming and French murderers and I really don't fancy being murdered. Then again, I really don't fancy finding my own way home either, so I let myself be steered.

We get back on the scooters and ride up Kingsland Road, then down another tiny alley, which opens up into a small courtyard.

It's the other side of London, where the shadows live; not as pretty as the other bits. Not as exciting. Here the backs of

80

buildings loom, jutting out at odd angles and studded with rickety fire escapes and huge ventilation units. There are two guys in grubby chef whites smoking by an open door. I hope they wash their hands before they go back to work.

'This is us,' Vic says and points to a metal door with 'KIM IS A SLAG' painted on it in crude white letters. It opens up to reveal a small but surprisingly pristine kitchen where I suppose they make their legendary tartlets. There's a little lock-up to the side too where they stash their mopeds while I pull out my phone charger from my bag, plug it into the nearest socket and take great whiffs of the air. It smells of sugar and chocolate, with just the faintest hint of cheese and coffee.

I realise I'm quite hungry and I perk up when Vic opens a huge, old-fashioned fridge, which makes a strange stuttering sound as it hums along as if one more pint of milk or packet of butter placed inside might finish it off all together.

He pulls out a plastic tub, takes off the lid and waves it temptingly in front of me. 'Mini quiche?'

Terry always says that real men don't eat quiche, but I'm not a man so I take one. Then I take another. And one more, because Vic keeps holding out the tub. I think he knows he's been a very, very bad man what with the whole Audrey business and impersonating Jean-Luc, because he doesn't say anything but starts making coffee while Jean-Luc fusses with his hair in the mirror over the sink.

It's all become quite awkward. What with the two of them not talking and me not knowing them well enough to make them hug it out.

Then my phone beeps and I get that now familiar panicky, pukey feeling that it might be Mark, but it's Emmeline.

U alrite? Did u dump Mark? Not sure ur at home. Am on nightbus. Going 2 club in town. Call me if u want. Hugs, Em xxx

I so want. I so do.

'Sunny! Are you all right? How much ice cream have you eaten?'

I jump down from my stool, take the tiny, teeny cup of espresso Vic offers me and wander out into the yard. 'I'm not at home! I've been trying to find Mark.'

'Oh, have you?' Emmeline sounds like it's taking all her powers of restraint not to shout at me. 'Please tell me it's so you can kick his arse.'

'Hmm, not exactly. It's not as black and white as that.' There's nothing for it but to sing her my sad song about my futile odyssey around North and East London for a boyfriend who slips from my fingers each time he's almost within my grasp.

'God, where does he get off screwing you around?' Emmeline shouts at one point, but mostly she manages to stay quiet until I come to the end. 'He kissed another girl. I saw the photos! She's kissing him and he's kissing her right back, and then he has the nerve to play you. Not cool, Sunny. Not cool.'

'I know, but he explained about all that and I'd have been fine with it, mostly, except now with him disappearing on me, I'm not fine. I think I'm actually starting to get quite cross.'

'I can't bear to talk about Mark for even a second longer,' Emmeline groans. 'Let's skip to the part where you've been hanging out with the Godards, shall we? So, what are they like? Are they nice or are they really up themselves? They look like they'd be up themselves. Arty boys usually are.'

'I thought you were gay,' I say to her. 'Why do you care?'

'That doesn't mean I can't appreciate the male form on an aesthetic level. Plus, Lucy says they're funny. But she's not sure if they actually mean to be funny. Anyway, like, now that you've experienced them close up, what would –'

'What about Mark? What should I do now? Go home or . . .'

'Well, if you're up, miles from home and drinking coffee, come clubbing with us, or else you could wait for a lead and then track Mark down but only if you promise me that you're actually going to stand up to him and . . . What's that?' I hear Emmeline say to someone, then a lot of excited squeals. 'Hey, Sunny, so, like, I'm going to put you on speakerphone . . . Now, how tall would you say the Godards are?'

I hear a general rumble of amusement in the background from whomever Emmeline's with. It sounds like the whole of the London roller girl squad. 'Well, I'm five seven and I've got to look up, if you know what I mean, but it's not about how tall they are.' I grin. I can't help it. I know what it's like to have a crush on a boy. To see him and immediately a grey, blah kind of day transforms into an amazing day bursting with possibility, the kind of day where anything could happen. To memorise every one of his smiles and replay them on long bus journeys or when you're in bed and drifting off to sleep, wondering if he had a smile that you hadn't seen yet, one that would be yours and yours alone.

God, I'd spent so long with that calibre of crush on Mark until he took me out of my daydreams and made them real. Like, my first day back at school after I'd had the norovirus. I'd still been feeling like I might throw up if I went within five hundred metres of the dining hall and caught a whiff of institutional mince, so I'd been cowering on a bench next to the playing field.

Then Mark and Archie had walked past in their footie gear and Mark had smiled at me. 'You all right, Sunny?' he'd asked and he'd carried on walking, not even waiting for my reply, but that smile, his noticing me, had felt like a jolt of adrenalin straight to the heart and suddenly I'd felt as if I could have run a marathon.

Maybe the reality never lived up to the feelings. Oh, those wonderful, tummy-flipping feelings . . .

'Sunny? You still there? What do you mean when you say it's not about how tall they are?' Emmeline asks. 'What is it about then?'

I shove all thoughts of Mark away and I grin again. 'It's about how *lean* they are, how messy their hair is, how French they might be.'

I wasn't crushing on either of them. Not when I was hoping that I still had a boyfriend. Anyway, memorising their smiles was as pointless as wishing on the moon. It wasn't just Vic who was out of my league, Jean-Luc was too. They were in a league populated by girls who looked like Audrey, who wore slinky dresses and high heels and danced like nobody was watching when actually everybody was watching because they were beautiful, free spirits. Girls like that.

I could never be a girl like that. Not sure I would want to be either. It seems like a lot of pressure, plus I can't walk in heels.

'So they are French, then?' Someone who isn't Emmeline wants to know.

'Technically. Well, Jean-Luc is. He only came to London last year. Vic says he's French too, but he's lived in London for ages so I think he's had to give back his official Frenchness certificate or something.'

'It sounds like you're having all the fun,' Emmeline says as I hear a noise behind me, and standing in the doorway of their little lock-up kitchen are both Vic and Jean-Luc, each holding a tiny espresso cup, their faces in shadow so it's impossible to know how long they've been standing there listening to me speculate on their Frenchness and, oh God, their *leanness* and . . . 'You all right, Sunny? You just moaned like you're in pain.'

'No, I'm good,' I mumble and my skin is so hot with shame that it's a wonder that I don't spontaneously combust. 'I wouldn't say I was having all the fun. Still can't find Mark, can I?'

'If you're round that way, maybe try the convenience store on Kingsland Road that has the raves,' the someone who isn't Emmeline says. Whoever they are, they're being very helpful. 'Every time I end up in there, I always bump into everyone I've ever known in my life, ever.'

'OK, I'll try that. What bit of Kingsland Road 'cause it's a pretty long road, isn't it?'

'Oh, you can't miss it.' Which actually wasn't that helpful at all.

'I'll text you when we get into town, which might be quite some time 'cause this nightbus is moving slower than the Ice Age,' Emmeline says.

I kind of want to stay on the phone for ever, which is ridiculous. But Emmeline hangs up and now I should walk over to Jean-Luc and Vic with my face still on fire.

I decide to stay where I am, so they're in shadow and I don't have to see them looking pissed off about me dissing their Frenchness, or worse – looking all arch and knowing and thinking that I fancy them.

I wave my espresso cup, then place it carefully down on the ground. 'Well, thanks for everything. I'm going to head off. Not actually going home now. There's a rave in a convenience store on the Kingsland Road. Maybe Mark's there. So, anyway, see you around, yeah?'

It was far better to face the collective wrath of the *garçons Godard* than walk down the Kingsland Road on my own, but I was making all sorts of bad decisions tonight and one more wouldn't make much difference.

'Don't be stupid!' Vic says, but I'm walking away – well, scurrying, if I'm being honest. I hear the sound of the big metal door of their unit closing, then I feel something bristly poke me between the shoulder blades.

'You forgot your broom,' Jean-Luc tells me. 'And your phone charger.'

'Don't you have something you'd rather be doing?' I ask, though I'm kind of relieved that I'm not on my own. 'I mean, it's Saturday night.'

'Saturday night is the new Sunday night,' Vic says and I don't even know what that means. 'I've never raved in a convenience store before and I like to try everything once. At least once. I mean, the night is young. We're young . . .'

'You're not that young,' Jean-Luc says. 'Sunny and I are younger. Much younger.'

'I'm twenty-one. That's young!'

'And I'm nineteen. I'll always be younger than you, old man,' Jean-Luc drawls.

'Yeah, says the boy who made me leave the picnic early because he wanted to come home and experiment with a new tartlet recipe involving chestnut paste. You're like a middle-aged housewife trapped in the body of a nineteen-year-old boy.'

'You're like an idiot trapped in the body of an idiot.'

They were arguing again, jostling again, and I have to tell them sharply to, 'Shut up and behave yourselves or I'm leaving you behind!'

I've never said anything that sharply before. It's like a huge leap for Sunkind. And it works. Vic and Jean-Luc stop arguing and we start walking.

THE HOT WING RAP

Written by Sunshine Williams and Emmeline Sweet

We need chicken
We need hot sauce
What we need
Ain't written in Morse (code)
Yo!

We like 'em spicy
We like 'em sticky
We eat so much
But we never get sicky
Yo!

Hot wings are neat
Hot wings are sweet
They give you a rush
That can't be beat

We love 'em eat-in
We love 'em on the go
We love 'em supersized
With fries on the side
Yo!

We got no time for breast or thigh
We ain't bothered about waiting in line
Got to get our fix or we will scream
Mouth on fire, we're living the dream
Yo!

Hot wings are neat
Hot wings are sweet
They give you a rush
That can't be beat

Hot wings! Hot wings! Hot wings!
(Repeat to fade)

MIDNIGHT

DALSTON

Dalston, in the London Borough of Hackney, takes its name from Deorlaf's tun, tun being a really, really olde English word for farm and Deorlaf being a name that never really caught on.

In around 1280, a leper colony was established in Dalston because it was out in the sticks, but by the eighteenth century it was a bustling suburban village. In 1880, the famous Ridley Road market started, which some say was the inspiration for the one in Albert Square in EastEnders *some one hundred years later.*

In 2009, the Guardian *decreed that Dalston was the coolest place to live in England but by 2011 Dalston was no longer cool, largely because Britney Spears filmed the video for her single 'Criminal' there.*

We turn the corner into Kingsland Road. It's a very, very long road that stretches from Hoxton, which is cool and hipstery and full of trendy bars and art galleries and raw food cafes that serve disgusting brightly coloured gloop made from locally sourced vegetables and seeds in jam jars, right up to Stoke Newington. Stoke Newington is full of middle-aged people who used to be cool and hipster-y and they think they still are, but they're totally not, even if they drink soy lattes in twee cafes strung with bunting and wear Ramones T-shirts.

My mum and Terry have a lot of friends who live in Stokey.

Anyway, we're not at the hip, arty, Hoxton end of Kingsland Road and we're not at the free-range, organic Stoke Newington end either. We're in Dalston, which is somewhere in the middle and it's actually kind of rough and bleak and there's lots of kebab shops and chicken shops and convenience shops that stay open all night.

Grizzled old men slump on the pavement, nodding off over cans of extra-strong lager. Three girls have a loud, shrieky fight with a lot of hair tossing and handbag hitting outside a minicab office. A gang of hoodies huddle and congregate on a corner, but they stop talking as we walk past.

Maybe it's because it's late and I'm wired from drinking espresso that tasted three times stronger than espresso should, but there's a sense of menace in the air and I'm glad I'm not on my own, even if the silence between us is awkward. Sort of spiky too.

'Don't be mad at me,' Vic suddenly says after three minutes of us not talking. 'That thing with Audrey. I can't help it.'

'Can't help what?'

'Don't even ask,' Jean-Luc mutters and I turn my head in time to catch his extravagant eye roll. 'Don't encourage him.'

'I can't help falling in love with beautiful women. I fall so easily and so hard. But there are so many beautiful women, Sunny, and another one comes along and I fall in love with her and then I forget about the beautiful woman I was already in love with. I don't mean to.' Vic shoots me a sidelong, sultry glance. 'I guess I have the soul of an artist or a . . . a poet knight . . . I guess I wasn't made for these times. I can't be in love with only one person at a time.' He sighs. 'It's just so plebeian.'

I don't really know what plebeian means – I think it's something do with being a bit pikey – but I know when someone is talking absolute utter bullshit.

'What*ever*!' I breathe and I forget that Vic is cool and sort of French and out of my league and mysterious. Those things don't really count when he's also being a massive tool. 'What a load of rubbish. You don't actually fall in love with them.'

'I do! One look, one smile, one snap of their fingers and I'm gone! My heart is theirs and theirs alone.'

'Until you see a prettier girl the next day and decide you want to sleep with her instead,' Jean-Luc says.

'So when you say "fall in love" what you really mean is "get into their pants?"' Typical! Boys are all the same. Total skeeves.

'You say potato, I say potarto. You say tomayto, I say tomarto,' Vic sings, like this is actually funny. 'Potato, potarto. Tomayto, tomarto. Let's call the whole thing off.'

Vic is no longer a sharp-suited enigma to me. He's starting to remind me of my little brother, Dan. Though Dan is only eleven, so he's got some time to go before he starts acting all skeeve-like, but he and Vic are both equally irritating. 'I am so close to smacking you right now,' I say.

Jean-Luc grins. 'That's a good idea. Do it. Go on. I won't stop you.'

'You don't understand what it's like to be ruled by your heart. To be a slave to your passion. A prisoner of your desires.' Vic draws himself up and sweeps out a hand to encompass his desires. He really is quite the drama queen. 'The problem with you British is that you're so cold. And you, Jean-Luc, you're too uptight.'

'I'd rather be uptight than *un imbécile ridicule* . . .'

'Actually, you're just being a player,' I say before they can have another jostling, snarky argument and also because this needs to be said and, for some bizarre reason, I've suddenly found the guts to say it. 'You can dress it up like what you're doing is beyond your control and that you're an incurable romantic, but really you're just hooking up with random girls. Then you don't even have the nerve to dump them. To say, "Oh, it was just a bit of fun, but let's not make this into anything more than it is." You don't even do that – you just disappear on them. It's well shady.'

'I don't do that!' Vic does a nifty quickstep that puts him in front of me so I have to come to a stop. 'It's a good thing to have a heart open to love.'

'Sounds like the only thing that's open is your flies,' I mutter. 'How do you think those girls feel when you give it all the chat, all those pretty words, sleep with them, then not even text? I bet each one of them feels like crap.'

'No! Sunny, no!' Vic tries to take my hand, but I yank it away from him. We're not talking about me and Mark. Not at all. But in different circumstances, if that girl hadn't turned up, if there'd been no kiss, I could be losing my virginity to Mark at this precise moment. So although I don't know what it's like to have sex with a boy – which is just about the most intimate thing you can do with another human being – and then get tossed aside, I'm beginning to understand what it's like to love someone who thinks of you as something less. Yeah, I know exactly what it's like to have a boy make you feel like shit.

Vic is still walking backwards in front of me. 'I only fall in love with girls who won't love me back. Believe me, they make that quite clear. I don't even get coffee or breakfast the next morning it's all, "Don't let the door hit you on the arse on your way out,"' he says. 'Most times we don't swap numbers so I can't text them. Audrey laughed when I asked for hers.'

'If I was a girl, I wouldn't give him my number,' Jean-Luc says. 'Look at his face! So untrustworthy!'

All this time, we've been making short work of the long, long stretch of Kingsland Road. But we still haven't cleared the dodgy-looking part and now I'm aware of three guys on bikes behind us. Like, really behind us. If I slowed down, I'd have tyre tracks down the backs of my calves.

I speed up. Vic and Jean-Luc speed up too, like we have some kind of hive mind thing going on, but maybe it's because they can hear the hissing too. Not so much hissing as a collective kissing of the teeth and that never leads to anything good.

'Yo! Why's a lighty hanging with a white boi?' Chills ripcurl down my spine. 'You too good for a brother?'

Jean-Luc stops, jaw tight. 'Don't say anything,' I whisper so quietly that I'm not sure he can hear me but then he takes my arm and Vic takes my other arm and we march down the road so fast that we almost skip.

'Yo, bitch! You wanna see what I'm packing? Once you go black, you never go back.'

Both Jean-Luc and Vic stop again. 'Come on!' I pull them along. I know it's not right for people to say those things. They might be black, but they're still being racist. Like all I am to them is the colour of my skin. Which I'm kind of used to but usually from the other side of the fence.

Still, both Mum and Dad agree that I should never engage when I'm in a tense situation. 'Walk on by,' Mum sings like Dionne Warwick because she always tries to inject a little light humour and musical stylings into her dire warnings, while Dad just lectures me on knife crime statistics.

Besides, someone at school's cousin was totally stabbed to death on the 29 bus when he tried to break up a fight. It was on the news and everything.

'Keep moving!' I force the words out between gritted teeth and they're riding in circles around us now, hoods pulled down low over their faces.

'Hey, baby girl, you want a real man?'

I can tell that we've now left the bad stretch of Kingsland Road because I see a guy with a pointy beard in a bowler hat riding a unicycle, but we're still being harassed by the hoodies who get nearer and nearer each time they cycle round us.

'Bitch, you need to suck on my dick!'

'*Assez! Ferme ta gueule!*' Jean-Luc snaps and he grabs the handlebars of the nearest bike. 'That's an unforgivable way to talk to someone.'

'Just leave it,' I whisper fiercely because his two friends have stopped and I wait for the flash of a blade, a pool of blood, but all six of us, three on one side, three on the other, are still. Watchful. Waiting.

'You should apologise,' Vic says thoughtfully. 'Then you should probably go home. How old are you anyway? Eleven? Twelve?'

I tense up, shoulders hitting my ears. Try to remember what I learned when I was earning my Brownies first-aid badge, though I don't think we covered multiple stab wounds.

'I'm not twelve. I's sixteen, innit.' He's indignant. Draws himself up to stand on his pedals. 'Course I am.'

'Bullshit,' Vic and Jean-Luc say in unison. They've picked a great time to get over their snit.

'Are you going to say sorry?' Jean-Luc asks. He and Vic are tall, wiry even, but they're pastry chefs and baristas by trade and I really don't fancy their chances. 'Or are we going to have to make you?'

'You can't make us do shit, man,' one of the others says but his voice is all squeaky like a) he really is eleven and b) he's secretly bricking it. 'You disrespect my blud and I cut you.'

'Yeah, right. If you were going to cut us, you'd have done it by now.' My God. That was me! Like my subconscious has decided it doesn't care about getting knifed. That it's fed up of doing nothing while I let yet more boys make me unhappy. Yay for my unconscious! Now it's my turn to draw myself up. 'For the record, I don't want anything to do with your penises, whatever colour they are. I mean, rude!'

'OK.' The smallest one immediately wilts like a week-old lettuce. His head hangs down. 'Sorry.'

96

Jean-Luc and Vic step off to the side like they know I've got this. That I have to deal with these three, if there's ever any hope that I might be able to deal with Mark when I finally catch up to him.

'Fuck that! I ain't saying sorry to no half-breed bitch,' the taller one spits and his two friends immediately shuffle their bikes away from him.

'Shut up!' one of them yelps and he gives me a wary side-eye, before he nods to his friend and they pedal off. 'We got to go now, innit.'

I hold out the broom in front of me, like it's an ancient fighting stick, and I can feel my hair ripple in the faint breeze and maybe for once in my life I'm being a bit of a badass. 'So, you calling a sister a half-breed bitch now, are you, bruv?'

'I ain't your bruv,' he says, but his voice has got all squeaky now too. I actually feel a little bit sorry for him. 'And I ain't apologising for shit.'

But not that sorry. 'Oh yeah, you're still a big man, even without your mates, aren't you?' I take a step nearer and I scrape his chest ever so gently with the bristly end of the brush. He gives a panicked cry, backs away onto the road and tries to do a wheelie but can't quite manage it.

'Bitch!' he shouts one last time as he pedals like his very life depends on it.

I turn back to Jean-Luc and Vic, who makes an 'I'm not worthy' gesture. 'I can't believe I just did that!'

'You know that we'd have been there if anyone went down,' Vic says. 'But you looked like you could handle it.'

'Yeah! I did handle it! One brush with my broom and he totally caved.' They fall into step beside me and we start walking

97

again. 'Just so you know, though, Vic, I still think you're a dick for the way you treated Audrey.'

'And I think you're a dick for giving girls my name. Despicable! Sunny, how do you say, er, *véreux*?'

'Er, you what?'

'You know, um, louche?'

'Oh, right! It's well shady. You knew you were doing something wrong, which is why you pretended you were Jean-Luc.'

'Well shady,' Jean-Luc says but it sounds ridiculous with a French accent, which Vic points out as we come across a crowd of people throwing serious shapes outside a convenience store that's pumping out deep, deep, *deep* house.

'At least I am French, not like you, *le rosbif*,' Jean-Luc is saying and they're obviously going to be at it for quite some time.

'This must be the place I was telling you about,' I say but they ignore me.

'For the last time, I am French! I'm as French as you are!'

'*N'importe quoi!*'

I leave them to get on with it and squirm my way through the people having it large outside. I can't quite believe what I'm seeing with my own eyes.

As advertised, it's a rave in a convenience store.

There are people queuing up at the counter to buy smokes and chewy and bottles of water, but in the aisles, amid the loo roll, the bags of crisps and packets of biscuits, and the cold cabinet full of milk and cans of fizzy pop and Polish sausages, people dance.

Like, really dancing. Like they're in a club with strobe lights and a smoke machine and the floor is heaving. Except they're dancing in a shop, under a flickering fluorescent strip, and having to sidestep people wanting a packet of Hobnobs and a jar of Nescafé.

There's even a DJ on the decks by an open doorway hung with plastic strips, which must lead to a stock-room.

It takes a while for my brain to buffer. Then I do a quick sweep of the store but Mark isn't here. I glance towards the counter and then I see *her* and my heart doesn't just sink, it plummets to the floor, then crawls somewhere to hide.

Sitting behind the till is Jeane Smith.

TV star. Newspaper columnist. Lifestyle blogger. Queen of Twitter. Empress of Instagram. Mad, bad and thoroughly obnoxious. I can't stand her.

She was two years above me at school, thank God she's left now, and she's friends with Emmeline, which means that even when she's talking to Emmeline, she ignores me. I haven't amassed enough cool points for someone like Jeane to acknowledge my right to breathe the same air as her.

But then again, Jeane has nearly a million followers on Twitter. She knows everybody. Or she knows everybody in London and I really need the services of somebody who knows everybody in London.

I pick up my heart, shove it back in my chest and join the queue at the counter.

Vic and Jean-Luc are still outside. They're jostling. Again. On a purely objective level, I can appreciate the hotness of the two of them jostling. I'm heartsore but not dead.

Then the couple in front of me pay for their Rizlas and a mountain of snacks because they're obviously going home to skin up. They *reek* of skunk. Just standing behind them is enough to get me second-hand stoned, but I'm not. I wish I were because it would be easier to act all cool and nonchalant as I smile at Jeane.

I say smile; what I mean is a forced facial grimace that I'm sure makes me look like a rhesus monkey. 'Hey, Jeane.'

'Hey,' she says, all narrow eyes and suspicion writ large, like I'm some kind of stalker when I don't even follow her on Twitter. I did but she didn't follow me back (not even after several three-way chats with her and Emmeline about everything from *The Great British Bake Off* to what Emmeline's roller derby name should be), so I unfollowed her. Like Jeane would even notice. 'What can I do you for, then?'

Maybe Jeane's career as a professional gobshite has crashed and burned because she seems to be working behind the till. I try another smile. I don't think I've ever despised myself more. 'We used to go to school together. I mean, you were two years ahead of me but, well, I'm best mates with Emmeline. You know, Roller Derby Emmeline.'

'Oh? Oh!' Jeane nods. She frowns. 'Hunny? Bunny?'

'Sunny!'

'Sunny!' says Vic's voice in my ear. He and Jean-Luc nudge past me. 'Get some chocolate, we'll get some crisps. Oh, Jeane! Looking quite lovely as ever.'

What I can see of Jeane, because most of her is obscured by the till, is wearing a blue check polyester overall. She also has most of her hair tied up in a scarf, but the hair I can see is aquamarine.

It's a whole lot of look.

I catch Jean-Luc's eye and his lips twist a crucial three millimetres. He waves at Jeane. '*Enchant*é,' he murmurs, then turns back to me. 'Crisps?'

'Doritos, if they've got them.'

'So, you're hanging out with the Godards,' Jeane says. 'How very interesting.'

'Not that intere—'

'You managed to find the only two boys in London with hair almost as big as yours. Your hair is really big,' she adds accusingly. 'I wish I could get my hair that big.'

If I had a pound for every time a white girl told me that she wanted hair like mine, then I'd have about a hundred and fifty pounds more in my Post Office savings account than I actually do.

'Actually, I only met them tonight. They're helping me find my boyfriend, Mark.' I thought I was becoming immune but just saying his name makes my insides lurch the same way they do when my mum texts me to tell me that we need to have 'a talk' when I got home. It's like my digestive tract has prophetic powers. Nothing signals doom, heartache and possibly being grounded like your stomach lurching.

It lurches now but Jeane just says, 'Yes, I know Mark. Boring. Emmeline loathes him. Says you could do so much better.'

It's nothing Emmeline hasn't said to me before but her taking those thoughts and sharing them with other people like Jeane makes my stomach lurch again. It's a minor violation of the girl code.

'Yeah, well . . .' I try to bluster, but the thing is, Emmeline was right about Mark. All those months when I'd pined for him from afar, she'd been all pursed lips and 'Really? Him?

101

You don't think he's kind of basic?' but I'd been too besotted to listen. Besides, Emmeline was gay, what did she know about what made a good boyfriend? A lot more than I do, it turns out. 'Maybe I can do better. But first I have to find Mark so I can . . . y'know. I'm going to find him and then . . .'

'And then what?' Jeane leans forward on her elbows and all but shoves her face into mine. 'Is this about those photos that did the rounds earlier?'

There's no point in trying to style it out. 'Yeah.'

'And you're totes going to kick him to the kerb, right? He cheat, he beat, he hit the street.' Jeane nods emphatically.

'He hasn't actually beat, but I think that maybe he might have cheat. He says that he hasn't but he's avoiding me and he wouldn't be doing that unless he knew he'd done something really, really . . .'

'Jesus! When you're done nattering, do you think you could actually serve someone?' snaps a man standing behind us. 'Haven't got all bloody night.'

Jeane gives a long-suffering sigh. She's really not cut out for customer service. 'Excuse me! A young girl's future happiness rests on the outcome of this conversation, thank you very much,' she says grandly and I turn round and I guess my face looks miserable enough that the man adjusts his heavy black framed, hipster-issue glasses and simmers down.

Jeane leans back and above the sound of the music she bellows, 'Frank! Can you take over for a bit?'

A good-looking Asian guy wearing surf shorts and an AC/DC T-shirt slides out from behind the decks and snake-walks down the aisle. 'I knew you'd get bored after ten minutes.'

'Not ten minutes. I stuck it for fifteen,' Jeane argues. 'Frank, this is Sunny, she has the biggest hair of anyone I know. Sunny, this is Frank, the genius who came up with the idea of having a club in his dad's shop. It's even been on TV!'

'Got a film crew coming from Tokyo next week too,' Frank says proudly as he shakes my hand, then looks past me. 'Right, who's next?'

Jeane steps out from behind the counter. I'd forgotten how small she is. Emmeline says she's stunted from never eating a single vegetable in her life. 'Why are you holding a broom?'

I start to tell Jeane why I'm holding the broom but I've only got as far as the barbecue part of the story when she holds up one stubby hand. 'Whatevs! Forget I asked. So anyway, back to your loser boyfriend. What are you going to do when you catch up with him?'

'Still haven't worked that one out,' I admit as we lean on the National Lottery stand. 'Hopefully, I'll launch into this amazing, heartfelt speech that makes him question his entire existence, or else he'll explain that sucking face with some . . . some *girl* pretty much just wearing knickers was all a big misunderstanding and then I'll forgive him because I'm completely ridiculous.' It was the truth. No wonder my stomach was lurching left, right and centre. 'Got to find him first, though.'

'Well, I can help you but only if you promise that you'll go with the first option, not the one where you roll over and play dead,' Jeane says sternly even as she holds her phone aloft.

Maybe I have been wrong about her. Though I haven't been wrong about how bossy she is. 'I'm not like you. The right words never make it from my brain to my mouth.'

Jeane shakes her head. 'Your hair is so fierce. You need to be more like your hair. Wow! Now there's a blog post. Hair as role model, discuss.'

'Jeane, not everything in life happens so you can blog about it,' I tell her, because my failures are my failures and not to be shared with the gazillion people who hang on Jeane's every word.

'That's more like it! I knew you had to have at least a little bit of edge to you,' she says. 'Now, I'll text my trusted peeps group and put an APB out on Mark. Bet we can find him wherever he is.'

'Oh! Would you? That's so kind!'

'Don't gush, Sunny. No one likes a gusher,' she says as her thumb moves over her phone screen at a speed that's hard to fathom.

I'm saved from thinking of something else really edgy to say to her because all the people dancing have suddenly stopped and instead are all clapping wildly and going 'wooh, yeah!'

I look round to see, oh sweet baby Jesus, Vic on top of the freezer compartment doing . . . I'm not even sure what he's doing. I think it's the Running Man. On steroids. His legs look spindlier than ever, especially when he keeps clutching an ankle on every third step. And his arms. Oh my days! They're pumping away like he's in a little rowing boat being chased by pirates.

He keeps pursing his lips and I can't decide if this makes Vic cooler than he already was or if he's dropped about ninety million cool points. One thing I do know: it's impossible to stay mad at someone who's doing the Running Man on top of a freezer unit.

Vic sees me grinning, waves and finishes off with a fancy little spin that any boybander would be proud of before he jumps down. 'Your turn,' he shouts. 'Come on, Sunny!'

'No, no, no!' I shake my head. I don't dance. Well, I do dance on proper dancefloors with my mates. Then I dance. But not here. Not now.

Except, everyone is looking at me. Clapping their hands. They don't even know me, but they've taken up the chant and now fifty strangers with nothing to do on a Saturday night but have it large in a convenience store all know my name.

'Sunny! Sunny! Sunny! Sunny! Sunny!'

I look to see if there's any way to make a run for the door, but of course there isn't because everyone's standing in a circle around me.

There's nothing else for it. I'm going to do it. I'm going to be fierce. 'Take this,' I say to Jean-Luc and hand him the broom.

Then I slowly advance into the centre of the shop.

'Sunny! Sunny! Sunny! Sunny! Sunny!'

I shut my eyes, take a deep breath and then I do a clumsy two-step shuffle and manage to kick the guy standing behind me. I come to the grindingest of halts.

'Come on, Sunny! You can do it, girl!' I'm back to hating on Vic, but then the music changes to something a little less deep and bassy and a bit more melodic and beat-y.

I do another two-step shuffle and I realise that I need to put all my faith in my legs and hope that they don't let me down.

I kick out my legs, arms pinned to my sides, and it's all a bit *Riverdance* but there are a few encouraging cheers now that it's clear I'm not going to wimp out. And I can do this.

I did seven years of dance: tap and modern, jazz and even a little ballet, until I decided I'd rather have a lie-in on a Saturday morning.

That's seven years spent training for this moment. I take another deep breath, and I start to click my fingers to the beat and OK, all right, apparently I'm doing the Charleston. Not just that bit where you cross your knees over, but the kicks and the arms, a bit of cakewalk and it's scary, but then it's not scary at all. It's kind of joyous and freeing to dance with everyone watching and 'wooh, yeah!'ing and 'you go, girl!'ing, because my body can do all sorts of incredible things to the music when I tell my brain to just shut the hell up.

If only my old dance teacher, Stacey, could see me now. She used to spend Saturday mornings bellowing in my face, 'Stop overthinking it! Move your feet! Faster, Sunny, faster! It's a foxtrot not a tortoise trot!'

Now I'm Ginger Rogers. I'm Josephine Baker. I'm Baby in *Dirty Dancing*. I'm a quicksilver sprite of a girl, whirling and turning until a boy I don't know suddenly glides into the circle and he matches my steps perfectly so we're dancing side by side in perfect harmony for what feels like for ever but is probably only a couple of minutes until I have to concede defeat and come to a panting, breathless halt.

The circle closes around my partner and I bend over, hands on my knees, and wait for my heart to stop hammering.

Someone presses something cool against my back.

It's Jean-Luc with a bottle of water that's about as welcome as, well, a bottle of cold water on a filthy hot August night when you've been dancing the Charleston in a crowded shop without any air con. 'Your turn next?' I manage to gasp. 'You can't let Vic outdance you.'

He shudders. His top lip curls. Eyes widen. 'I think you'll find that I can. Besides, I only waltz. You can't do the waltz in a store that sells Pop-Tarts. C'est une abomination!'

'Oh I'm sure you can,' I say and I swear Jean-Luc winks at me a split second before settling his features back into a medium-strength scowl. 'If you really put your mind to it.'

'Sunny! Girl, you got the moves!' Vic moonwalks over and gives me the finger gun. 'We should go proper dancing one night. Big band, you in a sparkly dress, me in a penguin suit.'

'Oh, so I'm going to be one of those lucky girls that you do keep in contact with then?' Dancing the Charleston and letting the music drown out the sound of the doubting voice in my head is giving me another shot of badassness straight to the heart.

'Sunny, you wound me,' Vic simpers. He clutches his hands to his chest. 'To the very core.'

'I've forgiven you for being a skeeve but you're on probation.'

I'm moist in all kinds of places where I don't want to be moist and my hair is wilting as I glug down the water in one long, glorious gulp. As soon as I'm done, Jeane beckons us over with a click of her fingers. She waves her phone.

'Your horrible boyfriend has been spotted in a chicken shop two minutes away,' she announces cheerfully. 'If I were you I'd throw hot sauce in his stupid, cheating face.'

'Don't throw hot sauce in his stupid cheating face,' Jean-Luc murmurs. 'It might blind him and then you'll be arrested by the flics.'

107

It seems from that advice that Jean-Luc isn't going to come with me and that's really all right. I can fling the hot sauce that are my angry words at Mark and then get the nightbus home, but Vic nods his head at Jean-Luc who nods his head too and raises his eyebrows and they're right by my side as I reach out to take Jeane's phone so I can see the text that says Mark is 'wit crowd of vile rah-rahs in chicken shop on Kingsland Rd, next 2 dodgy sauna.'

I have a very vague idea of where the chicken shop is. My mum had once gone to a party at Shoreditch House and got so drunk afterwards that, according to Terry, she'd banged on the door of a dodgy sauna and asked if they could give her a quick rubdown and then she'd gone into the chicken shop next door and asked how many chips she could have for a fiver. Way to keep it classy, mum.

'OK,' I say in a voice that sounds like I'm going to be kicking arses and taking down names. 'Er, so, um, would it be all right if you take my number in case you get any more texts?'

'Course it is,' Jeane says. 'I've just followed you on Twitter too, even though you're not following me. I don't know what *that's* all about.'

'Well, it's just –'

'I like you, Sunny,' Jeane makes it sound like a papal decree. 'When I saw you dancing I realised that I was completely wrong about you, which is weird 'cause I'm hardly ever wrong about people.'

'You make snap judgements about people all the time!' says someone behind me and I turn round to see Michael Lee, who'd also been two years ahead of me at school and was now at Cambridge studying something deeply brainy and *still* going out with Jeane, apparently. When they'd got together, it had been all that anyone at school had talked about for, like, months. 'Based on the most flimsy of evidence.'

'Just because I make snap judgements doesn't mean my judgements are wrong,' Jeane says as she plucks my phone out of my hand and puts her number in my contacts without even waiting for my permission.

'Wrong more times than you're right.' Michael Lee smiles at me in a vague we-know-each-other-but-I-can't-remember-your-name-and-I-don't-want-to-embarrass-either-of-us-so-a-smile-will-have-to-do way. 'I've kept a score if you want to see it.'

As we leave the shop, I hear Jeane squawk, 'No, you haven't. Have you? You'd better not have.'

FIFTEEN MINUTES LATER

Turns out there are three chicken shops on Kingsland Road in the vicinity of dodgy saunas.

They're all heaving. It's Saturday night. It's twenty to one. If you're going home, or going on somewhere else, you're going to need some chicken, definitely some fries and a really icy-cold drink in a cup larger than your head.

When we get to the last one, right next door to a dodgy sauna, I try to put on my fight face. I pouf up my hair, then clench my fists. But it's no good. It's been hours since I had a tuna-mayo baguette for lunch and since then I've only had two tartlets and three mini quiches. I have an ache that's less about my heart and my pride and more to do with the fact that I'm starving. My stomach *literally* thinks that my throat's been cut.

Besides, Mark isn't in the last chicken shop. In a way, tonight is like a metaphor for our entire relationship. This is our thing: I tag along behind Mark, but I'm never quite able to keep up with him.

But then I think about riding pillion on scooters and seeing off rude boys and dancing the Charleston and I think that Mark has never seen the best of me.

Anyway, I need hot wings. Extra-hot hot wings. With hot sauce. The Godards are appalled. 'The chicken isn't even free-range,' Vic tells me in a scandalised voice as I join the back of the long, straggly, shouty queue. 'How do you even know it's chicken?'

'The hot sauce . . . it's full of, how do you say, Vic? *Produits chimiques?*'

'Chemicals,' Vic grimly translates. 'E numbers. And the chicken is injected with water and hormones and antibiotics and God knows what else.'

'Stop trying to harsh my hot-wing mellow.' I thrust my shoulders back in annoyance. 'Are you ordering anything?'

'*Mais non!*'

'Never!'

'Well, I am, so just . . . just go and find a seat and leave me to my fast-food shame.'

It takes ages to reach the front of the queue. Ages until I have my hands on a box full of piping hot, possibly carcinogenic, hot wings and chips and a 7UP that really is as big as my face because I press it against my cheek as I fight my way out of the queue and look around for Vic and Jean-Luc.

110

There are tables and chairs on either side of the shop. The queue snakes between them and out of the door. It's noisy and chaotic, everyone yelling and pushing. A group of girls in tiny dresses and nosebleed heels gather round one of their friends and press tissues on her. 'He's a wanker,' I hear one of them say as I squeeze past. 'Never liked him anyway. Oh my God, you can do *so* much better.'

Jean-Luc and Vic have found a table right next to the door. Not just a table. Vic has crashed into his own personal heaven. There are already four girls sitting there but when I say girls, I mean four superhero-goddess-vixens, because Vic has a type and it's girls with legs like Victoria's Secret models. Girls with sass and style, and these four have sass and style up the wazoo. They're the kind of girls whose make-up – all contouring and thick, elegant sweeps of eyeliner and glossy lipstick – doesn't melt in the heat. Girls who can sit in a chicken shop wearing, like, evening gowns as if that was a perfectly all right thing to wear in a chicken shop.

'Oh, there you are,' Jean-Luc says and they all look at me with my wilting hair and my wet cheek from where I pressed my drink against it and I can tell that my shorts have ridden up *again* and the black and white stripy tee I'd started off the evening in is now more black and grey. 'You can have my chair.'

There's no way I'm eating food in front of these four goddesses. Especially not hot wings, which will end up smeared over my face. In fact, now I'm not sure if I even want to eat them in front of Vic and Jean-Luc.

'Or you can sit on my lap,' Vic says and he pats his knees and waggles his eyebrows like a pervy uncle.

I forget about the four goddesses. 'In. Your. Dreams,' I snap and take the chair that Jean-Luc is offering me. 'Thank you.' It's not enough to get me to open my box of hot wings, but I can wait. They'll go soggy, but I've eaten worse things than soggy hot wings.

Two of the girls murmur at each other as they stare intently at a phone, but the one nearest to me, whose platinum hair is so sleek and shiny that I wonder if it's real, smiles at me. 'Girl, you fierce,' she says in a voice that's a lot deeper than I expect. 'Gotta treat the pretty boys like dirt otherwise they gonna walk all over you like a Nancy Sinatra song. You dig?'

I get it! Hello! Not that it was my fault, but it's way past my bedtime and the lights are so bright and everything is so sharp and loud and hyper-real. But I should have known. Emmeline and I have *RuPaul's Drag Race* marathons each time we have a sleepover. These girls are guys dressed up as goddesses. Drag queens. Like women, but a little bit more.

I could say that I do dig, except usually I did let the pretty boys walk all over me like a Nancy Sinatra song and also I was slipping back into the Sunny who could do nothing but smile gormlessly, jaw agape. Because I am like a woman, but a little bit less.

'Oh sweetie, no need to look so scared. None of us bites,' says the person sitting opposite. She (Emmeline and RuPaul both say that it's only polite to use the female pronouns if the person you're talking about chooses to identify as a woman. Even if they might have a penis. Gender politics has a lot of rules. I can never remember all of them) is mixed race like me and she's wearing a silver sequinned shift dress and has a massive black beehive. It has to be a wig or a weave 'cause I know black-girl hair doesn't do stuff like that, but either way she's serving up some serious retro-glam realness. 'What are you doing with the broom?'

I can't even. 'It's a really long story,' I say. 'A very long, very boring story.'

'Best to skip it then. Now, you gonna share your fries with a sister or are we going to be having words?'

'What? Huh?' I shake my head to try to put my brain cells back in the right place. 'Yeah, sorry.'

I open my box of hot wings, then tear open the paper bag and spill out my fries. I didn't want to share them, but now I've suddenly gone all shy again. I hate when that happens.

I also hate the hands that descend on my food especially when two of the hands are French and they're aiming straight for my hot wings. Outrage makes my shyness melt away like spit on a pair of hot hair straighteners. I slap both the hands. 'Get off my hormone-enhanced chicken that's stuffed full of chemicals, you utter pair of hypocrites,' I tell them.

Jean-Luc looms over me. 'I gave you my seat,' he reminds me and tries to smile winsomely like he's been picking up tips from Vic who's giving me the first-gen version of the same smile. 'Anyway, if I eat a hot wing, then it's less hormones and er, *les produits chemique* for you to eat. I'm doing you a favour, *non*?'

'*Non!* And you can *non* too, Vic.' I snatch up a hot wing and wave it at him accusingly. He squeals at the thought of getting hot sauce on his white shirt, which is still doing a good job of staying blindingly white. 'You said you only eat free-range chicken.'

'I never said that. I just pointed out, as a friend, that the chicken here wasn't free range.' He sniffs plaintively. 'It does smell rather good for non-free-range chicken.'

113

'That will be the hot sauce with all *les produits chemique* in it,' I say and the, er, lady with the beehive and her friends grin.

'And she's back in the room,' she says. 'I'm Shirelle, this is Ronette, Shangri-La and Vandella. We're named after the four greatest Sixties girl groups.'

'No Supremes or Chiffons?' I ask because my mum hasn't met a Sixties girl group that she didn't love.

Vandella, who has a huge brown bouffant and has to be wearing two sets of false eyelashes, holds up one glittery-nailed hand. 'Oh honey, please! Who cared about the other two Supremes when Diana Ross was up front?'

'Actually, the reason that we don't have a Chiffon is because then we'd have three names beginning with a sh- sound and one Ronette,' Shangri-La, the platinum blond, explains. 'That wouldn't work.'

'Well, there was The Shaggs, though I s'pose Shagg isn't a very glamorous name,' I say and they all shudder and agree and I decide that I'm not going to be judged for eating hot wings in front of them, so I do, while Jean-Luc and Vic and our new friends talk about Sixties girl singers and how there were lots of amazing French girl groups in the Sixties and that it was a sacrilege that the rest of the world didn't know about them.

'*Un sacrilège!!*' Jean-Luc shouts at intervals. He's been dipping fries in hot sauce and I think the spice has gone to his head.

I catch Shirelle's eye and we both giggle. 'So, pretty girl, what flavour are you? I've got an Irish dad and a Trinidadian mum. Both Catholic. Lot of talk of hellfire when my grandmas get together.' She rolls her eyes. 'I used to dress up as a nun called

Sister Eviline. Trinidadian grandma thought it was hilarious. Irish grandmammy, not so much.'

'I'm Jamaican on my dad's side. My great-grandparents came over in the Fifties. Then on my mum's side, they're very middle-class, middle-England types. My grandma had a fit when Mum got pregnant in her second year at university and when she found out my dad was black she took to her bed for a week.'

'Oh God, no offence, sweetie, but she sounds like a bitch.'

'Nah, she's really all right. She lives in deepest Surrey so I don't think she'd even spoken to a black person before. But then it turned out that my dad was studying law and apparently I was an adorable baby so she got over it pretty quick. Still not over the Afro though, but then neither is my black grandma.'

'I'm loving the Afro. You make me want to grow out my hair too but, honey, there ain't world enough or time,' Shirelle says, and then she tells me that her non-drag name is Paul and when she was a teenager she had the New Kids On The Block logo cut into her hair.

'Who are New Kids On The Block?' I ask and I think she might cry because she gives this weird anguished moan but then we carry on talking about our hair.

We talk about the hair for ages. 'I'm thinking of experimenting with a flat twist, faux hawk for when I go back to school,' I tell Shirelle, and I'm showing her a couple of styles on my phone when it beeps.

U found Mark? We're in Soho. Come 2 The Dive w' us. U heard anything bout secret Duckie gig? Em xxx

Somehow I'd managed to forget about Mark for a good fifteen minutes. I'd even forgotten about Vic and Jean-Luc, who are explaining *their* haircare regime to Shangri-La and Ronette, who look repulsed because their haircare regime involves hardly ever washing their hair.

The three of us are a team now. We've been through stuff. Or rather, I'm going through stuff and Vic and Jean-Luc have stuck by me. I can't just dump them to hang out with Emmeline and maybe see Duckie.

Also, what if Mark is still in Shoreditch? I immediately crane my neck to see if I can catch sight of a shock of floppy blond hair in the chaotic press of people at the counter.

'What's up?' Vic asks. 'Is that a text about the dastardly Mark? Sunny's boyfriend's done her wrong,' he explains to our friends. 'We're on a mission to hunt him down like the dog he is.'

'Oh, honey, no! You sleep with dogs then you're always going to wake up with fleas,' Shirelle tells me. My face heats up like it's been slathered in hot sauce.

'It's not about Mark,' I say quickly because Shirelle's been great for hair talk but I don't want to have to have a sex talk with her too. 'It's from Emmeline. She's in Soho. Says that Duckie might be playing a secret gig.' I try not to sound wistful. 'Do you like Duckie?'

'Oh yeah. Me and Jane from Duckie go way back,' Vic says. He smiles a little smile that I don't think he should smile when there are other people about 'cause it looks kind of rude. 'Way, way back. But a gentlemen never kisses and tells.'

'Any fool can tell you're no gentlemen,' Vandella says and Jean-Luc snorts in agreement.

Vic pulls out his phone. 'I'll text Jane. Find out what's going on,' he says, like it's no big deal that he's had, like, *intimate* dealings with someone in a really amazing band who have been on TV and played proper festivals and that he can just get in touch with her whenever he feels like it.

'So when you went way back with Jane from Duckie, you didn't pretend to be Jean-Luc and then leave without exchanging numbers?' I ask.

'Not nice, Sunny. Not when I might be able to get you into a secret Duckie gig.' Vic stands up. 'Right, we need a new plan. We can't find your Mark, so all those in favour of going back into town, raise their right hand.'

'I thought we were going to get up early to make pastries?' Jean-Luc shrugs and raises his right hand. 'No need to get up early if we don't go to bed. *D'accord*, Sunny?'

I raise my right hand. '*D'accord*.' I get up too, then glance down at Shirelle. 'Do you fancy it?'

'Darling, kind of you to ask but we're heading into deepest, darkest Hoxton for a spot of karaoke.'

Shirelle and I exchange numbers. I even invite her to my gran's on Monday because Grandma always has an open house for the Notting Hill Carnival weekend, though I don't know what she'll do if Shirelle rocks up in full drag. She'll probably tell her she doesn't have the legs for such a short skirt.

Vic blows extravagant kisses at the girls, but it's Jean-Luc they sigh over when he gives them an elegant bow, then a mock salute. '*Mesdemoiselles*,' he says, all deep and smouldery and French. '*Ce fût un plaisir.*'

Outside is just as humid and dense as inside. 'We should get a bus then,' Vic says decisively. 'There must be a bus that goes from here to Soho. Doesn't the 38 stop in Dalston?'

We look up and down the road for a bus or a bus stop. 'We must walk back up Kingsland Road and get a 38 from the station,' Jean-Luc says, after looking at his phone.

Even fortified with hot wings and my body weight in 7UP, the thought of walking back up the longest road in London makes me feel exhausted. 'We could get another bus up the Kingsland Road,' I point out as Vic gets a text.

'No time! No time! Duckie are on stage in forty-five minutes. Doors close in thirty!' He finishes on a shrill note. He must really like Duckie or else Jane from Duckie was the vixenish, superhero, Amazon, girl-goddess that got away and he was still pining for her. 'Have we enough money for a taxi?'

We do but there's a massive queue outside the dodgy minicab office and as we start to argue about whether it's safe to get in a dodgy minicab, the bus we need sails past.

It's then I see them. The hoodies. The rude boys. The bruvas from before. They've not gone home but have got off their bikes to peer in at the window of the chicken shop and you can call it revenge, you can call it the meanest thing I've ever done, but I turn to Jean-Luc and Vic. 'Let's nick their bikes and catch up to that bus!'

'Sunny, we can't. It's . . .'

'C'mon!' It's a head-of-steam momentum that propels me forward to grab a bike, hop on and take off, with the broom wedged under my arm. 'Come on!'

They come on. It's stay there to face the wrath of hoodie or join me on my one-girl crimewave.

There's a shout behind me. 'Beeeeyyyyyaaaatttcccchhhhhh!' and I stand up on the pedals so I can go faster and not get a knife in the ribs.

Jean-Luc and Vic catch me up and I'm laughing so hard that it's all I can do to make my legs work.

I see the bus in front, getting ever closer. It pulls in to the next stop and I think we're going to make it but as soon as we're close enough to feel the hot kiss of its exhaust, it pulls away.

'You're a bad influence,' Vic gasps but he's laughing too. Even Jean-Luc is doubled up over his handlebars and we pause to catch our breath but there's an angry bellow behind us. The hoodies are gaining ground.

'Go, go, GO!'

We go. Cycling like bosses right down the centre of the road, getting beeped and sworn at by all the dodgy minicab drivers intent on doing illegal U-turns. I punch the air with the arm that isn't on broom duties when we overtake the bus and nearly fall off, but we've made it.

We jump off the bikes and dump them, dash the last few steps to the stop and bundle onto the bus, squeezing our way in so there's enough space for the driver to shut the doors as our three nemeses turn up.

My heart salmon leaps as they bang on the door. 'Don't let them on,' Jean-Luc shouts. 'They're very bad people.'

'No room, innit,' the driver says.

And as the bus pulls away and they stand there gesticulating and mouthing obscenities, I stick my tongue out at them.

119

A HISTORY OF MY HAIR

Nought to two – the fuzz years

Nothing much to do with my hair but keep it lint-free.

Two to eleven – the pain years

My hair grows in. Back then it's what my grandmother poetically calls the colour of mouldy hay. My mum would section and gather my hair into little Afro puffs. Not good enough for my Jamaican great-grandma. When they'd take me round for lunch every other Sunday, she'd cluck her teeth and shake her head.

'What have you done to that poor child?' she'd ask my mum, and Mum would say that that was how the other black girls at school wore their hair.

After lunch, Gramma would make me stand in the kitchen while she combed out my hair, which hurt. Then her friend Pat from next-door-but-one would come round and they'd braid my hair into tight cornrows. Really tight cornrows. They hurt too. On the way home, Mum would say that Gramma had no right to impose her will on my hair, but it would take a week of tantrums before she'd take out the cornrows because secretly she was scared of Gramma.

Eleven to fourteen – the relax years

Gramma goes back to Jamaica and my grandma, Dad's mum, decides that she's going to assume responsibility for my hair. This means that she straightens my hair with the same relaxer she uses on my cousins, even though my hair isn't as tight and curly. It's three years of hair breakage and her accusing me of washing my hair too much, until I've had enough. Drastic action is needed.

Fourteen and a half – the day of the weave

Deep into my Beyoncé phase, I beg and beg for a weave but Grandma says it won't take on my hair and Mum says I'm too young. In an act of defiance I've yet to rival, I save up my allowance and the sister of Alex's older brother's girlfriend says she'll give me a weave, but my hair is so broken from my gran's extra-strength relaxer that she has to hot-glue it into place. It's so heavy that it pulls out some of my hair at the roots and when my mum sees what I've done, she cries. She and Grandma bond over cutting the weave out of my hair. I am practically bald. There's never a good time to be practically bald but when you're fourteen that is definitely, totally the worst time to be practically bald in your life, ever.

I've been to a dark place.

Fourteen and three quarters to seventeen – the fro-yo years

Then my Uncle Dee, Dad's older brother, marries Yolanda (or Yolly as we all call her) and she takes my big bald self under her wing. Turns out Yolly'd had a similar bad experience with a blond weave. Once my hair starts to grow back, Yolly is the first person to tell me how beautiful my hair is (especially when the ends turn gold in summer), and says that I should think about letting it go natural. She's also the first person I've ever met who doesn't think of my hair as a problem that needs to be fixed.

So, now I have a big, beautiful Afro, and though I sometimes get snide remarks and side-eye from girls with weaves, and both my grandmas tell me that my hair sends out the wrong message, haters gonna hate.

I love my hair.

1.45 a.m.

SOHO

Rumoured to have taken its name from a former hunting cry, until the mid sixteenth century Soho was full of sheep and cows grazing its pastures.

Henry VIII, during a break from wiving it, had it turned into a royal park, and later lots of posh aristocratic types built houses there. But by the nineteenth century Soho was a seedy neighbourhood full of prostitutes and theatrical types. In the early twentieth century, intellectuals, artists and writers turned up to get drunk in its many pubs and restaurants.

In the Fifties, though, the beatniks arrived and coffee bars opened up where the kids could listen to beat poetry and skiffle. The famous Marquee Club opened in 1958, where the Rolling Stones played in 1962, but mostly Soho was notorious as a place full of sex shops, strip clubs and brothels.

Soho is now home to a vibrant gay scene centred around Old Compton Street, and a thriving Chinese community in Chinatown where the street signs are in Chinese and English. Two words: steamed buns. Three words: amazing steamed buns.

The bus is so crowded that we only stop to let people off, then we're at Dalston Junction station and we prise ourselves off the bus like peas popping out of a pod, just in time for a 38 bus to magically appear.

There's enough room for the three of us to squeeze onto a seat upstairs. I get stuck in the middle. 'A rose between two thorns,' Vic says and I say, 'Can you do something about your elbows before you end up puncturing one of my lungs?'

'Do something with your own elbows,' Jean-Luc says and then all three of us shove at each other to find a more comfortable position. I lose and with elbows pinned to my sides I text Emmeline.

Duckie gig is GO! This is not a drill! Repeat, Duckie is GO. KitKat club, Romilly St. Get there ASAP. Save us place in queue. Sunny xoxo

I rummage in my bag for powder, mascara and lipgloss and the boys do their hair. Then I get Vic to spray Elnett on my hands so I can do my hair too and the girls sitting in front of us ask if they can have a spritz. They're from Canada, abroad for the first time, and Jean-Luc talks to them in French, slipping into English for the odd word: 'Hampstead Heath', 'courgette', 'dickhead'. There's a hen party sitting at the front of the bus, all of them wearing clip-on veils and L-plates. They shriek and giggle and every time a guy goes up or down the stairs, they catcall: 'Oi, fitness! Where you going, fitness?'

Then someone at the back begins to play Pharrell's 'Happy' on their phone and soon everyone on the bus is singing along and the ones who don't, who huff and roll their eyes, they don't deserve to be here right now in this perfect moment. Then we switch it up a gear and start singing 'Uptown Funk' and an older man in a suit stands up like he's going to shout at everyone, but instead he conducts us so that each side of the bus has a different harmony to sing and Vic, of course – who else? – begins a Mexican wave and being on the top deck of the 38 bus is the best fun I've ever had on a Saturday night and we haven't even got to the Duckie gig yet.

It's five minutes before the Duckie list closes when we jump off the bus on Shaftesbury Avenue, which is so busy that it could be rush hour. People hurrying home after nights out, other people hurrying to the next party, the next bar, the next adventure.

We dart down Dean Street, weaving through rickshaws and black cabs, then onto Romilly Street, past where Kettner's used to be with its posh champagne bar where Terry's mum had her sixty-fifth birthday lunch and . . .

'Do you know where this club is?' I ask and Vic spins round.

'Not really, no. But this is a tiny street. It has to be here somewhere.'

'Sunny!'

At the other end of the street, blond hair reflected in the glow of the streetlight and waving frantically, is Emmeline.

All we've done since we left the chicken shop is dash but

it's one last frantic dash now that takes me to Emmeline and Charlie and some of the other roller derby girls and then we're all hugging and jumping up and down and, 'Oh my God! We're going to see Duckie!'

We clatter down a flight of metal steps to join the end of a short queue. 'They're only letting in fifty people, but we should be all right,' Emmeline says. 'Why have you got a broom with you?'

'Archie gave it to me.' It's all I need to say.

'Oh, Archie . . .' Emmeline sighs, then she anxiously eyes the people queuing in front of us. 'I hope we get in.'

'I know Jane,' Vic says with that tiny, secretive smile again. 'We'll be fine. Or I'll be fine. Don't know about the rest of you.'

'Although I could just say that I was you and then I'd be fine,' Jean-Luc points out.

'God, you're never going to let that go, are you?'

'Depends how many other girls you've treated abominably.'

'You all know Vic and Jean-Luc, right?' I say, because once they start with this, it won't be long before they're jostling again and the guy on the door is already looking in our direction.

Everybody kinda knows everybody already but formal introductions are made and Vic kisses everyone on the cheek and Jean-Luc kisses everyone on both cheeks. When Vic gets to Emmeline his eyes gleam.

'Sunny's told me so much about you.' His voice is as sweet and dark as the espresso we had earlier. 'But she never told me how beautiful you are.'

Jean-Luc and I both snigger. Charlie looks at her friends, as if she can't quite believe that anyone could deliver such a triple-cheese line with a straight face, and Emmeline pins

Vic with a look. I know that look. It's the look she gives me whenever I'm being a fool. It's usually accompanied by Emmeline saying, 'Sunny, ain't nobody got time for this.'

Not tonight though. 'I'm gay,' is what she does say. 'I'm very, very gay, so don't even try it on because it's never going to happen. Never.'

Vic's smile dims. He turns to Jean-Luc for some moral support but gets a shove instead. 'Oh well.' He shrugs. 'Can't blame a guy for trying. Any of you ladies not gay?'

'We're all total lezzers,' Charlie says, though I know for a fact that Lucy standing behind her got off with Charlie's brother's best friend a couple of weeks ago, but even she shakes her head.

'Yeah, total lezzer.' Then she folds her arms and looks at Jean-Luc. 'Though I could be persuaded otherwise by your better-looking brother.'

'He's not better looking than me!'

'I'm not his brother!'

'Don't start,' I beg. 'They've been like this all evening,' I add to Emmeline and I start to tell her about all the arguments that Vic and Jean-Luc have had while they insist that I'm exaggerating, until we reach the door . . . and the guy who's on the door.

He's been really friendly; smiling, even laughing as he catches snatches of our conversation and he's wearing a Duckie T-shirt, so he's one of us, he's cool. 'In you go, then,' he says and he starts to count us in. Charlie, Lucy, Preeta, Emmeline, Jean-Luc, Vic and . . . 'Sorry, that's it. We're up to fifty now. Not allowed to let anyone else in. Any more and it's a fire hazard.'

I'm left standing there with a handful of people who've joined the queue since we arrived.

'Oh, come on, we're all together,' Emmeline protests. 'Let her in. It's only one more person.'

'Yeah, one more person isn't going to make any difference if there is a fire,' Preeta says. 'Anyway, Sunny's skinny and so are Vic and Jean-Luc so really if you put the three of them together then they only count as two people.'

He holds his hands up. 'No can do. If the police were to come by and did a headcount, we'd be closed down.' He cringes. 'I don't make the rules. It's a health and safety thing.'

The people behind me aren't too happy about it either. They mutter but move back like they know they don't stand a chance and so it's just me staring forlornly at my friends on the other side of the door. 'Please. Come on, have a heart.' It's meant to be plaintive and ping on his heartstrings but it just comes out as a nasal whine.

'I can't. I'm really sorry.'

'Sunny, you go in and I'll wait out here,' Emmeline says, and I see the look Charlie gets like nothing, not even seeing Duckie play a secret gig, is any fun if Emmeline isn't there.

'Don't do that. You like Duckie even more than I do,' I tell Emmeline. 'If you dare take another step through that door, I'll never forgive you.'

'C'est bon. I'll give up my place,' Jean-Luc says, and I'm not even sure that Jean-Luc has heard of Duckie before tonight but it's not fair if he has to hang around outside when I've already derailed whatever Saturday-night plans he had.

Now Lucy's face falls at the prospect of missing her chance to convince Jean-Luc that she's not a total lezzer. Though, really, I don't think she'd be his type. I'm not sure what Jean-Luc's type is, but anyone who would get off with Charlie's brother's best mate, who tweets really lame pictures of every meal he ever eats, even if it's just a bag of Monster Munch, isn't that choosy. And Jean-Luc deserves someone who is a bit choosy. 'Sunny! *Allez! Allez!* How do you say in English? Get your arse over here.'

Jean-Luc clicks his fingers at me, but I stay where I am. 'No, it's all right. I'm fine.' I'm not fine but I try to put on a fine face. 'Really, it's OK. And I could get a text at any minute saying that Mark's, like, back in Camden with that *skank* in her short shorts, so then I'd have to leave anyway.'

The guy in the Duckie T-shirt looks a lot like he's losing the will to live. Or, hopefully, the will to deny me access to Duckie. Emmeline taps him on the shoulder. 'Did you hear that? She's having a really bad night on account of her boyfriend sucking face with a skank in short shorts . . .'

'Oh, Emmeline, don't say skank,' Charlie butts in earnestly. 'It demeans all women.'

'But she is a gigantic skank,' Emmeline insists. 'Show him the picture, Sun.'

I never want to see the picture again, but I unlock my screen and Mr Health and Safety sighs but edges nearer so he can see when I hold my phone up. 'That's my boyfriend kissing a skank in short shorts four hours ago. My boyfriend. And a skank. And I've been halfway round London to try to find him and I can't and now you won't even let me see Duckie. I swore earlier tonight that no man would ever be the boss of me again, so why are you trying to be the boss of me? God, I hate the patriarchy and all it stands for!'

'But I'm a feminist. I'm not part of the problem, I'm part of the solution.' His shoulders slump. 'This is so unfair. None of this is my fault so I'm going to turn my back and if you choose to sneak in when I'm not looking, even though I've told you not to, well, that's between you and your God.'

Then he turns his back on me and I dive through the door. I'm not entirely sure that I believe in God but if I do, he's totally benevolent and would be completely down with me sneaking into a Duckie gig in direct contravention of health and safety rules.

'Thank you! Thank you so much!' I call over my shoulder as I hear the door shut behind me with a distinct and final clunk.

The KitKat Club is the size of our lounge at home. There's a bar that's actually a table and a dustbin full of ice and bottles of lager at one end, and a raised platform, which is meant to be the stage, at the other end of the room. The club is heaving with sweaty people. If there was a fire, it would take hold in no time at all and we'd all be burned extra-crispy, health and safety regulations or not.

But what a lovely way to burn. While the others are still taking it in turns to raise their eyes to the ceiling and wail, 'I hate the patriarchy and all it stands for!' because apparently my feminist call to arms is comedy gold, there's a screech of feedback from the speakers and we see four figures run on stage.

'Hello, pop kids!' shouts Molly Montgomery, Duckie singer and the woman Emmeline and I would very much like to be when we grow up. 'Shall we turn this all the way up to eleven?'

All fifty-one of us scream our agreement at this plan. Then the drummer lifts her sticks and brings them crashing down on the snare drum in a four-four beat that matches the frantic thrum of my heart and Jane steps up to her mic and the lights hit the glittery aqua-green plate of her guitar and she makes a beautiful noise come out of it.

'Oh! My! God!' If Emmeline and I had a theme tune, then 'Girls Together Only' would be it and as soon as we hear those opening chords we grab each other's hand and run full pelt towards the stage.

Everyone else has the same idea and we don't get to the front but find ourselves in the middle of a melee of Duckie girls all dancing and singing, and Emmeline and I are still holding hands, and I'm still holding my broom, and we spin round and round, laughing and screaming, until we have to stop because I'm getting dizzy and Emmeline shouts that she'll totally wet herself if she carries on.

It's a short set and seems to speed by in five minutes flat. All too soon Duckie are ending with their cover of 'I Can Do Without You' from *My Fair Lady* and every person joins in with the jubilant cry of 'If they can do without you, Duckie, so can I!'

Molly brushes her soaked hair back from her face. She doesn't look sweaty, though. She's glowing like she's made entirely from moon rocks. 'OK, that's all. We haven't got time for any more. We're playing Reading in approximately sixteen hours and Jane really needs her beauty sleep,' she says.

Jane grabs the mic. 'And Molly is such a nana that she needs at least eight hours' sleep or she's an utter beast the next day.'

They leave the stage arm in arm but pretending to hit each other, and Emmeline and I also still want to be friends like that when we're all grown up, but for now I bend over and grab my knees because I've got a stitch from laughing so much and Emmeline rests her arms on my back and tries to catch her breath.

'You all right?' she asks at last when her breath's been caught and she's tugging me upright again. 'Like, really, how are you doing?'

'I'm kind of angry and sad, then angry at feeling sad every time I think about Mark, so I've mostly stopped thinking about Mark and as soon as I did that I started having fun,' I tell her. It's been at least forty-five minutes since I last checked my phone; I pull it out but there's nada. No messages from Mark and his silence is screaming a thousand words at me so it's impossible to actually make any sense of them. There are no new sightings of Mark either. Just a few late 'U OK, hun?' texts. 'Yeah, now I've looked at my phone, I'm angry, sad, angry all over again, so let's change the subject, shall we?'

'Well, not to ignore your pain, but I really need a wee,' says Emmeline.

It seems like the forty-nine other people in the KitKat are waiting for the loo too. Emmeline says she's in a thousand agonies and crosses her legs as we wait. The effort to control her bladder makes her eyes cross too and to take her mind off it I tell her about the hoodies and having to deal with Jeane on my own and dancing the Charleston and meeting Shirelle and finally nicking the hoodies' bikes.

'You did all that?' Emmeline asks. She's in the cubicle now and I can hear the effort in her voice as she tries to pull her denim cut-offs down her sweaty legs. 'That doesn't sound like you.'

'I know, right!' I tug at my hair, which is drooping slightly. 'Who knew I had it in me, eh?'

'I think that you should keep channelling whatever you've been channelling tonight.' Emmeline unlocks the cubicle door and stands there, her cheeks red from all the effort involved in having a good wee. 'Seriously, I was worried that you were at home crying and instead you've been having adventures.'

'I kind of have, haven't I?'

'Also, we need to talk about you and the Frenchies. Normally, you're not like that with boys.' Emmeline catches my eye in the mirror as she washes her hands. 'If you were as ballsy with Mark as you are with Vic and Jean-Luc then he wouldn't treat you like dirt.'

'He's only treated me like dirt tonight,' I protest.

'He doesn't treat you that marvellously the rest of the time.' Emmeline rolls her eyes. 'Dude! He went to a polo match on your birthday. Who goes to watch polo anyway, but on your girlfriend's birthday?'

'But that was because his grandfather's some big cheese in the polo world,' I explain, much as Mark had explained it to me.

'It's a family tradition, Sun,' he'd said. 'We always have a big picnic for the opening match of the season. It'd be like missing Christmas. I'd risk getting cut out of my grandparents' will.'

When he'd put it like that I'd had no choice but to let it go, to forgive him, but now I wonder if he was lying then – if he'd taken a posher, more suitable girl to the polo and snogged her there too.

I'm getting cross again. It makes my palms itch. 'Oh no. You need to cut him off,' says a girl who's been waiting for the loo, though I'm starting to come to that conclusion all by myself. 'Never go out with a boy who a) goes to polo matches and b) bails on your birthday.'

'Total dealbreaker,' says another girl. 'Is he, like, really posh or something?'

'No,' I say automatically despite the whole polo thing.

'Yes,' Emmeline says. She turns to our audience. 'But he pretends not to be by talking in this rubbish mockney accent.'

'He's not that posh,' I insist even though that's not really true, but Mark's failings are becoming more and more obvious and they don't reflect that well on me. 'His mum's posh but his dad isn't.'

'He's still a wanker, though,' Emmeline says and I can't really disagree about that, and then one of the girls says that she was going out with this boy who got off with another girl *on her actual bed* during her actual birthday party.

Then the other girl says that her ex-boyfriend borrowed a hundred quid from her the day before he dumped her by text, then left the country.

'Boys are more trouble than they're worth,' I say. 'It would be much easier if they were more like girls.'

The four of us take a moment to muse on the evilness that is boy but then the door opens and a crowd of girls push in. There's only three but the loo is tiny so three feels like a crowd.

'Which one of you is Sunny, then?' demands a mardy-looking blond girl.

First rule of life. When someone mardy-looking is asking after you, you keep your mouth shut. I look at Emmeline and she got the same memo, because she mimes zipping her lips. 'We don't know no Sunny,' she says.

'It's *her*,' says one of mardy-looking blond girl's mates and she points at me and then the mardy-looking blond girl throws her drink over me.

134

It happens in slow-motion. I see this arc of lager coming towards me and I stand there and because it's not really happening in slow motion, but at normal speed, it hits me full in the face. Right in the eyes. In my hair. I can taste it in my mouth when I cough and splutter and my black-and-white stripy T-shirt is covered in brown sticky splodges.

'What?'

'What the fuck?'

'What did you do that for?'

Emmeline and the two girls we've been talking to are instantly furious and indignant, but I just stand there spluttering and trying not to cry and wondering what on earth I could have done to make someone I don't even know throw their drink over me.

'If anyone's a skank in shorts, it's *her*,' mardy-looking blond girl says and Emmeline's in her mardy face in a second.

'She's not a skank and you're going to be so dead in about a minute.' The girl visibly gulps and takes a step back. Sometimes I forget how big and fierce and terrifying Emmeline is to people who haven't known her since she was seven. 'What the hell is your problem, bitch?'

Our two new friends have fled and it's just me and Emmeline and these three other girls. The other two girls are flanking their mardy-looking friend and eyeing up Emmeline like they're wondering if they could take her down. They couldn't. Emmeline would *destroy* them.

'I don't even know who you are.' I find my voice. It's very squeaky. 'What gives you the right to . . .'

Mardy-face manages to step away from Emmeline so she can hide behind her friends, who stand there, arms folded,

135

gamefaces on. 'Tabitha is my best friend so that gives me the right to deal with some slutty *skank* who has the nerve to tell everyone that Tab's a *skank* just 'cause she wears shorts. Like, hello! It's the middle of summer! Especially when that same slutty *skank* is trying to get with Tab's boyfriend.'

'I don't even know a Tabitha.' I pull at my damp T-shirt. 'Maybe next time you should ask for some ID before you throw lager over someone.'

'You're Sunny. I know exactly who you are because when we went to Camden to find Mark earlier, this girl called Martha tried to imply that you were hooking up with Mark.' Mardy rolls her eyes like it's the most ludicrous thing she's ever heard. 'She even showed us a picture of you and Mark at a barbecue on her phone while Tab was in the Ladies. Like, because you and he were in the same place at the same time doesn't prove anything.' She paused to suck in a breath. 'And then some of my other friends were waiting outside but they couldn't get in and they heard you calling Tab a skank. Repeatedly. Though you're the skank who tries to get with other people's boyfriends. So that gives me the right to throw beer over you, *bitch*.'

I'm angry again. Sad isn't figuring too highly. I advance on her; I'm pretty sure that murder is written all over my damp face. 'Is that a fact, bitch? Because if you want to start something then I'll finish it.' I hold out my arms and beckon her with my fingers, in time-honoured 'Come and have a go if you think you're hard enough' fashion. 'Go on, I dare you! Give me your best shot, *bitch*.'

Her gaze skitters to the door, but she'll have to go through me first to get to it She licks her lips. She's scared and I'm not surprised 'cause I'm scaring myself. All this rage. I don't know where it's come from. Maybe it's always been there, humming along, bubbling through my veins, and I've tamped it down because I didn't want to be the angry black girl.

'I will totally end you,' she says but she's too posh to carry it off and I decide that I could smack her. Just once. Because she totally deserves it and I am done with being treated like dirt by people who think that I'm lacking balls and a backbone. I raise my hand, I really do . . .

'Right. OK. No one's ending or finishing anybody else.' Emmeline pushes in between me and Mardy Blond Utter Bitchface. 'No more skanks and bitches. Time out, ladies. Time bloody out. What's your name, anyway?'

The girl sulkily says her name's Flick, because posh girls always have stupid names and I snort much like Jean-Luc and Emmeline tells me to wash my face.

I have to scrub my face with damp loo roll so it isn't sticky any more and what's left of my make-up comes off with it so my skin is raw and tight. Like I've been crying for ages, which I haven't, it just feels like I have.

'I don't know who died and made you the boss of the whole world,' I tell Emmeline.

'Yeah. You're so aggro,' Flick says, but I'm not ready to bond with her over how bossy my best friend is so I stare at her, trying not to blink, until Emmeline nudges me.

'So, the thing is that Martha, who really needs to keep her nose out of other people's business, wasn't *implying* shit. Mark *is* Sunny's boyfriend, not your mate Tabitha's,' Emmeline says reasonably even though there is no reason here. 'You've been going out since last Christmas, right?'

'Since bonfire night, actually.' Because that was the night we'd first kissed. Lit up by sparklers and Catherine wheels and Roman candles. And afterwards my lips were sore and my throat ached from the woody smoke of the bonfire. But mostly I remember kissing and Mark tugging off my woolly gloves so he could take my hand in his as he walked me home. We'd kissed again on the corner of my road and then we'd made a definite date to see each other, instead of me spending my spare time hanging around places where I thought that Mark might be.

Funny that there didn't seem anything wrong or desperate about that plan of action back then – after all, it had worked, but now I cringe at what a sap I'd been.

'Really?' Flick sounds like she doesn't believe a word of it. ''Cause Tab's been going out with him since Easter and they hooked up loads before that. I'm not making this up!' she adds hotly when I roll my eyes. 'It even says that they're in a relationship on his Facebook.'

'Well, that's funny because his Facebook says he's in a relationship with me.'

I pull out my phone and she pulls out her phone and her mates and Emmeline gather round us and I think oh God, if Mark has changed his relationship status tonight because he knows I'm onto him and he wants to get in there first and that skank and her mardy friend Flick and her other posh friends all think I'm a delusional saddo who's stalking Mark, I will cry. Then I'll lock myself in the toilet and never leave.

I wait for Facebook to load. I can hardly swallow – all the moisture has suddenly disappeared from my mouth and I don't think I can speak as I see the familiar blue header. Then, with fumbling fingers because all the moisture that was in my mouth has migrated to my fingertips and the sweat is making it hard to operate a touchscreen, I call up Mark's profile.

The relief nearly makes my legs give way. 'There!' I say and I shove my phone at Flick's face. 'In a relationship with Sunshine Williams. Satisfied!'

'No, I'm not satisfied,' she says and she thrusts her phone in my face. 'That's not Mark's Facebook page. *This* is Mark's Facebook page.'

I don't cry, which is a miracle. Actually I kind of want to laugh but all that comes out is this weird noise like a death rattle. My worst fears, the ones I'd been ducking away from all evening, were all true and I was sad again. So sad. So fucking sad. And also I think I might puke.

My face falls, collapses, and Flick puts her arm round me and then her two friends say that they never liked Mark anyway.

'There's just something about Mark, isn't there? Something not quite right. He's always been a bit shifty and we've known him since prep school.'

'Oh God,' I say, eyes smarting. The words don't really want to come out. 'I'm such a twat. All this time . . .'

Emmeline pushes Flick off me because she's my best friend and she has prior claim on putting an arm round me. Such is the gravity of the situation that even Emmeline, who doesn't do hugging, is doing hugging. 'Sunny, don't you dare blame yourself.'

'Yeah! You're not a twat. It's him! It's Mark!' Flick says. She looks down at my lager-splattered T-shirt. 'Look, dude, I'm really, really sorry about throwing a drink over you. I was just standing up for my friend.'

'It's all right,' I say, because that bit of it is. It's the Mark stuff that is never going to be right, not until I fix it. 'And I'm sorry I kept calling your friend a skank. God, I really have to stop calling people skanks.'

'I'm going to text Tab,' Flick decides. 'Tell her what's really going on. You know she's actually with Mark right now, even though she loves Duckie. Mark said that they were just shouty girl music and she cried off.'

She shares an exasperated, long-suffering look with her two friends, Chessie and Santa. 'Since she's been seeing Mark, Tab's become really, really not fun.'

'I'm not saying anything. Not a word,' Emmeline says, but then she gives me an exasperated look too. 'It's just that when you're with Mark, you're not a fraction, a smidgeon, a mere bloody soupçon as much fun as when you're not with him. He sucks all the fun out of you.'

'Yeah. He's such a fun-sucker,' Flick breathes and then she says that she'll buy me a T-shirt from the merch stand so I don't have to spend the rest of the night in a lager-stained top.

We troop out of the Ladies and even though Duckie have long finished playing, people are throwing themselves about the dancefloor in all kinds of gay abandon as the DJ plays something loud and fast and screechy.

It takes all of five seconds to establish that there's no merch stand.

'I'm wearing a cami underneath so, like, I can totally give you my top,' Flick says earnestly (now that she's not being mardy, she's being very sincere and very earnest). 'Honestly, it's no biggie.'

Flick is wearing a little drapey black top that probably cost a lot of money from somewhere really fancy. Also she's tiny and elfin, like she only eats quails' eggs and caviar, so I'm not even sure that I could get my head in the neckhole, never mind the rest of me. 'No, you're all right,' I say, but I look down at my ruined T-shirt and for some stupid reason I feel like crying again.

It makes no sense. And then I see Jeane bearing down on us and that makes me feel like crying too.

'There you are!' she shouts, like she's been looking for us for hours. 'Emmeline, love your hair. When did you cut a fringe in? Flick, Santa, Chessie, still working that whole *Downton Abbey* meets Riot Grrrl aesthetic, I see.'

Not only does Jeane really know everyone, she also has strong opinions on what they're wearing. 'And Sunny, the girl of the hour! Honestly, how long does it take to have a wee? What were you all doing in there? And you've still got your broom.'

'Well, we were doing stuff. It turns out that Mark and –'

'Oh, whatevs! I can't bear to hear another word about him. He's so dull. What did you two actually talk about anyway?'

Jeane doesn't even wait to hear my reply (for the record, Mark and I talked about plenty of things, though admittedly in the last few weeks it was mostly about when I might be ready to have sex with him) but grabs my hand and drags me across the club, the others following in our wake. Considering she's small, she's also very strong, like a sturdy little pit pony. She has my wrist in a vice-like grip as she pulls me past the makeshift bar and into a little alcove with a sofa where Jean-Luc, Vic and two other girls are staring at an iPad.

'Sunny! You've gone viral' Vic's gaze quickly glides over me, then comes to a halt on someone obviously far more pleasing to his eyes. 'Emmeline, you're looking even lovelier than you did before. Are you still gay?'

'I'm actually even gayer.' Emmeline's glee makes her words bubble. 'I don't think my gay levels have ever been this high.'

We're getting way off message here. 'Never mind that. I've gone *what*?'

'Viral!'

The iPad is handed over. It's paused on a YouTube video. A freeze-framed blur on the screen. I press a finger to the play arrow and the blur becomes a girl dancing down the aisle of a convenience store; legs snapping and kicking, feet tapping and sliding, arms freewheeling. There's even jazz hands, but if you're dancing the Charleston then jazz hands are allowed. They're kind of mandatory.

'Jeez, Sunny, you never used to dance like that at dance classes,' Emmeline says. 'You barely scraped through your level-three tap.'

It's like I'm watching a girl who looks like me, dresses like me, but unlike me she has the confidence to launch herself in the air and land where she damn well pleases, then carries on dancing, a huge grin on her face.

This is a girl who's got it going on.

Nobody would dare mess with a girl like this.

And I *am* this girl and I am done with being messed around.

Tonight I am going to rule the streets.

Tonight I'm taking chances and no prisoners.

Tonight I am going to lay waste to evil, two-faced, two-timing boyfriends.

'Serious moves,' Flick says. 'I didn't know you were a dancer.'

'I'm not . . .' I still can't tear my eyes away from this other Sunny and it's only when she stops dancing and melts back into the crowd that I look up and glare at Jeane, who takes one look at my face, then hides behind Jean-Luc. 'So who gave you permission to film it, Jeane, 'cause it sure as hell wasn't me?'

Jeane peeks out from behind Jean-Luc's shoulder. He wriggles said shoulders. 'I didn't film it. Frank filmed it.'

'It's on your YouTube channel! I didn't sign any photo release forms.'

'I'm only giving the public what they want,' Jeane says. 'It's been up an hour and it's already had over a thousand views.'

I don't know how I feel about that. Mostly nauseous, I think. A thousand people I don't know looking at me. Seeing how my thighs jiggle when I quickstep. Making judgements about me.

I scroll down to the comments. 'I'd hit that!' 'Urgh! What a show-off!' 'Damn! Baby's got back!' I am going to have to shut this shit right down.

Except, Jeane refuses to cooperate. She embarks on a loud rant, with a lot of dramatic hand gestures, about public domain and how in a media age everyone has to expect to see their image plastered all over the interweb. And besides, everyone secretly, deep down, longed to be famous. 'The law is on my side,' Jeane finishes at last. 'Anyway, why wouldn't you want your dance-off on You Tube? There is nothing about it that's any less than amazing.'

'*So* amazing,' Flick breathes in my ear.

So much for ruling the streets. 'At least disable the comments.'

143

'First rule of life, Sunny: never read the bottom half of the internet,' Jeane says grandly.

'I'm not having a whole load of pervs perving on me. Disable the comments right now,' I growl and something in my throat pings when I do. 'I'm not just some inanimate girl-shaped blob that people can do whatever they like to, regardless of my feelings.'

'I suppose you're talking about that Mark again.' Jeane sighs. 'Fine, I'll disable the comments.' She snatches back her iPad like she doesn't trust me to drop it from a great height. 'Happy, now?'

No. Not happy. Not even a little bit. All that joy at seeing Duckie had washed away as soon as the lager hit my face and everything that has happened since then, well, it just . . .

'Aw, Sunny, *tu es si triste. Qu'est ce qui s'est passé?*' I'm standing close enough to Jean-Luc that he can reach out and tip up my chin with a careful finger. 'You look like you've been crying. This isn't just about the video, *non?*'

'*Non,*' I agree. My eyes smart again and I try to open them really wide but that doesn't work.

Emmeline gives me another reluctant side-hug. 'Sunny, he's not worth a single tear.'

'I know.' I toss my head back, the threat of tears banished. 'I am done crying over that loser. He's going to be the one crying by the time I'm finished with him. And then I'm going to drink his tears and steal away all his power.'

She stares at me. 'You all right, Sun?'

'Never better,' I tell her and when I smile it's all teeth, and Emmeline backs away and Flick shoots me a fearful look. No one has ever given me a fearful look before, apart from the one time when I had the aforementioned norovirus and I'd been sent home from school and was seconds away from exploding out of both ends and Mum couldn't find her doorkeys. Good times, man.

'I really am sorry I threw my drink over you,' Flick says. Then she hits the highlights all over again for the benefit of Jeane and the two girls she's with.

Meanwhile Vic gives me a sip of his water and tells me that he, Vic, would never cheat on a girl. 'I might not be good at staying in touch, but I don't cheat,' he says and I scoff and Jean-Luc gives one of his trademark snorts and Flick is *still* going on about the two Facebook pages and, 'I texted Tab, didn't want to ring her in case she was still with Mark, but she hasn't replied and I think we're going to have to do an intervention on her. Also, Molly, don't suppose you have a spare Duckie T-shirt – I'll pay, but Sunny's top is looking rather gross and, God, I'd be totally *mortified* if I were wearing a gross T-shirt, well, in front of you guys. Big fan. *Big*, big fan.'

I was just about to inform Vic that I now have a zero-tolerance policy on boys who treat girls badly, but that can wait. I whirl round so fast I almost get whiplash so I can get a proper look at the two girls that Vic and Jean-Luc and Jeane have been hanging out with.

I glance over at Emmeline to see if she's noticed and she has, because her mouth is hanging open and she's got this dumbstruck look on her face like when she's spent a solid hour watching videos of kittens dressed up in outfits on the internet. 'I'm too scared to look,' she whispers and Emmeline isn't scared of anything. She plays roller derby, for God's sake.

'You need to close your mouth,' I whisper back and I can't believe this is happening.

But it is. It really is. It's Molly and Jane from Duckie, both wearing dresses made out of silver material with little red rocket-ships all over it. Molly's brown hair is plaited, twisted and pinned in two Princess Leia coils above her ears and Jane has platinum-blond hair, way platinum-er and blonder than Emmeline's, in a wispy pixie cut. They look amazing. They also look a little weary because Flick's still talking in her deadpan, earnest, posh voice. Boy, can that girl talk.

'. . . and I was like totally pissed off about having to go to Paris for Mummy's birthday but then I found out that Duckie was playing at this club in Saint-Germain-des-Prés and so I skipped out on her birthday dinner to see you play. She was furious but it wasn't like it was an important birthday. She was only forty-seven or forty-eight or something, so, like, whatever. Anyway, where was I? Oh yes, Mark. Poor Sunny. When my sister broke up with her boyfriend, Mummy sent her to a grief counsellor. I could get his number for you.'

Flick pauses for breath and I have to make her stop or condemn us all to yet more earnest, posh fangirling. Also, I'll have this encounter to look back on for years to come and when I am a grizzled old lady I don't want to say to my grandchildren, 'So, did I ever tell you about the time I met Jane and Molly from Duckie and all anyone could talk about was how my first ever boyfriend had been cheating on me?'

'I'm so over Mark,' I say quickly because Flick opens her mouth again like she's got her second wind. 'So over thinking that I'm less and that it's OK for other people to think that too. Not any more. I am powerful and strong and I believe in myself.' I shut my mouth, because Emmeline is doing a weird flickery thing with her eyes like she knows if she doesn't stop me right there, I'm going to ramble on and on.

It's too late. 'It's like RuPaul says, if you can't love yourself, then how the *hell* you gonna love someone else?'

Emmeline grips my hand. 'Oh God,' she whimpers at me. 'First Flick and now you. Please stop talking.'

'Can I get an Amen up in here?' Molly Montgomery out of Duckie says in a really crap impersonation of RuPaul and then Jane, Emmeline and I all raise our hands and shout, 'Amen!' because how can we not?

And if anyone knows a better way to make the acquaintance of your number-one girl crush then I'd like to hear it.

'You're definitely better off without this Mark,' Molly says and she flashes me a toothy grin. 'And if you need a quick way to get over him, I find writing really shouty songs about toxic boyfriends particularly cathartic.'

'Yeah! Dick rhymes with all sorts of handy things,' Jane adds. 'Once we even rhymed it with guitar pick.'

'Or "You make me absolutely sick",' I suggest. 'Sorry, I'm feeling quite stabby.'

'Honestly, Sunny, girls should never apologise for owning their feelings,' Jeane says, and she should know because Jeane's never apologised for anything in her life. 'Even if your feelings are about Mark.'

I'm saved from having to come up with a snappy reply that doesn't make me seem like a total bitch in front of Jane and Molly by Flick getting a text from Tab.

'It's a lot of emoji.' She squints at her screen. 'Three angry faces. Gun. Bomb. Hammer. I don't think she's taking it that well.'

Flick's phone beeps again. 'Tab again,' she murmurs, glancing down at the screen. 'Oh. Oh! Oh goodness, how bloody dare he? She says Mark denied everything, then dumped her.'

She holds up her phone and I squint and see the word. Dumped. Six letters that hit me right in my solar plexus. If my solar plexus is right in the middle of my gut, which I'm pretty sure it is.

All night I'd been treating this Tabitha as an anonymous skank in short shorts when really we were sisters under the skin. Related by betrayal. Connected because we'd both known the touch of Mark's hands, his lips, listened to him tell us that we were the only girl in the world.

'No way!' I gasp. 'He better not have. He doesn't get to dump her. Not when he's been cheating on her. On us. We're the ones that get to do the dumping. That's basic good manners. Oh God, I am going to dump his sorry arse like it's never been dumped before. Mark is going down!'

'Attagirl!' Jane claps her hands. 'You find this so-called Mark and make him regret the day he was ever born.'

'Well, we were all meant to be meeting in this club in Mayfair,' Flick says. She runs an eye over me, like I'm an item that won't scan at the self-service checkout. 'I'd better go on ahead. Run interference. Tell Tab that you're cool and that you're totally on board with the making Mark sorry that he was ever born. Only thing is that this club is members only.'

'Members only! Shmembers only!' I put my hands on my hips. 'They'd better let me in or I'll make them sorry they were born too.'

I wasn't sure who they were, but if they tried to stop me from a face-to-face confrontation with Mark then they'd wish they'd never tried.

'Now *these* are the feelings you should be owning,' Jeane says and Vic promises me that we'll storm the door, British Bulldog style, if we have to, and Jean-Luc says that he'll create a diversion by talking French to them very loudly and with a lot of hand gestures, and Molly says we can have a lift in the Duckie van but we need to leave now.

Only Emmeline seems uncharacteristically reluctant to seek vengeance on Mark, which is ironic considering that she never liked him in the first place. 'Oh? So you wanted to take Mark down tonight then. Like, right now?' she asks with a frown. 'Because I was kinda hoping that we could go home and take him down tomorrow. It's just that it's nearly three in the morning and I'm tired and I'm not wearing trainer socks and the backs of my heels are really rubbing.'

She sounds really whiny. In fact, she sounds a lot like me, as if we've been bodyswapped in a *Freaky Friday*-style cosmic accident.

'C'mon, Em! Where's your fighting spirit?' I pick up one of her limp hands to gee her up but it's like holding a dead fish. 'I have blister plasters and you can sleep when you're dead.'

Emmeline sighs. 'OK, but if a night bus to Crouch End suddenly materialises in front of me then all bets are off.'

WHAT THE HELL AM I DOING WITH MY SATURDAY NIGHT?

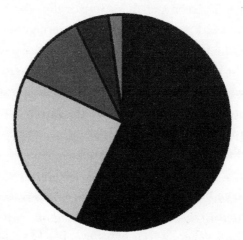

 Channelling Inigo Montoya from *The Princess Bride*

 Owning my feelings

 Fangirling Duckie

 Broom management

 Kind of needing a wee, to be honest with you

2.53 a.m.

MAYFAIR

One of the richest areas of London, and the most expensive square to land on in Monopoly, Mayfair took its name from the annual fortnight long May Fair that ran in the area from the late seventeenth century onwards.

Much of the area was owned and developed by the richer-than-God Grosvenor family in the mid-seventeenth century, who were then awarded the dukedom of Westminster, which was nice for them. Mayfair quickly became the most fashionable district in London and was the haunt of king of the dandies, Beau Brummel, famed for his elaborate neckcloths, who used to sit in the window of the gentlemen's club Whites and pass judgement on the outfits of his friends as they passed by. Kind of like a Regency-era Sidebar of Shame.

Famous Mayfair residents include several prime ministers including Sir Winston Churchill, the composer George Frideric

Handel and the two greatest Madges that ever Madged: Madonna and Her Majesty the Queen who was born in a house on Bruton Street.

It's almost too amazing to comprehend. I'm wearing one of Molly Montgomery's spare T-shirts. A T-shirt owned and previously worn by Molly Montgomery. It's yellow and in big black block letters it says: A CITY BUILT ON ROCK 'N' ROLL IS STRUCTURALLY UNSOUND.

If that wasn't enough, more than enough, Molly has given me her address in Brighton, so I can post the T-shirt back to her. 'I'm sure you're not a stalker,' she'd said, which goes to show how little she knows about me.

I'm wedged into the back of the Duckie tour van, with all four members of Duckie, Emmeline, Charlie, Vic and Jean-Luc. Preeta and Lucy had begged off and got the nightbus home, Emmeline and Charlie looking longingly after them. Flick and her friends had planned to come with us but when Jane opened the doors of the van and a smell of stale lager and cheesy feet wafted out, they backtracked. 'Actually there isn't much room, we'd be better getting in a nice black cab,' Flick had said, but she'd promised on her pony Melisande's life to text me once she'd spoken to Tabitha and found out Mark's location.

Once we get past Piccadilly Circus, it doesn't take very long to career around the tiny, twisty roads that run parallel to Piccadilly and all the while I'm clenching my fists and thinking about what I'm going to do to Mark. Probably going to start off by bellowing, 'Oi! I want a word with you!' then after that I'll kick it freestyle. I may even *kick* Mark freestyle, though

Emmeline says that violence is only the answer when you're playing roller derby.

Right now, though, Emmeline looks like she might be rethinking that philosophy. Her eyes promise death by unimaginable pain as Vic gestures at her and Charlie and says, 'So you two, then? You a thing or is it just a phase you're going through?'

'Right, well, first of all sexual identity is a fluid concept and not a fixed point on a graph, and secondly, it's none of your bloody business,' Charlie says. She gestures at Vic and Jean-Luc. 'Anyway, what about you two? Are you a thing or is it just a phase you're going through.'

'We're cousins,' Vic says, while Jean-Luc shakes his head and sighs and probably wonders why he ever left Paris. 'And if I were gay, he wouldn't be my type. Too moody, too bony, not pretty enough.'

'Prettier than you,' Jean-Luc mutters, though I'm not sure that technically he is. If there were a scale of prettiness, Vic would probably get a higher score than Jean-Luc. When Vic smiles, his eyes light up and his whole face is this lovely, welcoming thing. Jean-Luc hardly smiles at all.

Tomorrow, Emmeline and I must sit down and talk about which Godard is foxier, objectively speaking.

'If you're so pretty then how come you haven't hooked up with a single girl since you rocked up at St Pancras?' Vic wags a finger at Jean-Luc. 'Or is the only thing that gets you hot your choux pastry?'

'*Casse-toi!*' Jean-Luc says without much heat. Then he smiles. No, it really isn't as pretty as Vic's smile, but there's something wicked about it, which looks a lot more fun. 'Ah Jane, I was meaning to ask, how long were you and Vic dating?'

'You what?' Jane's sitting up front but now she turns around. 'Me and Vic? Something get lost in translation?'

'Vic says –' Vic clamps his hand over Jean-Luc's mouth so he can't actually speak.

'Ignore him. His English isn't too good.'

Jane pulls a face. 'I'd say his English is excellent.'

'Honestly, Jane, he's a bit touched in the head. Lot of inbreeding on that side of the family so . . . Ow! Get your hand out of my face!'

Even sitting down in a moving vehicle, Vic and Jean-Luc are tussling. 'That's actually quite hot,' Charlie murmurs to Emmeline. 'With the suits and everything.'

'Hmmm. I know. And the hair and the swearing in French. At least, I think it's swearing.'

'So, Jane, Vic says that you and he go way, way, *way* back,' I pipe up from the cheap seats, by which I mean sitting by a wheel arch with a guitar case pressing into my kidneys. 'But that a gentlemen never kisses and tells, even though he's no gentleman.'

Jane bares her teeth. 'Yeah, I guess we do go way back, right back to the time I first met him, which was when I commissioned him to make my wedding cake. Great cake, but then he tried to get off with my Auntie Cheryl at the reception.' She throws her head back and the only word for the sound that comes out of her mouth is a guffaw. Maybe two words: hearty guffaw. 'Didn't go down too well with my Uncle Ron, did it, Vic?'

Vic succeeds in batting Jean-Luc's hands away. 'It's not my fault. *Ma chère* Cheryl, she's a hell of a looker for a woman her age.'

'You biddy fiddler,' Emmeline mutters and there's a collective gasp because Emmeline went *there*, then Molly starts laughing and I'm still giggling when we get dropped off across the road from The Ritz.

My grandmother has been promising to take me to The Ritz for afternoon tea for as long as I can remember. That we'll get all dressed up in vintage frocks and do it properly, but every time she does come up to town, we always end up spending hours in John Lewis so she can buy boring things like embroidery yarn and moth strips and it never happens.

It isn't happening tonight either. We congregate on a street corner and everyone looks at me expectantly.

'So, what's the plan then?' Charlie asks. 'We just gonna hang around waiting to get a text from this Flick?'

That was the plan but it sounds a bit crap when Charlie says it. Also, I wasn't in the mood for hanging about. I was in the mood for action. For doing, not loitering aimlessly on street corners.

'Why are you doing that funny dance?' Vic asks and I realise that I'm swaying from foot to foot and, oh God, screwing up my face and making little panting noises as if I'm one of the pregnant women from *One Born Every Minute* and I'm on the home stretch. I am doing . . .

'The wee-wee dance,' Emmeline exclaims and she could have been more discreet about it, even if she is right. Emmeline has seen my wee-wee dance before. Many many times before.

I ignore Emmeline and look up and down Piccadilly in the hope that there's a Burger King or a McDonald's still open so I can buy the cheapest thing on the menu, then rush off to relieve my agony. Yes, it was already fast approaching agony now.

'What's the wee-wee dance?' Jean-Luc asks. 'Is it some English thing?'

'I need a wee, all right?' There's no time to dress it up, say that I need to powder my nose or splash my face with cold water. I need a toilet and I need it now. Yesterday. 'Oh God, how I need a wee!'

I'm already speedwalking down the road. I can feel everything sloshing about in my bladder. It's very unpleasant.

'But why didn't you go before? You were in the bathroom for ages,' Charlie asks accusingly as the others catch up with me. 'What were you doing?'

'Having lager thrown over me, mostly.'

'I'm not surprised you need a wee,' Vic says. 'That drink you had in the chicken shop was bigger than your head.'

'Yeah, thanks for reminding me.'

We're heading further and further away from Piccadilly Circus as I desperately look for the sight of those glowing golden arches; a beacon of hope for my poor bladder.

'Why isn't there a MacDonald's when you need one?'

'There is. We're going in the wrong direction. It's by the station.' Jean-Luc squints at his phone. 'Oh, *tant pis*, it's closed.'

I am going to have to do the unthinkable. I look around for an alley. Better, a tiny alley off an already tiny alley so I can urinate in the street like someone off their nuts after binge drinking all night. Though can't you be arrested for public urination? And we've been through all kinds of stuff together but I don't know Jean-Luc and Vic *that* well and they are impeccably turned out and I don't want them to think that I am the kind of person who happily pisses in the street whenever the need takes her.

I can tell Emmeline is thinking the same thing for she looks around too and then says to me, 'Shall we take a little walk together, Sun? See if we can't find, you know, a public convenience that no one knows about.' She does air quotes round 'public convenience' so I know that what she really means is we'll find somewhere, anywhere, for me to go and Emmeline will shield me during my escapade of shame and then we'll never say anything about it ever again.

Except Charlie shakes her head. 'Well, there won't be a public convenience open, will there? They'll all be closed.'

I know Emmeline likes Charlie but she's really starting to get on my nerves with all the naysaying. I close my eyes and squeeze every muscle I have. God, it is either piss in an alley or wet myself. Lesser of two evils? I can't decide.

'Oh, we're right by The Ritz. They must have a loo for a lady in distress.' Vic takes my hand and starts to take me across the road.

'They're never going to let us in The Ritz!' Emmeline says, as she scurries to keep up with us. 'Just look at us!'

'Our money is just as good as anyone else's,' Vic declares. 'Not that I'm planning to book a room or anything but maybe we could order a glass of water.'

'Or a small cup of coffee?' Jean-Luc suggests hopefully.

'Please stop talking about liquid,' I beg as we get nearer and nearer to the imposing building that's lit up and glowing like it should have a discreet sign by the door that says, 'No riff-raff.'

'Can you hang on just a little bit longer?' Vic asks.

I can barely speak. 'I hope so or I might just die of utter humiliation.'

'Nothing to be embarrassed about,' Vic says, because we've already established that he's beyond embarrassment. He doesn't even know what it means. 'One time, we got held up on the M6 for hours due to a pile-up and I had to piss in an empty milk carton.'

'It wasn't empty,' Jean-Luc recalls with some disdain, and I would laugh but all my muscles are still on clench setting as we walk through one of the arches, because The Ritz is so grand that it has its own covered walkway to protect its guests from the elements, and right up to the door. Through the glass, I can see a huge ornate chandelier that sparkles in the dark night. My eyes follow the path of the plush red and gold carpet, which opens out into a circular foyer. Maybe not even a foyer. Cinemas have foyers, even the really grotty ones. This is something grander. A vestibule maybe. Or a rotunda. Whatever it's called, it's like looking into a Fabergé egg or a beautiful music box. I half expect to see an impossibly delicate ballerina slowly spinning round and round instead of a gilt-edged marble table topped with a huge vase of white flowers.

A man in a pinstripe suit strides down the carpet towards us.

Usually there are smart uniformed doormen outside but even The Ritz locks its doors at this time of night and the man bearing down on us, a quizzical expression on his face, will take one good look at our dishevelled appearance – even Vic's shirt has lost its snowy whiteness by now – and tell us to piss off. But he'll probably be more polite than that.

I try not to jiggle as he unlocks the door and as soon as it opens, my mind is set. I'm going to storm the gilt-edged citadels of The Ritz. By the time he catches me, I'm sure I'll have been able to find the Ladies and lock myself in a cubicle.

The door opens just enough for me to be able to wedge myself through it and I take a step forward and that's it! I'm off! I push past the man and everything is a red and gold blur as I race across the lobby. I don't know where I'm going, but I see a sign to a restaurant and where's there a restaurant, there has to be public toilets. It's the law. Both my grandmothers and Terry's mum have told me and countless cafe owners this on numerous occasions and I'm hobbling down the corridor, dimly aware of people behind me, my knees locked together, and I come to another door . . . and thank God.

I hurl myself through the door. Then hurl myself into a cubicle. I don't even bother sliding the lock but fumble with the button and zip on my shorts and yank them down, while I hop from foot to foot.

Then I plonk myself down on the loo. Ah! Bliss. Sweet, sweet bliss.

TWO MINUTES LATER

How could I ever have known when I set out for the arduous trek to Crystal Palace all those hours ago that at some point during the night I would end up peeing in The Ritz?

159

'Peeing in The Ritz,' I sing under my breath to the tune of 'Putting on The Ritz', but there's no one to share the joke with. If I could ever tell Terry about this night – maybe years from now when I can't be grounded or have the Wi-Fi password withheld – he would think it was hilarious.

It *is* hilarious. I've just peed in The Ritz and now I'm in a pastel pink powder room with a quite disturbing mural taking up one wall that features a frond-encrusted pond with lily pads and a woman peering through the fronds, while on the other side a man peers at her like a gigantic perv. The more I look at it, the less sense it makes.

Besides, I have more important things to do, like wondering who or what is waiting for me outside the door. Could I be arrested for trespassing? Would they let me off with a caution? It's best not to think about it at all, so instead I slather myself in really expensive hand-lotion, not just my hands but my arms and legs too. Underneath the mural is a plush pink sofa and I think about sitting on it. Then I think about lying on it. Then I think about curling up and going to sleep on it because now that I no longer need to pee, I'm feeling quite tired.

There's a knock on the door. 'Miss! Miss! I'm going to have to ask you to come out now.'

One more generous squirt of hand lotion, then I slink out to find a security guard standing by the door.

I try to remember that no man is the boss of me. I'm a warrior. Tonight I run this town. 'Oh God, please don't have me arrested,' I squeak. 'Normally I'm a law-abiding citizen, I really am, but the circumstances were beyond, *beyond*, extenuating.'

I could swear that beneath his peaked cap he winks at me but his face remains blank. 'I'm going to have to ask you to vacate the premises, miss,' he says in the same neutral voice, and as long as I'm not being arrested I'm more than happy to be escorted back to the front entrance where Jean-Luc appears to be remonstrating with another security guard and the man in the pinstriped suit.

'*Mais c'est une question de vie ou de mort,*' he says, throwing his hands up. '*Mon amie est bouleversée. Qui sait ce qu'elle pourrait faire? Elle a un historique de maladie mentale!*'

'I'm so sorry. So, so sorry,' I call out. 'I can't think what came over me. I promise I'll never do it again.'

'Yes, well, if you do, I'll have to ban you from every Ritz in the world for life,' Pinstripe Man says, but he doesn't seem that cross about it, just shoos us out the door and locks it behind us.

'High five,' Charlie says and she looks at me with proper respect like I didn't just storm The Ritz but stole a priceless antique on my way out the door too. 'Dude, high five. I can't believe you did that.'

We high five. All of us, except Jean-Luc, who shakes his head. '*Non.* I don't do high fives.'

'Are you all right now?' Emmeline asks.

I nod. 'Much better. Let's not talk about it any more. Not ever again. I'm going to check my phone and see if Flick has texted me.'

First we cross over Piccadilly. It's deserted now; a ghost road through the centre of town. It's hard to believe that in a few short hours it will thrum with life, carrying people in cars and buses and taxis from Piccadilly Circus to Hyde Park

Corner. That Sunday shoppers and tourists will amble along the pavement, staring into shop windows and buying silly hats from souvenir stalls. Now all is still, all is quiet, apart from Charlie who says, 'Flick is never going to text you. Those posh types always stick together.'

She's so negative. I'm starting to think that maybe she and Emmeline shouldn't get together if she's not going to be supportive of Emmeline's best friend's lifestyle choices, and also Charlie knows nothing because as I extricate my phone from the depths of my bag, it beeps.

'Ha!' I say. 'See! The girl code trumps poshness every time. And . . . oh! It's from Mark.'

Just seeing his name on my phone screen has my stomach lurching all over again, but I'm a warrior who isn't afraid of a little thing like a text.

Everyone crowds around me to see as I open it.

Babe! U mad at me? Don't be. That girl Tab is cray cray. SO ARE ALL HER FRIENDS. Believe nothing they tell u.

'Urgh, he is the worst,' Emmeline mutters.

'Now that he's dumped this Tab, he's trying to keep his bases covered, making sure he's still got you in reserve,' Vic says. 'Don't let him suspect a thing.'

Hey! Met girl called Flick. Said some pretty shady stuff about u.

Mark texts back immediately. For a change.

162

Please say u don't believe her.

NO! You said nothing happened. I trust u. I love u. U know that. Where u at?

On way home. Unless u still up for it? Literally & figuratively?

Now I kind of wish everyone wasn't still crowded around me so they could witness this little exchange. Emmeline snatches my phone so she can squint at the text in disbelief. 'Unbelievable. He really thinks he's still going to get into your pants. Come on, just dump him so we can all go home.'

'I'm not dumping him over text. We agreed that was a shabby thing to do.'

'No, we agreed that it was a shabby thing for *him* to do. Just tell him you know everything, make some mid-level threats and finish it,' Emmeline flails her arms in a half-hearted fashion. 'I'm *so* tired.'

'It's not *that* late,' I say, although it is. I've never been up this late before but now I'm high on righteous anger and adrenalin. I snatch my phone back from Emmeline.

There's nothing I want less than Mark rummaging about in my pants, but I need to keep stringing him along for the time being so that when I dump him I can look him right in the eyes as I administer the fatal blow. Still, I don't want to appear too eager and also Mark's track record of being where he's said he'll be is appalling.

Know it was nothing but still quite upset about seeing u wit other girl. Going home now. U heading north? Want 2 get bus together?

'*Mon dieu!* Experimenting with chestnut paste would have been more thrilling than this,' I hear Jean-Luc say, but I ignore him as Mark replies in an instant.

Heading west. Staying with Pa. G'ma's bday 2morrow. Sure I can't make it up 2 u tonight? Could stay over at mine?

Emmeline's whining in the background. Jean-Luc is muttering in French. Charlie is flat-out demanding to go home and only Vic is being any real help.

'Say that maybe he could change your mind,' he advises me. 'If he thinks you're gagging for it, pardon my French, he'll give you a location, we can go there and then the arse-kicking can commence.

'You won't kick his arse, though, Sunny,' Emmeline says and she suddenly collapses her legs so she's sitting on the pavement, but that's not enough because then she lays down and flails again. 'I want to go home! Everything hurts and I told you I had blisters from not wearing trainer socks and you promised me plasters and you never gave them to me and I want to go home.'

I know how she feels. I'm sympathetic but resolute as I fish in my bag. 'You want plasters? Here! Have the plasters. But I've come this far and I'm not going home until I've confronted Mark. In person. That'll show him!'

'*Mais non*. What exactly is it going to show him? Let's all go home!' Jean-Luc tries to pull me away even though I try to dig my heels in. He's surprisingly strong. It must be all that beating eggs and creaming sugar and grinding coffee beans. For a moment, I want to sink into his arms because I am actually quite tired myself and my feet are sore too, though you don't hear me complaining about it.

Only for a moment, though. Then I'm standing unaided. 'I'm going to show Mark that I won't be ignored. He can't treat me like this. You can't, like, be with someone, do stuff, say stuff, for all of it to be a lie. Like, it was never real. I thought it meant something and all the time he was playing me! Can't you understand how that makes me feel?'

I don't get it. I never have. Like, my parents. My mum and dad. Except, they've never been mum *and* dad because I can't remember them being together. They've always been mum or dad.

But they were together for four years. Lived together. Spent all those months and weeks and days and hours and minutes together. Told each other their secrets. Cried in front of each other (though I can't imagine my dad ever crying). Looked after each other when one of them was sick. All the things that being a couple are and then it just ended and now they've never spent a single minute together where it was just the two of them.

They only talk about me. About my university tuition fees and whose turn it is to have the pleasure of my company on birthdays or major public holidays and all the other stuff; the secrets and the looking after each other, it's simply stopped.

What happened to all those feelings they had for each other? Where do they go?

So, yeah, I'm going to smoke Mark out because this needs to be finished on my terms. When he's standing in front of me, sickened and ashamed, because I've made him acknowledge what he's done, how he's hurt my feelings.

Emmeline doesn't get it when I explain it to her. 'Dude, you're being ridiculous,' she snaps.

'My feelings are not ridiculous!'

She rolls her eyes and clutches at the pavement that she's still sprawled on. 'God, will you stop banging on about your feelings? There is no point in all of us staying here. Anyway, even if Mark does agree to meet you, all you'll do is burst into tears. Again.'

'No, I won't! Anyway, you're always telling me that I should be more decisive. Well, I've made a decision and I'm sticking by it. I'm staying out until I find Mark and then I'm going to tell him exactly what I think about him.'

'It's a bad decision,' Emmeline spits out as she struggles to her feet. 'You don't even know where he is, do you? You don't have a plan and I can't even believe that we're still talking about this.'

I've come too far to back down now. Me and Emmeline are nose to nose, both of us breathing hard. 'Well, thanks for all your support, Em! It's good to know who your friends really are.'

'I am your friend, you div. I'm trying to be supportive but you're making it really difficult. If this is the new, improved Sunny then I have to tell you that she's a bit of a twat!'

'I am not a twat.'

'Yeah, you really are and I'm going home. I've had enough of this! Charlie! Come on! We're going!'

'Fine! Go!' I shout after Emmeline as she storms off. Though she doesn't so much storm as hobble. Charlie follows her, though she pauses to give me a reproachful look. 'I don't care!'

Except I do care because it's Emmeline and she's my best friend. And though I am *not* a twat, maybe I've been a little inconsiderate of how tired Emmeline is. She gets really cranky when she's sleep deprived. One time, when we were in Year Three and at a sleepover, she locked herself in the toilet and refused to come out because everyone else was making too much noise and watching Hannah Montana DVDs when Emmeline wanted to sleep.

'Should I go after her?' I ask Vic, who shrugs. Emmeline isn't moving very fast and I could easily catch her up. 'I should go after her . . . Oh! I'm beeping! It's Mark.'

He's sent me a snapchat and 'Woah! What even is *that*?'

It's a photo of Mark with his hand delving into the front of his jeans and the caption: 'Sure u won't change your mind?'

Jean-Luc actually says, '*Ooh la la!*' and Vic sniggers and says, 'Even I wouldn't stoop that low,' before the picture disappears.

In its place is a text from Flick.

Sorry for delay. Tab in hysterics. Mark & pals in Chelsea. Club called Plebs. Will put name on door.

She's even included a Google Maps link.

There's no time to race after Emmeline now. I can already feel the adrenalin start to kick in again. Vengeance shall be mine.

'OK. So we're on?' Vic asks.

'We're *so* on.'

Jean-Luc is slightly off. 'Chelsea is *miles* away,' he moans. 'And this could be um . . .' He snaps his fingers. Not in a crisp, clicky way but in a way that suggests that even his fingers are a bit tired. 'A *double bluff*?'

'Double bluff. It's the same in English,' Vic says. 'That Flick. How trustworthy was she?'

'I don't know,' I say, doubt starting to creep in.

It could be a double bluff. Then again, it might not be. There's only one way to find out.

'We're going to Chelsea,' I say firmly and I ignore Jean-Luc's bitten-off groan and the way his lips twist in an entirely different way to Vic's. There's a French word for it. A *moue*. Yeah. Jean-Luc is moueing or pouting. Even Vic is looking a little battle weary, but he straightens his shoulders and smiles brightly and I'm starting to feel like I can never go home again.

Anyway, Chelsea isn't *miles* away. We get on the tube at Green Park, go one stop to Victoria, then change onto the Circle line, one more stop and we're at Sloane Square. Couldn't be simpler.

Except the Circle line isn't running, which is just ridiculous. What even is the point of having the tube run all night if you're going to leave out major bits of it like the Circle line? So, we have to get the Piccadilly line to Knightsbridge and then figure it out from there. They shouldn't call it the night tube. It's false advertising. They should call it 'a small part of the tube that runs all night.'

'How I wish that we'd never caught up with you at Clapham North,' Jean-Luc grumbles as we walk to the right platform.

It's the first time I've been on the tube after-hours since it started running all through the night, and it feels strange. It's quiet. Hardly anyone about as if each station is inhabited by ghosts who keep the trains gliding along the humming tracks in the small hours. It's as if we're not really meant to be there, under all that harsh strip lighting so our skin looks ashen, our eyes huge, everything kind of hyperreal.

Or maybe I've just been awake so long that life has got trippy.

I'm bookended by Godards as we sit and wait for the train. 'But we did catch up with Sunny at Clapham North and now we're having adventures,' Vic says and I shoot him a grateful smile because Jean-Luc has had a face like thunder ever since we travelled down the first escalator at Green Park. Not just thunder but ominous dark clouds and hail stones too. 'Anyway, we couldn't have left you on your own. Imagine if something had happened to you. All the free pastries and coffee in the world wouldn't make it up to *la belle Hélène*.'

I squirm a bit. My midnight curfew is shot to pieces and lying dead on the floor. Then I unsquirm. Like, she and Terry are ever going to find out. Unless . . . 'You won't tell my mum about tonight, will you? I mean, technically you're accessories after the fact.'

'I prefer to think of us as willing accomplices,' Vic says. 'Though it shouldn't be this hard to track down one boy.' Vic rests his sharp elbows on his bony knees, then rests his chin on his hands. It looks very uncomfortable. 'Is he always this difficult to find?'

I think about all the times I waited for Mark to call me. The many times I stood outside various North London landmarks:

the Crouch End clocktower, Kenwood House on Hampstead Heath, Camden Town tube station, because he was running late. Never where he'd said he'd be at the time we decided on.

I could think about the good bits, and there were lots of those, but there was also the endless waiting for Mark and the endless rehearsing of what I'd say to him when he finally surfaced. But as soon as I tried out the first fumbling, stumbling sentence, he'd say, 'Babe,' all sorrowfully and give me a flash of that grin and hold my hand and then I'd feel grateful that he'd bothered to turn up at all.

In some ways, Mark was a bit like Emmeline. It's hard to be around people whose star always burns brighter than yours does.

Except, now Mark's star had burned itself out.

'I am sorry that I've dragged you on this mad chase. Have I been a real pain in the arse?'

Jean-Luc and Vic don't even have to think about it. 'Yeah,' they both say in unison, then stand up at the same time too as the train comes roaring out of the tunnel.

'Major pain in the arse, Sunny. Just as well you're funny and you dance a mean Charleston, otherwise we'd have left you in Camden,' Vic says as we sit down on the train, me in the middle again. 'And pretty too, not that I ever judge a woman based solely on her looks because that would be wrong.'

'Such a pity that we didn't leave *you* in Camden, Vic.' Jean-Luc reaches around me to dig Vic in the ribs.

They bicker quietly in French all the way to Knightsbridge and are still going at it as we emerge from the station. All this forward motion and getting on and off tube trains has been great for distracting me, but now, as we get on a bus that will

170

take us down Sloane Street, I'm beyond nervous. There needs to be a new word for how I feel.

If I'd found Mark as soon as I'd left the Duckie gig when my blood was up and the demands of my bladder were making everything just a little bit urgent, then I would have been devastating. Mark would have been devastated. I'm still hazy on the details of this devastation, even hazier now that we jump off the bus at the top of the King's Road and we're moments away from a bar called Plebs. Where I will confront Mark and try to come up with words that will put a hard, gnarly knot in his stomach too. That makes his heart hurt. That makes him look deep within himself, at the way he treats people, and for Mark to realise that he doesn't like what he sees.

I'm not sure that I know any words that can do all of that. Still, I've got to try, otherwise this night was all for nothing.

First, I have to find Mark – and then the blue dot and the red arrow on my Google Maps matches up and we're here.

LONDON CALLING

A playlist (compiled by Sunny, Terry and *la belle Hélène*)

'Waterloo Sunset' – The Kinks
'Girl VII' – Saint Etienne
'A Rainy Night in Soho' – The Pogues
'Warwick Avenue' – Duffy
'The Underground Train' – Lord Kitchener
'London Pride' – Noël Coward
'Hey Young London' – Bananarama
'Mayfair' – Nick Drake
'London Town' – Laura Marling
'Bar Italia' – Pulp
'Galang' – M.I.A.
'Maybe It's Because I'm a Londoner' – Hubert Gregg
'Hometown Glory' – Adele
'LDN' – Lily Allen
'West End Girls' – Pet Shop Boys
'London Calling' – The Clash

3.45 a.m.

CHELSEA

In 1536, Henry VIII acquired the manor of Chelsea as a good place to put Anne of Cleves, the wife he really wasn't that into.

Chelsea continued on the up and up. Its famous King's Road began life as Charles II's private road linking St James's Palace to Fulham, but by Victorian times Chelsea was better known as an artist's colony. Whistler, Sargent, Rossetti all slung paint around in SW3.

Chelsea became popular again in the Sixties when it was home to boutiques like Granny Takes a Trip and Mary Quant's Bazaar and its streets were packed with girls in miniskirts and men with shaggy hair. The punks moved in during the Seventies, and in the Eighties the debutantes and aristos who had always lived in Chelsea took over again. They were known as Sloane Rangers, best personified by Lady Di before she became a princess.

These days, Chelsea is best known for the reality show Made in Chelsea, *even though it's a well-established fact that the greatest thing to ever come out of Chelsea is the Chelsea Bun.*

Plebs.

It's spelled out in icy-white neon letters. A bar buzzing with people. Through the window I see girls with glossy limbs artfully arranged on leather sofas, guys with hair slicked back and one too many buttons on their shirt left unbuttoned.

This has to be a trap. There's no way that Mark and even his poshest friends from his old life would hang out here. They might be rich but these people are beyond rich. Like they have Ferraris bought for them when they pass their driving tests and black Amex cards instead of an allowance.

'I think this is a trap,' I say.

'It probably is.' Jean-Luc isn't exactly helping. 'I don't trust people who are so shiny-looking.'

'Oh it will be fine.' Vic marches up to the entrance, and the bouncer, who's wearing a much nicer suit than he is, simply opens the door and lets Vic walk straight in.

I have no French blood in my veins. Not one ounce of *je ne sais quoi* or *savoir faire* or anything else, so I shuffle up to the door and squeak, 'I'm on the list, my name's Sunny.' I gesture at Jean-Luc who's now slouching so hard that his neck has completely disappeared. He looks like a skinny, big-haired tortoise. 'He's with me.'

The bouncer gives me a hard 'what the hell?' stare, but then he glances down at his iPad (they don't do clipboards in

SW3 apparently) and my name must be on the list, because he opens the door for us too.

The first thing that hits me is the noise. I'm bludgeoned by a wall of sound. There's shrieking, shouting, laughing to the beat of the clink of glasses. A DJ in his booth high above the crowd spins what he probably calls 'smooth grooves'.

Vic has disappeared. I don't know where to but Jean-Luc and I do a quick circuit. It's quite hard as there are lots of little cubbyholes that lead off the main bar and they're all reserved for private parties. The people in the invite-only cubbyholes look at us like we've just farted and they can smell it from where they're sitting. I try to text Flick but using Google Maps has absolutely wiped what was left of my phone battery.

Once we're back in the main bar I realise that I'm the only brown person here. The only person wearing a crumpled T-shirt that proclaims that a city built on rock 'n' roll is structurally unsound. The only one wearing scuzzy Adidas trainers, which have greying tide marks on the white rubber bits from all the times that I've got caught in the rain and squelched my way home.

But mostly I'm the only brown person in here.

'Shall we get a drink, then?' Vic is back. 'Whose round is it?'

Getting a round in is the least I can do. 'Mine. As long as I can get served.'

'You'll be fine.' I wonder if anything phases Vic apart from the girls he's wooed and then shooed. 'Just get me the cheapest lager they've got.'

'What do you want?' I ask Jean-Luc.

Jean-Luc sniffs. 'Lager, I suppose.'

It takes me ages to get served. Again, I can't help but wonder if it's because I'm the only brown person in the place.

That's not why the barman gives me serious shade, though. It's not to do with being under eighteen either, because he doesn't even ask. He just tells me that the two cheapest bottles of lager will be twenty-one pounds and thirty-eight pence and when my eyes bulge and I shriek, 'How bloody much?' he says that one pound and thirty-eight pence of that is the service charge. One pound and thirty-eight pence for getting two bottles of lager out of a fridge and popping the tops off.

And he gives me even more shade when I ask for a glass of water. 'Tap water,' I say, even though I die inside when I'm out with my mum and she orders tap water in a restaurant because she makes such a big deal out of it and I don't see what difference it makes to order a two-pound bottle of fizzy water, but now I'm saying 'tap water' and, by God, I mean it.

'We don't serve tap water,' he says. Ordinarily I'd be tongue-tied and unable to make eye contact because the barman is really fit. He looks like he models really tight T-shirts and sunglasses and hair products when he's not a barman. It's not even because I suddenly remember that I'm a warrior and I take shit from no one.

No, the reason why I'm channelling my inner badass is because he's just served me the two most expensive lagers in the world and so I look him right in his beautiful, soulful, shade-throwing eyes and I say, 'You have to serve me tap water. It's against the law if you refuse me. I could die of dehydration and my dad's a barrister.'

After that, he serves me tap water with a tight smile. Even puts ice and a lime wedge in it and I carefully carry my precious cargo back to Vic and Jean-Luc who are sitting on a sofa, legs crossed, pointy feet pointing in different directions. Jean-Luc looks like he wishes I'd got a side of razor blades with his lager.

He takes it from me without a word of thanks, then sits and stares at it like he expects the bottle to share some Yoda-like wisdom with him. 'Ah, young Jean-Luc, the force it is not strong in you.'

Vic looks round eagerly. 'So many beautiful women in here. I don't know where to start.'

There's nowhere for me to sit because it's a two-seater sofa, though it would probably be horrified to be called a sofa because it's white and leather and so minimalist it doesn't even have arms that I can perch on. So I lean against the wall with my dirty trainers, sipping at my tap water, being brown, and I'm glad Mark isn't here. This is not how I wanted things to go down.

'You know what? Should we just go home after you've drunk your lagers?'

Jean-Luc's eyes get very squinty. 'We come all the way to Chelsea for nothing?'

I lean further into the wall but it doesn't swallow me whole, which would be helpful. 'Er, yeah. Looks like it. Sorry.'

'Are we going?' Vic stops looking so chipper. 'But we've only just got here. What a waste! Let's stay for a little bit or at least until I've separated that blond girl over there in the jumpsuit away from the rest of her herd.'

'I hope you give her your real name,' Jean-Luc says as he levers himself up. 'This lager tastes awful. That girl over there keeps sticking her tongue in her boyfriend's ear but she keeps looking at me at the same time. *C'est l'endroit le plus horrible du monde. Allons-y!'*

He tries to stalk out but some guy in white jeans, loafers and a pastel-yellow shirt unbuttoned to show off far too much of his chest hair is in the way. They do this awkward dance until Jean-Luc leans in and says something to the guy, who immediately backs away, hands held up in surrender.

'The thing about Jean-Luc, Sunny, is that he's great until, all of a sudden, he's not great,' Vic says. He takes a casual swig of his lager. 'Very moody. I keep telling him that he should get his blood-sugar levels checked.'

'I'm sure that always lifts his spirits.' I feel very moody myself. I've been up tonight, coasted all sorts of big feelings, but now I'm coming down. I'm broke. My feet hurt. I feel like I'll never be clean again and the thought of having to get from Chelsea to Crouch End by public transport at gone four in the morning with a very moody Frenchman (I have a feeling from the way the blond girl in the jumpsuit keeps giving Vic these sultry looks that he won't be coming back to North London with us) makes me want to lay down on the floor and cry. 'I can't believe we came all this way for nothing.'

Vic takes one last gulp of his lager, then gets up. 'I wouldn't say it's been a completely wasted trip. So, you're all right to go home then, are you? I think it's time I moved in for the kill.'

I can't see Vic's face as he's turned away from me but the blond in the jumpsuit can and she obviously likes what she sees because she licks her lips and tosses her hair back, and I hate to interrupt but needs must and all that.

'Hang on. Let me do one more sweep.' I know in my bones, that Mark isn't here, but my bones are weary and aching so they might not be that reliable.

I push my way around the bar again, peeking into all those private rooms, catching my breath each time I see a boy with floppy blond hair. I feel quite faint, because there are a lot of boys with floppy blond hair, but none of them is Mark.

Until, suddenly, one of them *is* Mark.

I'm at the back of the room when I see him heading towards the door. Just another floppy blond head in the crowd, but then he turns, raises his hand at someone out of my eye line and my heart suddenly slam-dunks against my breastbone.

Mark says run and I run.

Except he doesn't even know I'm here, but I run anyway, hurdling over a footstool that's in my way, grabbing hold of Vic, who's mid-prowl towards the girl in the jumpsuit, by his sleeve and pulling him with me. He's not very happy about it.

'Sunny, what are you doing?'

'He's here!' I say, my eyes locked on Mark, who's now slipping out the door. 'He's getting away.'

We bundle after him, picking up Jean-Luc, who's loitering by the cloakroom until I yank his hand and pull him out of the door while Vic shouts something at him in French.

Too late! We get outside just in time to see Mark climb into the back of a black cab and slam the door as it pulls away from the kerb.

I don't dither. It's obvious what I have to do. Another black cab is dropping off more posh kids and one of them very kindly keeps the door open for me as I jump in, still clutching a Godard in each hand so they have no choice but to jump in with me. And then I say three words that I never thought anyone said outside of movies. 'Follow that cab!'

FIVE MINUTES LATER

We are in a cab. A black cab. I had no other choice.

Even though black cabs are ruinously expensive. That's what my mum says, but I think it's because my dad always takes black cabs and it's a dig at him. In the past, whenever he's queried the cost of my Spanish exchange trip or my dance lessons or why I need new shoes for school when I only just got a pair (because I really wanted them and lied and said they fitted when they didn't and then my feet were *riddled* with blisters and one of them got infected, hence new shoes, and really infected blisters were punishment enough), my mum always says bitterly, 'Huh! And this from the man who takes black cabs like they're bloody buses.'

Now I'm in one and it's lovely. Very comfy. Lots of leg room so Jean-Luc and Vic, who's sitting on one of the tip-up seats opposite me, can stretch out their legs and the cabbie, Stan, says that he's been cabbing for twenty-seven years and he's always wanted to hear a passenger say, 'Follow that cab!'

The streets are just a shadowy blur of plane trees and big stucco-covered houses and Vic points out a pub where he was once thrown out for standing on a table and singing the Marseillaise when France won the rugby but Jean-Luc slumps in his seat, until his chin rests on his chest.

'You can't find a person who doesn't want to be found,' he says eventually. 'We should go home. This Mark . . .' He sniffs.

It must be a Parisian thing, these sniffs that say so much. 'Why must you chase him? He's not chasing you.'

'God, that's a bit harsh,' Vic says and Jean-Luc shakes his head.

'No. I mean . . . all this energy, Sunny, all this effort, he doesn't deserve it. He's a . . . c'*est un salaud*. You're too good for him, too good to be chasing after him, *non?*'

'But I'm not chasing after him because I want him back. I'm chasing him down so I can tell him exactly what I think of him. I always let people walk all over me, squash me down until there's nothing left. Even when I feel like I'm shouting no one hears me, so I don't want to wait until I see Mark around. It could be days from now, and then it will seem like I'm being pathetic for not letting things go, but I'm not pathetic. I'm sick of people thinking that I am. Can't you understand that?'

Jean-Luc gives another Parisian sniff. 'Ha! You're the least pathetic person I've ever met.' Somehow he makes it sound as if it isn't a compliment. As if I'm as bossy as Jeane. Or as belligerent as Emmeline. I wish.

'I haven't had such a crazy Saturday night in ages. Maybe ever,' Vic says cheerfully. 'Such fun. Like a scavenger hunt but without a prize at the end . . .'

I hold up my hand. 'The prize will be my liberation!'

They both pull matching identical expressions of not being impressed by my liberation, which is odd, what with them being French. The only bit of French that I properly know off by heart, after all, is '*Liberté, égalité, fraternité ou mort*'. It's their national motto. I know this because it came up in an episode of *Pointless* one time. 'I'd rather have hard cash than liberation,' Vic says.

'Or alcohol. Or chocolate.'

'Standing up for myself for once in my life is a fantastic prize. If I can stand up to Mark then I can stand up to anyone.' It's true. Once Mark starts on the 'babes', each one sounding more reproachful than the last, I begin to relent. Then he touches me on the arm and does this thing with his eyes; looks at me like I'm the reason that the sun came up and that he got out of bed in the morning and I'd forget all the promises I made to myself. I'd still be mad at him but he'd be standing there all golden and glowing and focused on me and I'd panic and get frightened that he'd slip from my grasp.

Maybe that's why Mark is so elusive, so hard to find – because he's turned himself into a prize. A trophy boyfriend. But if Mark is a trophy it's the kind that looks good when someone else stands on the winners' podium and holds it up high so the sun glints off it.

Then when you get to wrap your own hands around the trophy, at first you're excited that you've won and dazzled by the way it shines. It takes a while before you notice that your trophy isn't made of anything precious. It's cheap metal that tarnishes quickly and the words you thought were engraved were just stamped on and are already starting to fade. This thing that you'd worked so hard to win is flimsy and cheap and it doesn't take much to break it.

'Really? So will you be able to stand up to *la belle Hélène*?' Jean-Luc pulls another sceptical face. 'C'*est impossible*.'

'So impossible. The things she makes us do. She hasn't paid for a cup of coffee in months,' Vic tells me. 'She's robbing us blind!'

That sounds like my mum. Obviously being a badass is in my genetic make-up; you only have to look at the women on both sides of my family to know that. Maybe my badassness was a dormant gene.

Suddenly Jean-Luc is right up in my face, so close that if we both blinked at the same time then our eyelashes would brush against each other's. So close that if we both pouted then our lips would brush against each other's. He still smells of sweet things. 'Sunny, I implore you. This is so silly. Let's go home.'

Home does sound kind of tempting but . . . 'I'm a warrior and warriors don't go home!'

Jean-Luc subsides back in his seat and I'm sure he'd be muttering in his native tongue if he weren't scowling so hard.

Anyway, I have better things to do, like keeping a close eye on the cab in front (Stan helpfully tells us that the other driver is 'going all round the houses, cheeky git') and stare at the meter and wonder why it keeps going up another thirty pence in the time it takes to blink. No wonder my dad bitches about new school shoes. He must be on the verge of bankruptcy if he takes taxis everywhere.

'Looks like our friends in front are stopping,' Stan says as the cab we've been following pulls up outside a huge house and a gang of boys, all with low-slung jeans and blond hair, pile out. I'm keen to pile out too but we need to pay the fare. The journey has only taken five minutes but costs nearly thirteen quid. I fumble in my purse and think I might cry, but Vic swats my hand away and thrusts a twenty at the driver. 'Make it up to fifteen, mate,' he says. 'You can buy me another drink, Sunny, some other Saturday night, then we're even.'

Vic helps me out of the cab and we're on a residential street, wide and tree-lined, built in the days when houses had four storeys because people had staff, who'd slave away in the basement and sleep up in the attics, and needed a wide turning circle for their horse-drawn carriages.

We're standing outside one of those huge four-storey houses where a party is raging and disturbing the tranquillity of a sleepy Sunday morning. People and loud music spill out onto the street, cigarette butts and bottles adorn the flowerbeds and the door's wide open. Normally I'd never go where I wasn't invited but the boys from the cab have already disappeared through the open door and been swallowed up by the crowd. And it isn't like there's someone standing there ticking names off a list.

'Shall we, then?' I jerk my head in the direction of the door.

'I'll say!' Vic is rubbing his hands together as his eyes sweep over a gang of girls sitting on the garden wall. 'I have to hand it to you, Sun, you know where the pretty ladies hang out.'

He offers his arm, which I take, but we haven't taken a single step when there's a small explosion behind us.

'*Non! Non! Non!* Enough.' I turn to see Jean-Luc hugging a lamp-post like it's the only thing holding him up. 'You can't just disappear into a house. Anything could happen. You may run into an – an – er, *meurtrier avec une hache* . . .'

'I doubt there's any axe murderers in there. Just a lot of pissed-up toffs,' Vic says. 'Plus some lucky young lady who's going to enjoy the pleasure of my company.'

'And Mark is in there,' I remind Jean-Luc, who's now clutching the lamp-post like it's his only friend in the world and groaning like he's in pain. 'Look, this isn't going to take long. I'll go in, find Mark, destroy his entire belief system with my pithy character assassination, hopefully even make him cry, and then we'll go home. It will take half an hour, tops.'

It sounds so simple when I put it like that. The simplest thing ever. I'm getting fired up all over again for the – what? Ninth time that night. Jean-Luc isn't fired up, though. He looks like he's just been doused with a bucket of cold water. 'Pffft! I don't believe you.'

That stings. 'Oh Jean-Luc, don't be like that!'

'I'm going home,' he insists. 'I can take it no longer. *Assez!*'

'Whatever. Go home then, Mr Buzzkill,' Vic says. He makes a shooing motion with his hands. 'Off you go. You've got that app I put on your phone. It will tell you what bus to get.'

'*Mon dieu!* Apps!' Jean-Luc seems like one exclamation away from a full meltdown. He launches himself off his lamp-post. 'Fine. You keep chasing your hateful boyfriend and Vic, you go and have sex with some poor girl who doesn't know that you're *un salaud. Ça va! Je peux prendre soin de moi-même!*'

Then he storms off. It's such good storming-off that all Jean-Luc needs is a sweeping cape that he can swish behind him as he storms. But I can't help feeling a little guilty. Well, actually, a lot guilty.

'Vic, we can't just abandon him!'

Vic is climbing the steps. 'You heard him; he'll be fine. He's a big boy. He can look after himself. Come on. Let's go hunt for bad boyfriends.'

First I make Vic give me Jean-Luc's mobile number, but I don't even have enough juice to send Jean-Luc a text.

'Honestly, he'll be all right,' Vic assures me as we walk through the door. 'I'll text him your number so that once he's got over himself, he can let you know that he's still alive. If I had a pound for every time he's gone home early on a night out . . .'

'Technically it's not night any more. It's morning . . .'

'Or stormed off in a huff, I'd be a rich man.' Vic puts an arm round my shoulder and presses a kiss to my forehead, and I do have the faintest of stirrings as Vic's *leanness* presses against me for a few blissful seconds. 'Don't worry, Sun. I've got your back.'

I'm glad of Vic's arm round me because the house is dimly lit and Jean-Luc was right: we don't really know what we're walking into. The only light is coming from these fancy spotlights embedded in the walls at ankle height and the gleam of pearly white, perfect teeth as we push our way through the other partygoers. They all have good hair too. Boys and girls. Blond and ripply and sunkissed from days spent lazing about on beaches and the decks of private yachts.

I've noticed that before, that all posh people look the same. Sleek and rangy. They all sound the same too. Loud and entitled. This crowd are mostly wearing distressed vintage T-shirts of bands they've never heard of, because they might be posh but they'll never really be cool.

It's the world's way of restoring order, I suppose.

It reminds me of the time Mark was wearing a Trojan Records T-shirt when we bumped into my uncle Dee in Notting Hill and Dee sat Mark down and grilled him about Lee Perry, The Cimarons and the Ska revival, until Mark

186

was forced to admit that he didn't even know what Trojan Records was.

Uncle Dee had told me afterwards that Mark was no good and I should get rid of him as soon as possible.

Better late than never, right?

TEN MINUTES LATER

Vic and I forget all about finding Mark. We walk through the house, goggling and marvelling at all the sights. Even the entrance hall looks like a really chic art gallery. There's a huge ugly painting that takes up most of one wall. I couldn't even say what it was meant to be because it's all splodgy black lines on a murky grey background. The floor is marble and there's a huge staircase that sweeps down it and a queue of people waiting patiently to slide down the banisters.

There's a state-of-the-art kitchen that looks like the interior of a spaceship, despite the bottles and teenagers that clutter every surface. The dining table is the size of an Olympic swimming pool, though a boy and girl are rolling about on top of it as they snog furiously.

'Whose place is this?' I ask and Vic shakes his head.

'Someone very rich. Richer than God.'

We don't go upstairs because it seems kind of rude to wander in and out of bedrooms, even if we have gatecrashed a party that we haven't been invited to, and anyway, the downstairs is entertaining enough.

Our basement is a horrible, dank, cobwebby space at the bottom of a rickety flight of stairs where we and Max from the

187

top-floor flat stash our bicycles and bulky items. This basement goes down three floors and has a gym, a cinema, a nightclub with a light-up dancefloor and a wine cellar.

Vic's eyes are practically bulging out of his head. Not from the house and all its grandeur but because there are so many girls milling about, all long of leg and tanned and with tousled hair that they toss back at every available opportunity. I get a mouthful of someone else's hair twice and yet it's still impossible to find Mark. The house is so big and there are so many boys who look similar to him and as we come up the stairs from the basement we run into another gang of them. They all have fair hair and they're talking in loud voices like they've all got their earbuds in and one's wearing a pink polo shirt with a popped collar and when someone calls out, 'Giles?' two of them turn round and – but wait!

It's coming back to me now. All those hours ago at The Lock Tavern when I was being given the lowdown on Mark's Chelsea friends. Loud voices. Pink polo shirt. Popped collar. Giles times two.

'Cover me,' I hiss at Vic like we're two cops on a stakeout and I don't stop to think about the consequences – that's been an overriding theme tonight – I march over with Vic at my heels.

'Don't do anything silly,' he says. 'There's a lot of them and I'm too pretty to die.'

I ignore him. 'Where is he?' I demand, tugging at a pink polo shirt. 'Where's Mark?'

'Who wants to know?' one of the Gileses asks and all of them are suddenly surrounding me. Not in an aggro way, not exactly, but they're not altogether friendly.

His girlfriend wants to know, I'm about to say, but who can even guess what Mark might have told them? 'I'm a friend. A North London friend,' I hastily improvise. 'We're at school together.'

'Right. So, do you know that Sunny girl?' pink polo shirt asks. 'What a home-wrecking little harpie she is. Made up shit about Mark. Made Tab cry. Flick seems to like her but really, Flick prefers horses to people anyway so how much does she –'

'Enough!' I hold up my hand for silence and I think it must be the murderous look on my face that gets him to shut up. 'Are you even for real?'

I'm on the verge of going into one. Going full Khaleesi on their arses. But in a split-second epiphany I realise that Mark can't know that I know that he's a dirty, dirty cheater. He also doesn't know about my transformation from pushover to powerhouse, and if I give his Chelsea friends any hints then my plans for vengeance will all have been in vain, that crucial element of surprise ruined.

'That really doesn't sound like Sunny. She's cool. Super cool,' I say fondly. 'We have a saying in North London. WWSD. What would Sunny do? And she's totally going out with Mark so I don't know what the deal is with this Tabitha girl.'

One of the boys pushes forward slightly. I would have said that I was the brownest person present but he has such a deep tan that actually I think he might be browner than I am. 'Tab and Mark are a thing. *Were* a thing.' He frowns. 'It's so complicated. Because they just broke up. Not sure who dumped who but Tab threw a drink over him. So, were you in The Lock Tavern earlier? What are you even *doing* here?'

He doesn't sound hostile but perplexed that someone from North London might be partying in his hood. 'Yeah, I was in The Lock earlier – it's how I recognised you – and then I headed over here because I'm Poodle's cousin,' I say vaguely because, I mean, there's bound to be someone here called something ridiculous like Poodle and I must be right because the Gileses are both nodding. 'Anyway, Poodle's gone home and I need to get back to North London and I was hoping that Mark could lend me some money for a cab.'

They shake their heads. No can do. 'Mark isn't with us,' Giles One says. 'He was with us, but then he had to go back to the club we were in earlier because he'd left his phone behind.'

That makes me feel better about Mark's phone silence but then I feel worse because Mark's friends are offering to give me money or order me a car on account ('Like, seriously, it's OK, my dad never even checks the bill') and they're actually really sweet. Not the arseholes that Mark said they were and they might be posh but that doesn't make them bad people and when I insist that I can sleep over at Poodle's because my mythical cousin doesn't live that far away, they offer to walk me over.

'Oh no, you're all right,' I say.

'We're going now anyway,' Giles Two says. 'But we should all totally meet up before school goes back, yeah? That George guy said that come the revolution, he'd see us all hang. He's freaking *hilarious*!'

I snort with delighted glee. We all hug. Who'da thunk it? Then they all leave and I turn to Vic who was absolutely meant to have my back and he's not there. He's gone, leaving no trace.

I can't find him anywhere. I even go upstairs, cringing as I have to open doors that I really wish I'd left shut because some of the sights I see are not for my innocent young eyes.

As I'm coming down the stairs, I see Vic standing by the front door, foot tapping impatiently, a girl draped all over him.

'Sunny!' he calls out as he catches sight of me. 'At last! Time we called it a night, don't you think?'

'But what about . . .'

He's not even listening to me because the girl, I can't see that much of her face because her long brown hair obscures most of it, is whispering in Vic's ear.

'What was that, *chérie*?' he purrs. She whispers again. 'Oh, you really are a very naughty girl.'

Then he turns back to me, all brisk and business-like. 'You'll be fine. It'll be light soon.' He dips his hand into his jacket. 'Here's twenty quid to get you home.'

I trip down the stairs. 'I thought you had my back.'

'Oh, but you don't need me to have your back,' Vic says as he tries to thrust the twenty at me. 'You're a powerful woman. A warrior.'

He was quoting my own words back at me and it was infuriating. 'Now, I have to see this young lady home because she's not a warrior.' He waggles his eyebrows at the girl and judging from the way she's still clinging to Vic, it does look like she's incapable of walking unaided. 'But we've had fun, Sun. It's been real. Let's do it again sometime.'

He shoves the twenty at me again and I take it because it wasn't just a line when I said I needed some money to get home.

'Well, bye then,' I say. 'I can't believe you're bailing on me.'

191

Vic cuffs me under the chin while the girl he's picked up pushes back her long curtain of hair so she can shoot me evils. At least *I* don't have split ends. 'You'll be fine,' he says again and then he's gone.

And I had been fine except now I'm not. My phone's dead. I've rowed with Emmeline and I've rowed with Jean-Luc and driven them away with my obsessive, blinkered search for Mark who's disappeared into the ether yet again, Flick is MIA and now Vic's deserted me too.

I'm on my own on the other side of London, though actually I don't even know my exact location and I'm tired and my legs ache and I'm coming down fast. So all I want to do is curl up on the floor in the foetal position. I sit on the stairs because instead of being fierce and taking no prisoners, I'm now that girl who always sits on the stairs and cries at parties. I'm not actually crying but it feels as if the tears aren't too far away, and then I hear a voice say, 'Sunny?'

I look up to see a blond girl standing there. Pretty. Wearing a tight white vest and black short shorts. Nibbling her bottom lip as she sees my eyes do a quick up and down. I know her from somewhere, I just can't think where that somewhere is.

'I can't believe it's you. *Here*.' She's got one of those voices that is so la-di-dah, the words so clipped, that it's almost like she's talking another language. Then her face hardens as if someone's poured wax over her features. 'You called me a skank!'

'Sorry. Who are you?'

'I'll tell you what I'm not. I'm not a skank,' she says furiously and it's all starting to make sense now. 'I was just kissing my boyfriend. I just didn't know he was your boyfriend as well.'

TWO SECONDS LATER

I cringe and then I look again, just to be sure. At those long legs in those short shorts and it's not until I mentally superimpose a hand sliding into the waistband that I figure out who she is. I'm seized by an urge to stroke my chin in a pensive manner and say, 'So, we meet at last,' like a Bond villain, but I manage to restrain myself. Instead I come out with a tentative, 'Tabitha?'

'Who else would I be?' She puts her hands on her hips. 'And for your information, the reason I wear short shorts is because my legs are my only good bit. If I play them up, then no one notices the rest of me.'

'Are you kidding? You're beautiful. Do you not have mirrors in your house?' I look round the entrance hall. It's getting light now and surely Tabitha can see how she looks in the many shiny surfaces. I never noticed when I was looking at the photos because all I could see was Mark's hand on her arse, the kiss, his other hand caught in her super-shiny, long blond hair, but Tabitha's beautiful. Big eyes, tiny nose, a pouty little mouth – I bet she never has to take selfie after selfie, tilting her face this way and that, until one's acceptable enough to post. I bet every selfie she takes is perfect.

'I'm really not. Two of my friends at school are models and Mummy was a Bond girl. I know pretty and it doesn't look like this.' Tabitha points to her incredibly aesthetically pleasing face. 'But I thought that maybe I was a little bit pretty when Mark kept wanting to hook up with me. He *is* pretty.'

She sounds wistful. Like, despite everything, she still loves him. I can kind of understand where she's coming from.

I pat the stair next to me and Tabitha sits down. 'Mark rocks up at our school and he's instantly popular and everyone likes him and when I realised he was interested in me, it made me feel popular and cool too,' I tell Tabitha, though it's something that I haven't even told Emmeline. 'It's this thing I do, right: I always latch on to people that are cool and hope it will rub off on me a little.'

'But you are cool!' Tabitha flings out a hand, which I suppose is meant to encompass my alleged coolness. 'I've been hating on you all night. Not just because I thought you were trying to steal Mark and you called me a skank but because after I dumped Mark, I met up with Flick and she was all, like, "Oh, Sunny's so cool," and then she showed me that video of you dancing the Charleston in a supermarket. I mean, that's peak cool. And you're mixed race or whatever, so that automatically makes you cooler than most other people.'

'You can't say stuff like that. It's actually quite racist,' I snap.

She holds her hands up in protest. 'But I was complimenting you! How's that racist?'

'You can't make sweeping generalisations about people based on their race or their skin colour. It's like me saying all white people can't dance. Anyway, not all black people are cool. My grandma isn't, that's for sure.'

We're both bristling. 'I'm sorry,' Tabitha says with a little huff. 'But I think you're cool and Mark's cool so it makes sense that he'd be into you, with his DJing and everything.'

I snort so hard that a bit of snot flies out of my nose but I don't think Tabitha notices. 'Let me tell you something about Mark's so-called DJing. He downloads DJ playlists off of the internet, and when he gets a so-called gig he just hooks his iPad up to the PA system and double clicks. He doesn't even own any decks. DJ, my arse!'

'So, you're not still, like, having feelings for him?' Tabitha asks.

I do a quick check on my heart. It's still there. It's beating quite fast because it's had one shock after another tonight, but it's not aching in my chest like it did before. 'I have feelings for Mark but they're more murderous than anything.' There isn't even a trace amount of love for Mark left in my system. Maybe it never had been real love if I'd fallen out of it so quickly. But how could I call it love if the boy I'd loved had been lying to me with every kiss, every compliment, every time he'd taken my hand?

I look at Tabitha. 'What about you, then?'

'No. We had a furious row when Flick sent me that text about his two Facebook accounts. He tried to deny everything.' She reddens and picks at her cuticles. 'Then when it was obvious I was seconds away from dumping him, he dumped *me*.' She sniffs, like the tears aren't far off and I know what that feels like. 'It's all come out of the blue. I thought me and Mark were solid, yah? And now suddenly we're over, finished, like, even if he begged me to take him back. You can't stay with a boy who treats people like he's treated us. Mummy's on her fourth husband. I really don't want to be like Mummy.'

I'm about to empathise with Tabitha and maybe pile into Mark a little bit more, but then a disembodied voice comes out of nowhere and shouts, 'Everyone out! The po-po are coming!'

It scares the crap out of both of us. I clutch my heart, which is now racing at dangerous speeds. 'What the *hell*?'

'Oh my God!' Tabitha gasps, with a hand to her heart as well. 'Their house intercom must be hooked up to a hidden speaker system,' she says at a less shrieky volume. 'We have one at home too, but it's not so terrifyingly loud.'

'The police are coming, that's terrifying enough,' I say as I press my elbows in and try to make myself as small as possible so I don't get mown down by the hordes of people suddenly streaming down the stairs. They're joined by yet more masses coming from every direction, all heading for the door and pushing and shoving each other out of the way. Everyone's panicking and there's a lot of shouting and screaming and honestly it's about the most exciting thing to happen since I arrived at the party.

I stand up, all set to join the bottleneck that's formed at the front door – things wouldn't end well if the police turned up and I was the only member of the ethnic minorities represented – but Tabitha grabs my hand.

'This way,' she says, pulling me through a little side door and down a small corridor. 'Servants' quarters.' We come to another door, which leads into a second, smaller, grottier kitchen and out the back door into a little yard. Tabitha unlatches the gate that opens on a mews at the side of the house. We're out of danger.

'Cool moves, Tabitha,' I say and she grins.

'My best friend from prep school used to live there. Not sure who lives there now, or even whose party that was, but *I* live a few streets away. You can crash at mine.'

'Oh I can't.' It would be too weird. The whole night had been stuffed full of weird, but crashing at the house of my boyfriend's other girlfriend (technically she was his ex-girlfriend, but only as of a couple of hours ago) was next-level weird.

'But you must. I mean, you're miles away from home,' she says as we start walking. 'What's it like to live in North London anyway?'

She says it like North London is some kind of dystopian wasteland. I tell her about Crouch End. About our street with the secret field at the end of it and the cakes from Dunns, the bakers, and that the dude who plays Doctor Who used to live on Archie's road, but Tabitha just gulps and says, 'So, you live in a flat. Not a house?'

'Actually, I think it's a maisonette,' I say and she gulps again. 'You know, Mark lives in a flat too when he's slumming it in North London?'

Tabitha sighs. 'So, what are we going to do about him? We should do something, right?'

'I'm going to take him down,' I say and I'm relieved that the Sunny of before hasn't left the building. 'You in?'

'The thing is, I'm not good at confrontations,' Tabitha says. 'I hate scenes and people being angry with me so I'm in in spirit, but I wouldn't be much practical help in a taking-Mark-down scenario.'

'Oh.' That was all right. In my still-hazy plans to take Mark down I hadn't planned on having a sidekick, but it might have been nice. 'Well, I suppose . . .'

'But I have the means that will help you take Mark down.' Tab rummages in her bag and pulls out a phone. 'His phone.' She holds it up so I can see the Chelsea FC logo on its rubber case.

197

Was she kidding me? Was this all some elaborate double bluff after all? I come to a halt. Hands on hips, scowl on my face – Jean-Luc would be suing for copyright, which just makes me madder when I think about how I dragged him on a wild good chase, and for what? No wonder he stormed off. 'How dumb do you two think I am?'

Tabitha looks like she might throw up. She was right about not liking confrontation. 'I d-d-don't think you're dumb.'

'That isn't Mark's phone. Mark's phone is in an Arsenal case,' I bite out.

'But Mark doesn't support Arsenal. He supports Chelsea.'

Oh. Oh! Terry would say that supporting Chelsea was the worst betrayal of all, but Tabitha and I wouldn't agree with him. We both look at the phone and then at each other.

'Two phones!' we say.

I had wondered how Mark, of all people, had juggled two girlfriends, even two different Facebook pages with different passwords, for months and now it was obvious how. Two phones.

It all makes a sick, dull sort of sense. 'What a git. What a sneaky, slimy git.'

Tabitha sniffs. 'Takes after his father, obviously.'

'What's that? I know his parents are divorced but what's that about his dad?'

Tab looks like she might burst from all the secrets she knows about Mark. 'It was a huge scandal,' she tells me breathlessly. 'He headed up the asset management division of a big American bank . . . He was involved in some kind of insider trading. Not insider enough because he ended up making some very bad investments. Very bad. He got sacked. My stepfather said he was lucky not to go to prison and they had to sell their house and Mark had to leave Harrow . . .'

'He said his dad wouldn't pay his school fees once his parents got divorced. Made it sound like he didn't fit in there anyway because he was such a rebel.'

'Hardly! He was captain of the rugby team.'

'Mark doesn't play rugby. He plays football.'

We both look at each other again, then shake our heads. 'He's such a liar. Though I do feel a bit bad that they lost all their money. No wonder his mum is so bitter and mean.

'Oh no,' Tab assures me. 'She was bitter and mean long before they lost all their money.'

We carry on walking. 'How come you even have his phone in the first place?'

Tabitha smiles proudly. 'I stole it out of the back pocket of his jeans. He didn't feel a thing.' She waggles her fingers. 'I'm the best shoplifter at St Mary's.'

'Well, I don't want to be an accessory or a fence or . . .'

'Sunny! If you really are on this vengeance mission to take Mark down then you need the phone.' Tabitha shoves the phone at me so I have no choice but to take it. 'Trust me on this.'

I weigh the phone in the palm of my hands. It's tempting but . . .' I don't even know his passcode.'

'I do. It's one, two, three, four.' Tabitha rolls her eyes. 'For that alone he deserves to have his phone hacked, and there are things on it we can use to get back at him.'

I'm not gonna lie, I'm intrigued. 'Yeah? What kind of things?'

We sit down on a low wall that skirts the manicured lawns of a mansion block and Tab unlocks the phone, goes into the photos and . . .

'Oh my days! Why has he taken so many pictures of his dick?'

Tabitha giggles and keeps scrolling. 'No, wait. There's one where he's resting his sunglasses on it. Here it is.'

'Ewwww!'

'We could send it to everyone in his address book?' Tabitha suggests. 'That includes both his grandmothers and his old housemaster and nanny.'

I rub my hands together in delight. 'Yeah! Let's do that . . . oh, but no. That's not fair on his grandmothers – I mean, there are some things you just can't come back from, and he's underage.'

'So what?'

I shudder at the thought. 'We'd get done for circulating child porn.' Worse than that. 'And we'd be put on the Sex Offenders' Register and that would totally stuff up our chances of getting into our first-choice universities.'

'You're right.' Tabitha subsides with a little sigh. 'Any other ideas?'

'Well, I have to find him first anyway. It's not like he's been calling me on his Arsenal phone, is it?'

And right on cue as we get up off the wall, Tabitha's phone rings. My heart skips half a beat.

'Mummy? Why are you yelling at me? Oh God! I am home. Well, I'm on my way home. I'm literally, like, five seconds from home.' So not Mark, then. If my mum wasn't in France, she'd be on the phone too, demanding to know why it was gone five in the morning and I *still* wasn't in my bed. In fact, she'd probably have the police and Interpol scramble a few helicopters and drones to track me down.

Tabitha walks as she talks and rolls her eyes in an exaggerated fashion as I hear a voice squawking at her. 'God, it's not *that* late. Yes, I suppose it is, but another way of looking at it is that actually it's quite early.'

It is early and nearly light outside. The sky is a beautiful pale blue. Birds are tweeting in the trees. It's breezy but already close like it's going to be another hot day.

There are no signs of life on these streets with their big houses all painted fantastic colours: yolky yellow, a sea green that makes me think of the nineteen-thirties lido we went to every day when we were on holiday in France last year, a smudgy purple, Calpol pink, a deep, dusky blue that reminds me of my grandmother's collection of Wedgwood china.

'Mummy! God! I'm practically walking through the front door!'

I don't even know where we are and I can't even load up Google Maps and then I wonder what people did before Google Maps existed – they must have got lost all the time. Then we turn a corner and then another corner and suddenly I know where I am.

Not in Chelsea at all, but Notting Hill, which means that, in a way, although I'm miles from Crouch End, I'm not that far from home.

GRANDMA PAULINE'S
PINEAPPLE PUNCH RECIPE

1 litre of full-fat milk
1 can (400 mls) of coconut milk
1 litre of pineapple juice
1 pinch of ginger
1 pinch of cinnamon

Mix together in your biggest bowl and serve with a whole lot of love.

5.30 a.m.

NOTTING HILL to LADBROKE GROVE

The first official mention of the place we know as Notting Hill is in 1536 as Knottynghull and may be a reference to a Saxon king called Cnotta. Bet he was a lotta lotta fun.

In the nineteenth century the area was unofficially known as the Potteries and Piggeries. The local heavy clay was used to make bricks and tiles, and many pig farmers, moved on from Marble Arch, had settled there.

The Ladbroke family, who gave their name to nearby Ladbroke Grove, built all sorts of big fancy houses in Notting Hill, but really rich types didn't want to live somewhere so far from the centre of town. Poor loves.

The area was quickly taken over by slum landlords who would cram several families into one house. Then, in the Fifties, immigrants from the West Indies settled in the area, which led to racial tension and riots.

The poor living conditions began to improve with the creation of the Notting Hill Housing Trust in 1963 and the first Notting Hill Carnival, which celebrated the culture of the area's new residents. Now poshos and poors, Trustafarians and Rastafarians live happily (mostly) side by side.

Tabitha and I hug it out and make plans to hang out and debrief once the Mark business is done, then she goes her way and I go mine.

I'm on Ledbury Road and if I keep walking, then take a couple of right turns, then a left and straight on, I'll come to my grandparents' block of flats. It's a fifteen-minute walk, tops. Fifteen minutes is all it takes to get from a multi-million-pound Notting Hill neighbourhood to a council estate in Ladbroke Grove.

I've done this walk with Mum many times over the years. We spend ages poking about in the vintage shops so she can sneer at the mark-up. And back in the day we'd stop in at what was then my great-grandma's flat long enough for a cup of tea, a slice of her everyday fruitcake and for her to say that we should have rung first because she was in the middle of watching *Deal or No Deal*.

It's my grandparents' flat now and, boy, are they going to be surprised to see me on the doorstep. Like all old people, apart from Terry's mum who lazes in bed until eleven most days, they both get up really early. Gramps works the first shift at

Park Royal bus garage and Grandma is a carer who starts her round at six. Except, it's Sunday and neither of them work on a Sunday, because it's the day of rest. 'If God wanted us to go to work on a Sunday then he'd never have invented the Sabbath,' Grandma is very fond of saying, but they'll still be up at first light even though if God had wanted us to get up early on a Sunday, he'd never have invented the lie-in.

The night has gone on for so long that it's hard to believe it's morning. I've seen five-thirty in the morning before but from the other side; getting up to see the sunrise when Mum has one of her notions and drags us all to Parliament Hill Fields. Five-thirty in the morning has a completely different vibe when you haven't slept: a grungy, grimy, grody vibe that can only be achieved by wearing the same pair of knickers for nearly twenty-four hours.

Because it's now officially morning, I try to tell myself that the occasional person I see up ahead or on the other side of the street is a virtuous early riser and not a night-dweller up to no good. I also try to tell myself that I really haven't got that far to go, but every step takes every ounce of energy I have and lasts for at least a minute and just generally hurts.

It's best not to get too fixated on how many steps I have left to take (about seven hundred and fifty, by my estimation.) Instead I think about what I'll say to Grandma. Something along the lines of, 'Oh, so I couldn't sleep and I thought I'd surprise you. Surprise!' Then I'll have to say, 'Actually, about going to church, well, I'm not really dressed for it and I'm having serious doubts about organised religion.'

Ultimately, my protests will be ignored. Grandma will run me a bath and Gramps will make me egg and toast soldiers, then they'll insist I go to church with them. There is a slim chance that they might take one look at me – I have to be looking very rough by now – and send me straight to bed, or else I could go home to my own bed, which would take at least an hour. AT THE VERY LEAST.

I come to a halt to ponder my dilemma and it's then that the first one drives by. I stop and blink. Maybe I'm hallucinating. Then the second one slowly rolls past, and another one and I see it's a whole procession of vehicles. Flat-bed trucks that look like birds of paradise and exotic flowers. Open-top buses bedecked with tinsel and bling. If I listen very carefully I can almost hear the steel drums, see those beautiful women who look like butterflies dancing in time to the beat.

How could I have forgotten? It's Carnival weekend! On Bank Holiday Monday, we'll all descend on Grandma and Gramps because their flat is on the Notting Hill Carnival route. All my aunts and uncles and cousins and step-aunts and step-uncles and step-cousins, all my grandparents' many friends and the little old ladies that Grandma cares for and any of Grandpa's workmates who aren't on shift will pile into their flat, watch the floats roll past and drink Grandma's legendary pineapple punch and eat her jerk fried chicken.

But that's tomorrow and this morning Notting Hill is still hungover from yesterday's party. The road's empty of traffic because the road is still closed off. Most of the shopfronts have been boarded up. There's a mountain of bulging refuse sacks lining the pavement waiting to be picked up by the binmen who must be stuck behind the stately procession of floats returning to the start of the Carnival route.

And still they keep on coming. A truck swathed in yellow, red and green streamers. A pimped-out ice-cream truck. A lorry that looks like a tropical rainforest, steel drums mounted on either side.

There's something otherworldly about the floats. I gaze at them in dopey disbelief because it really feels like the universe has created this dream, this mirage, just for me, though I'm still not ruling out a hallucination.

I smile but at the same time, for some strange reason, I kind of want to cry, and then I see a man on a silver float waving wildly, his shiny bald head gleaming in the early morning light. 'Sun-ra! Sunny! Is that you, girl?'

He leans forward to make sure that it is really me, then holds out his hand. I stumble towards him. I have to jog to keep up with the float but as I draw level I reach out and my uncle Dee and another man haul me up.

'Sunny! What the hell are you doing hanging about on street corners at five in the morning. Have you been up all night? Stupid question, of course you have. Look at the state of you!'

'Grim,' says the guy who'd helped hoist me up. Like I need the validation. I really don't.

Even the sedate, slow pace of the float makes me dizzy and Dee grabs hold of my arm to steady me. He's not looking quite so pleased to see me now. In fact, he's looking quite a lot like my dad when he's interrogating a hostile witness. I don't want Dee to look at me like that, not when bumping into him is the best thing that's happened in hours.

'Can I have a hug, please?' My voice is all wavery and I still think I might cry but then Dee's arms are around me and I'm pressed up against his white T-shirt and he smells of fabric softener and cocoa butter and it's almost as good as coming home without the journey of AT LEAST AN HOUR that would actually take me home.

The hug doesn't last nearly long enough before Dee lets go, but only so he can put his hands on my shoulders and peer at my face. My face that has had sweat, make-up, tears and lager run down it at various times during the night and now aches just from the sheer effort of blinking and breathing in and out.

'What's up?'

'Oh nothing. I couldn't sleep. Thought I'd surprise Grandma,' I mumble.

'Yeah, right. Do you want to have a bit more time to work on that because it smells like bullshit? You've been up all the night, haven't you? With that dickhead who doesn't know who Trojan Records are? And then he just left you to wander the streets on your own?'

'He left me quite a bit before that,' I say and I sniff, but it's weird. I don't actually have the energy to cry any more. Which is a first.

'What's he done?' Dee demands. He can be quite scary when he's in demand mode. He's a social worker who works with young offenders ('There but for the grace of God,' he always says) and if he gives them the face that he's giving me then I bet they don't dare reoffend. 'Did he hurt you? Because if he did I will kill him.'

Dee's quiet voice is worse than anyone else yelling at me.

'Oh, not like that. No! But he really, really hurt my inside stuff. My heart and that. Except, now I'm just really angry. Except, actually I'm too knackered to be angry.'

I'm too knackered to go into much detail either so I just give Dee the headlines, leaving out details of underage drinking, bike stealing and anything else that could harm my defence. 'And so when I realised where I was, I decided I could just go to Grandma's.'

'You can't go to Mum's, Sunny,' Dee exclaims. 'She'll ferret the truth out of you, then make you go to church as penance, and you know that she'll grass you up and tell your mum.' He smiles. 'So, what time's your curfew again?'

I'm too tired to glare either. Best I can do is a half-hearted pout. 'It's flexible during the holidays, and anyway, she didn't say *not* to stay out all night. She was more concerned about Gretchen Weiner's anal glands and that I might have a party and post the details on Facebook and have two thousand people turn up and trash the place. So really, in the grand scheme of things, staying out all night isn't *that* bad.'

'It's not good either.'

I sigh. 'Like you never stayed out all night when you were my age. Or worse.'

He dips his head. 'True, that.'

My dad might have been a straight-A student, but Dee sounded like he'd been much more fun when he was a teenager. Maybe a bit too much fun.

My all-time favourite Dee story, which he only told me because he drank too much rum and Coke last Christmas, was about the day he ended up taking part in the Poll Tax riots in the late Eighties. I'm not sure what a Poll Tax is or how this riot differed from other riots but at the time Dee was working in Tower Records in Piccadilly Circus. At lunchtime, he popped out to get a sandwich, saw that people were rioting, decided to join in for a bit, then went back to work, where he was sacked on the spot because someone had seen him chucking a brick through one of Tower Records' windows.

Great-grandma had got their pastor to come round and they'd all kneeled down on the living-room carpet to pray for Dee's soul.

I guess the praying must have worked because these days he's a fine, upstanding citizen but not in a dickish way. Like, now he cocks his head, thinks things over and says, 'Well, it's not up to me to tell your mum and you're in no fit state to deal with your gran so you better come back to ours.'

FIFTEEN MINUTES LATER

Dee and his wife Yolly live with Vivvy, Dee's stepdaughter, and my cousins, Elle and Perry, on the same estate as Grandma.

When Dee unlocks the front door and I step into the hall, which is just a hall, not a foyer or vestibule or art gallery, the air is thick and stuffy. Dee says the Carnival was still going on when the others went to bed and it was too noisy to sleep with the windows open. He opens them now and I want to sleep and I really want to have a shower but the most important thing is to charge my phone.

'I'm going to bed. Staying up all night was much easier when I was your age.' Dee shakes his head and tuts because I'm sitting on his sofa and my head keeps sinking back into the cushions and it's quite hard to stay vertical. 'You, you're a lightweight.'

'Funny, 'cause I feel like dead weight.' The sofa's swallowing me. I elbow myself back up. 'Can I have a shower?'

Dee says I can but I have to be quiet and not wake up Yolly because she'll kill me and there'll be nothing Dee can do to stop her, and then I can crash in the girls' room.

Pulling off my grungy clothes and having a two-minute lukewarm shower is as good as ten hours' sleep. I put on the dressing gown hanging on the back of the bathroom door and pad softly into the girls' room.

The sun is streaming in from behind the curtains and I gag on the fetid stench of Body Shop white musk perfume with base notes of hairspray and Play-Doh. Vivvy's half of the room is a shrine to Jourdan Dunn and Elle's is where pink plastic crap goes to die. It's a huge source of aggro that fourteen-year-old Vivvy has to share a room with three-year-old Elle.

I weigh up my options and decide that Elle's bed is the best bet. That kid can sleep through anything. One time when they were on holiday in Spain, the fire alarm in the hotel went off and no one could wake Elle up. When they got back to England, Yolly took her for a hearing test. Elle's hearing's fine, she just really, really, really loves sleep. She's tangled up in a pink flowery sheet, one fist clenching and unclenching, fat little cheeks bulging on every exhale because she's a total mouthbreather. She doesn't even stir when I shove her right over and get into bed.

This is going to be good. This is going to be monster sleep. I might even sleep so much that when I wake up it's Monday morning and time to head over to Grandma's.

Yeah, come on, sleep, show me what you're made of.

211

I rest my head on Elle's pillow, take a couple of deep breaths and my eyelids are drooping, arms and legs slackening. Oh yes, this is what I'm talking ab . . .

ONE MINUTE LATER

There's an angry bee buzzing somewhere in the room. It sounds like it's right next to me and I should be so tired that even an angry bee couldn't come between me and sleep, but it's right there. In my ear. Like it's about to sting me. I've never been stung by a bee, or even a wasp before, so it would just be my luck to have a fatal allergy to getting stung. Like Macaulay Culkin in *My Girl*.

'SHUT UP!' I open one eye and roll over. Vivvy is sitting up. 'TURN IT OFF!'

'Turn what off?' I grunt.

'Your phone. But first tell whoever's texting you to SHUT UP!'

'What?'

Vivvy lays back down so she can flail her limbs in fury. She's worse than Yolly if she gets woken up too soon. Right now, she's full-on body spasming in rage.

'I'm gonna get out of bed and *stamp* on your phone,' she hisses. 'I swear I will.'

'My phone's downstairs, charging.'

'Then. What. Is. That. Noise?'

'Um, an angry bee?'

'For fuck's sake!' Vivvy throws back her sheets, gets her legs tangled up in them, which sends her temper up by approximately eleventy billion more notches. Then finally

212

she's out of bed and stomping the seven steps that takes her to my side. I shrink back. Vivvy is so mad, there's no telling what she might do.

'Your phone. In your bag. Down there.' It's like the mad part of her brain has overriden the bit that forms whole sentences.

I look down at my bag, which I'd dumped on the floor next to the bed. 'My phone isn't in there,' I insist, but I pick it up and as I do, it buzzes again. 'How weird.'

'Oh God, I hate you!' Vivvy snatches my bag from my puny grip, plunges a hand inside, rummages a bit and pulls out a phone.

I'm just about to say that it's not my phone and then I remember whose phone it is. It's Mark's phone. 'Oh, that phone,' I say in a tiny voice and Vivvy makes this growly noise in the back of her throat and I shrink even further back and almost push Elle out of bed.

Miraculously, Elle is still asleep. I think Yolly needs to get her hearing checked again.

'It's my boyfriend's phone,' I tell Vivvy, who stands there in rumpled, cupcake-patterned vest and sleep shorts, her hair in twists. 'Ex-boyfriend.'

She stares at me, like she doesn't even know who I am. Then whatever demon has possessed her decides to move onto its next victim and she gives me a sleepy smile. 'Oh, hey, Sunny. Your hair is well big.' She gestures at the phone. 'Is that the boyfriend who doesn't even know about Trojan Records? Dee said he was a dickhead.'

'Thanks for that,' I say. Sleep has abandoned me. I don't understand how I can stay up for nearly twenty-four hours and still be in control of all of my faculties. Or about eighty-three

213

per cent of them. All I can think about now is Mark's phone and what I'm going to do with it. Right on cue, it buzzes again.

Babe. Don't be a h8er. Let's sort shit out. Mark x

He was texting his own phone, so which babe did he mean? Did he know that Tab had stolen his phone? Or did he think it was some *other* girl that he'd been seeing that Tabitha and I didn't know about? Or maybe he had some kind of personality disorder (which, yeah) that made him send semi-apologetic texts to himself.

'Sorry I got my bitch on. Did I swear? Don't tell Mum if I did, yeah?' Vivvy gets back into bed. 'Really, your hair is *so* big. Turn the buzzy thing off on that phone, OK?'

Then she's gone. Her head crash-lands on the pillow and she's asleep. I hate her a little bit in that moment for being able to get to sleep so easily, but not as much as I hate Mark. And really Tab was right, compared to what he's done, putting in his passcode and having complete access to his phone doesn't even come close.

I begin with the texts that arrived in the last five minutes.

Yo, Tab, u klepto! U got my phone?

Tab! I no ur mad @ me, but stealing my phone is wrong.

We both said stuff. That Sunny girl is cray cray. Don't believe what she told Flick. Flick is a stirrer. We talked about this b4. Shouldn't let her come between us.

Still luv u. Know u luv me 2. Text me!

Babe, I really am sorry but need my phone back ASAP.

This is too good an opportunity to pass up.

Mark has messed with me all night. Wrong, Sunny! So wrong. He's been messing with me for months and I know I still have a world of hurt to travel through. That it's going to take a while to get over this. But right now is not the time. Right now is the time for payback.

My thumbs hit the keypad.

Still mad at u. Not sure u deserve 2 have ur phone back.

He replies immediately.

Babe! After all we've been through. Let's not fight. Where are u? Really need my phone.

What about ur 2 Facebook pages? Only liar has 2 of them.

No biggie. One FB page 4 my proper crew and other one 4 North London poors. Only put Sunny as my relationship status to get her to stop bothering me. I swear.

You never even hooked up with her?

No way! Prefer vanilla to chocolate.

I suck in a breath. That's what happens when you ask questions that you really don't want to know the answers to. My heart throbs a warning to let me know that it's still tender and bruised and can't take any more pain.

Where r u?

Putney. But really need my phone, babes. Can't u jump in a cab?

What was Mark doing in Putney? God, if he could just stay in one place then this whole night would have been over at eleven. Gone to Camden, met Tab, dumped him, went home. It wouldn't have made for such a great story but right now I'd be on my sixth hour of sleep and not feeling like someone had pulled out my insides and replaced them with a load of mouldy old socks.

Still, better late than never at all.

Not coming 2 Putney. As if! Try again.

Babe! Got 2 get train 2 Godalming 4 big family lunch. Don't make me travel all way back 2 town. Please!

Elle sighs, wriggles and turns over. Vivvy has pulled the sheet over her head and all that's visible is one lone twist. It looks like a fluffy caterpillar resting on her pillow.

I sigh too. I realise now that we always did what Mark wanted and I always went along with it.

Well, this was the last time. Mark didn't always get what he wanted.

Royal Festival Hall. Final offer.

He could easily get to Waterloo from Putney and just bloody deal with it. Forcing Mark to go out of his way, to come back into town, might not seem much to the casual observer but to me it was huge. Total game changer.

Fine. Outside RFH 1 hour. Laters. M xxx

I pick up my bag and tiptoe out of the room. Then I look down at the borrowed dressing gown and tiptoe back in.

As I stand over Vivvy's bed, I don't think I've ever been so scared in all my life. This is what it must feel like to wake the kraken.

I gingerly prod a bit of her. I think it's her shoulder. 'Vivvy? Really sorry, don't hate me, can you lend me something to wear?'

She doesn't stir. I give her another prod. 'Vivvy. Wake up! Gently, in your own time, but the next ten seconds would be good.'

'Oh God! What is wrong with you?' She flings back the sheet. 'What is your problem? Why are you ruining my life?'

It takes five precious minutes for Vivvy to flail and rage and threaten to kill me before she stops behaving like a tool and starts rooting through her drawers.

Vivvy only ever wears one outfit: leggings and an outsize hoodie. Yolly says it's because she's embarrassed about her body blossoming into womanhood. Quite frankly, I'd be embarrassed about growing hips and boobs if my mum described it as blossoming into womanhood.

Now Vivvy makes a big deal out of letting me have her rattiest pair of leggings – they have holes in them and saggy knees ('No, it's all right, you don't have to give them back. They're a present') – and a pair of navy-blue granny pants out of an unopened pack of three that her nan had given her for her birthday, but she flat-out refuses to let me borrow a hoodie.

'They've all got sentimental value,' Vivvy says as she clutches a sky-blue Superdry hoodie to her chest like I'm about to snatch it from her and run for the hills. 'For real, Sunny, letting you take one would be like giving you one of my children.'

'But it's a loan. And I'd take good care of it. I'll give it back to you tomorrow, all freshly washed. So it's like giving me one of your children so I could, um, you know, babysit it.'

'No, I can't. It's nothing personal, but you're young and irresponsible.' She looks at me standing there in her ratty leggings and my bra, which has seen better days. Much, much better days. 'You could borrow something of Elle's. She wouldn't mind.'

We glance over to the bed where Elle sleeps on. Yolly should probably also get her checked out for narcolepsy while she's getting her hearing tested.

'She's *three*! Nothing of hers is going to fit.'

'Yeah, but she's a really fat three-year-old.' Vivvy has the grace to look slightly ashamed. 'Mum says she's just going through a chubby phase. We're not allowed to mention it in front of Elle in case we give her an eating disorder. She says so much stupid stuff.'

I give Vivvy side-eye and she gives it right back to me. 'My mum says a whole bunch of stupid stuff too. The sex stuff is proper cringe. I think she's trying to scare me into never doing it.'

'Don't talk to me about sex stuff.' Vivvy shudders. 'Gross. Look, there must be something of Elle's you can wear. One of her dresses would do as a T-shirt, right?'

Elle's little wardrobe is pink. So is everything in it. I reject anything glittery or with flowers appliquéd onto it. Also anything featuring Disney characters. I'm left with a flowy cotton sundress; it's white with huge cerise polka dots on it. It comes to my navel, chafes on the armholes and gives me a monoboob.

'It doesn't look *that* bad,' Vivvy says, even as her eyes widen in horror. 'You can well style it out.'

'Jesus! Stop being so tight and lend me a hoodie!'

'I can't. I want to, but I just can't,' Vivvy informs me sorrowfully. 'Honestly, you look all right. Anyway, it's not like you're going anywhere special. Only to meet that Mark so you can dump him. Why do you need to look hot to do that?'

I didn't *need* to look hot, but I also didn't want to look like I'd just escaped from a CBeebies set. Even new, improved Sunny who Charlestons in convenience stores and vanquishes vengeful hoodies wouldn't be able to pull off a sassy 'This is me and this is my ass walking away from you' speech in a sundress meant for a three-year-old. And let's be clear about this, I want Mark to be overcome with not just shame and regret but also for him to replay the moment I stomp away from him over and over again for years to come and to think,

219

'Not only was Sunny an excellent human being, far too good for me, she was also well fit.'

I also quite want to be able to move my arms. 'I swear, Viv, if you don't lend me a hoodie, I'm going to wake up your mum and tell her that you dropped the f-bomb because you totally did.'

Vivvy gasps and clutches at her hair. 'Why would you do that? Why are you being so mean? You're never mean.'

'I'm not being mean,' I say firmly. 'I'm standing up for myself and I'm going to be doing it quite a lot from now on so get used to it.'

'Seems more like bullying to me,' Vivvy grumbles but she's moving towards her chest of drawers again, face furrowed with indecision. 'Bullying is well worse than saying the f-word.'

'We could go and ask your mum if she thinks it's worse than refusing to lend me a hoodie when you've got . . . like, *hundreds* of them in there!'

'Not hundreds.' Vivvy rifles through her bottom drawer where I guess she stashes her least favourite hoodies and finally pulls out a khaki one. 'You can borrow this, I suppose.'

I know Vivvy loves an outsized hoodie but this could double up as a tent if ever the Royal Marines were short of one.

'My auntie bought it when she went to America. She forgot that their clothes come up bigger than ours. I still want it back, though!'

'Fine. Whatever. Thanks.' I tug off Elle's dress – it takes most of the skin under my arms with it – then I pull on Vivvy's hoodie. It makes me look like I'm pregnant with triplets.

'It's quite thin material so at least you won't be too hot in it,' Vivvy helpfully points out. 'It's quite a hard colour to wear, isn't it, khaki? Do you think that's why they make soldiers wear it? So they concentrate on fighting rather than how fit they look.'

'I don't know. Maybe it's because it doesn't show up the dirt so much."

Time is marching on like khaki-clad soldiers on parade. It takes another two minutes of begging to get Vivvy to part with a pair of trainer socks so I can pull on my sneakers and finally get going.

The house is still as I creep down the stairs, but not silent. I can hear the click of the boiler. The hum of the fridge. All those noises that houses make that are comforting and familiar. Our house creaks as the sun comes up and the radiator in the hall always rattles if you come down the stairs too fast. But I don't want to think about our house because now I remember that it mostly resembles landfill. Landfill left by meat eaters. Oh God . . .

But now I'm also thinking about eating so I go into the kitchen. Grab an apple and a carton of juice out of the fridge and write on the whiteboard, 'Had to go, but will see you all tomorrow. Love, kisses, hugs, Sunny ♥xo.'

I'm almost out the door when I remember my phone. The battery is now on 77%, which is good and I have three texts from Mark, which is bad. I can't even look at them. Oh, the idea of them. Of Mark's thumbs hovering over the screen, thinking of words designed solely to hurt me.

I stuff my phone back into my bag and open the front door onto the chalk-bright morning.

TO-DO LIST

Dump Mark.

Dump Mark in a devastating, understated way that he'll think about for at least five minutes every day for the rest of his life.

Text Emmeline to apologise for acting like a tool.

Text Vic to ask for Jean-Luc's number.

Text Jean-Luc to apologise for acting like a tool.

Go home.

Do not go to bed.

Feed Gretchen Weiner.

Varnish shed.

Collect all bottles that once contained alcoholic beverages and put them in the recycling.

Ask Max from top flat if I can tell Mum that it's his recycling if she gets suspicious. She will DEFINITELY get suspicious.

Ditto for rubbish bag containing empty meat wrappers.

Gather up all the dirty plates and cups and run the dishwasher.

Unload the dishwasher.

If Emmeline hasn't replied to my text, bake her a cake. She always responds well to baked goods.

(If cake-baking is a possibility, do it before I run the dishwasher.)

If Jean-Luc hasn't replied to my text, run the English through Google Translate and send it again in French. *En Français*, even.

Really, do not go to bed.

Don't even lie on the sofa or any other horizontal surface.

Burn scented candle in kitchen to get rid of the stench of cooked meat.

Don't forget to blow out scented candle.

Put back the bottle of perfume borrowed without asking from Mum's dressing table.

Also her black lace dress.

Do one final sweep.

Text Mum and ask what time they'll be back.

Set alarm clock for half an hour before ETA.

Go to sleep.

6.25 a.m.

SOUTH BANK

The sun has always shone on the north bank of the Thames, which was why St Paul's Cathedral was built on that side of the river. But the south bank, shunned by the sun, has always been a darker place.

In the Middle Ages, its shadowy shores were the perfect location for entertainment that was frowned upon by genteel folk. Bear-baiting, prostitution and theatricals were all popular with the poors. But by the eighteenth century, even the aristos liked to slum it at the famous Vauxhall Pleasure Gardens, where many a young maiden was totally ruined by sneaking down one of its tree-lined paths with a pompadoured rake and without her chaperone.

In 1951, the Festival of Britain (exactly one hundred years after the Great Exhibition, which saw the creation of Crystal Palace) was held on the south bank, after a huge project of slum clearance and development. The Royal Festival Hall was the centrepiece of the new exhibition and was later joined by the Queen Elizabeth Hall, the Hayward Gallery and the National Theatre.

These days the south bank is no longer the poor relation to the north bank, which might have Cleopatra's Needle, but it doesn't have two cinemas, the London Eye and a skate park, so it can just get over itself.

Working out how to get from Ladbroke Grove to Waterloo is more than my brain can handle. I stare at the tube map outside Ladbroke Grove station but it's just a squiggly collection of brightly coloured lines doing all these weird fandangos that don't make any sense.

Finally, I decide to take the tube to Baker Street, then change onto the Bakerloo line (the Bakerpoo line as we call it because it's brown and even this morning I laugh when I think about the word 'Bakerpoo'. But I laugh to myself in my head. Not out loud. Well, only for a little bit).

As the tube rattles through tunnels, I keep catching sight of my blurry reflection in the window opposite. I'm all sunken eye sockets and drooping mouth.

Across from me is a man in TfL uniform and a grey-faced girl wearing a Subway T-shirt, who looks even more exhausted than I feel. People going to work. Normally I can't even think of getting out of bed until at least ten on a Sunday – if Mum isn't there to wake me I've been known not to get up until Terry's taking the Yorkshire puddings out of the oven for lunch.

I'm beyond tired now. Tired has ceased to have any real meaning. It's just a word that doesn't come close to describing my gummy eyes and the way my jaw is locked and how, even though I just had a shower, I still feel like I have gunge collecting in all my crevices. Then I think of how Emmeline calls the fetid-smelling grey gunk that collects between your toes if you don't take your trainers off after cross country but spend the rest of the day wearing them along with the same sweaty socks toe jam. Once we saw this film where a man kissed a woman's feet, really went to town on them, and we discussed for a long time afterwards which would be worse: blow jobs or toe jobs. We never did decide.

And that's another thing about my new state of next-level tiredness. I can't hold on to my thoughts. Each time a new one comes along, it slips from my grasp like when you're trying to eat penne pasta. My grandmother says that the only polite way to eat it is to slide the tine of your fork through the tube, instead of stabbing at the pasta. It's very hard to do, especially if you've overdone it with the pesto.

I have to stop my thoughts rambling. I need something to distract me – and then I remember the texts from Mark. I should read them before I see him. So I know exactly what I'm getting myself into. Because, for all my fighting talk, the thought of seeing Mark makes my insides feel as if they've been hollowed out.

Babe. Guess you're asleep, but just wanted 2 say I love u. We cool, right?

Then another text, sent ten minutes later.

Sunny, going 2 my grans 2day. Shall we hang 2 morrow so I can make it up 2 u, cause we're cool now, innit?

And finally.

Babe! We cool? xxx

Get him! He is unreal. Acting like we'd just had a silly disagreement. Thinking he's totally got away with it, even as he was texting Tab at the same time. Playing us both for a fool because he still thought he could play us both. That we'd fall for it because he's such a prize.

I'm so blind with fury that I don't realise that we're at Waterloo until the carriage doors close and I have to stay on until Lambeth North, then go back one stop.

Then I get out the wrong exit at Waterloo, though it's a miracle at this point that I'm actually, like, able to put one foot in front of the other and walk. Going down stairs is really tricky. I keep freezing up because my brain has forgotten how to process the instructions on going down stairs and pass them on to my legs. Exhaustion and fury are not a good combination.

It's way past the hour since I agreed to meet Mark. Or rather that 'Tabitha' agreed to meet him, but as I stagger up the steps at the side of the Royal Festival Hall, then round the corner, there he is, sitting on a bench.

He's posed just so. In profile. Shades on. Hand pushing through the utter floppy blondness of his hair.

I last saw him yesterday lunchtime when he went home to shower after we'd painted the shed. But yesterday lunchtime was a lifetime ago. Yesterday lunchtime, I was still loved-up.

The Sunny of yesterday lunchtime – someone needs to give her a stern talking-to. And the Sunny of this morning suddenly gets this jolt at the sight of Mark. Not a good, heart-skippy, skin-singing, nerve-ends-tingling sort of jolt. It's more like I'm going into anaphylactic shock from a nut allergy and someone's just stabbed me with an EpiPen.

Adrenalin floods my system. It's fight or flight – the body's natural response to acute stress. Yesterday lunchtime Sunny might have fled but Sunday-morning Sunny is spoiling for a fight.

It's easy now to make my feet march over to Mark and when he looks up and does a really good impersonation of Edvard Munch's *The Scream* painting, I know exactly what to say.

'I know you prefer vanilla, but *tough*. You've got chocolate, which is actually a kind of racist way to describe your mixed-race girlfriend. Correction. Your mixed-race ex-girlfriend.' I sit on the bench and I go down hard, banging him with my elbow, crowding him, forcing him to shrink, to take up less space. 'Tab says hi, by the way, and that you're still dumped. And just in case you didn't pick up on the subtle way I brought it up, I'm here to dump you too. You're dumped.'

Mark lurches forward, then lurches back. He's tanned, always ruddy-faced like he's been racing across a field or surfing or doing something that a boy in an Abercrombie & Fitch advert might do, but now he's pale. Not even pale, but grey. It doesn't suit him. 'Look, Sunny . . .'

'I know! I got those three texts you sent me. I can't tell you how special that made me feel. Just after you sent Tab those texts asking to get back with *her*. Get your hand *off* me.'

Mark is touching my arm. Like he's still allowed to touch me when he isn't, not any more. And suddenly I'm glad that

I've had no sleep and I feel like I'm wearing my skin the wrong way round because I don't care any more. Not about my stupid clothes or that I might cry or what Mark might think of me.

Not caring what people think of me is amazing. I wish I'd figured this out years ago.

It means I can look at Mark, whose mouth is clamped shut but who is watching me warily, and say what I really feel in my heart; deep down, past the ventricles and veins, at its thudding epicentre. 'I know it's not the answer to anything but, God, I'd love to punch you in the face,' I say viciously.

I've never said anything viciously before. It doesn't feel as amazing as not caring, but whatever. I'm still feeling it.

'Sunny.' Mark whispers my name. His hands are curled against the edge the bench seat like he's about to launch himself up off it and go far, far away. 'Don't be like this. It's not you.'

'You know nothing about me. You only got, like, sixty per cent of me. I was always on my best behaviour, because I was scared that if I was anything less than perfect you wouldn't like me. You didn't like me anyway! I needn't have bothered.'

'It's not that. Of course I liked you. I loved you. I still do. Oh, what's the point?' Mark sighs heavily. 'Can I just get my phone back?'

'You mean your *other* phone?' and then I don't say anything because I'm so angry, I can't even speak.

Mark pulls an agonised ouch face but says nothing. Then, 'I am sorry, Sun.'

'You're sorry that you got found out. You're not sorry about how you cheated on me. Lied to me. Like, for *months*. Are you even a little bit sorry about that?'

'Well, I'm trying to apologise, aren't I?'

'Try harder. A lot harder.'

'I can't do anything right, can I?' Mark folds his arms with a little huff like he's the injured party. Like I'm the one in the wrong. Like I'm goading him to the very edge of his nerves with my utter unreasonableness. Now, this is the bit where I usually apologise for my sins. For complaining when Mark's late. For being upset that he tells me how the film ended. When he says my new trainers make my feet look huge. When we're out and his eyes settle on other girls. So many different ways I let him make me feel less and each time I'm the one who says sorry.

Not any more.

'No, I don't suppose you can do anything right when you're a lying, cheating, two-faced, evil, cheating, deceitf—'

'You already said cheating once and I wouldn't say I was evil. Not per se.' Mark pulls his brows together and sticks out his bottom lip. Not in an exaggerated way but a subtle way that hints of great sensitivity. That look has always done for me, but something has changed. I don't think it has anything do with sleep deprivation either.

It's more than that. It's like my cells and molecules and all the science bits that you can never see have rearranged themselves as I've travelled through the night. I look the same and I talk the same but somehow I don't feel the same and Mark's look of reproach isn't doing anything for me any more.

'Tab said . . .' I swallow hard as I remember exactly what Tab told me. 'You've lied about everything, even about what football team you support, so don't give me that "I'm actually a nice guy really" bullshit. You're not.'

'I'm sorry,' he mutters, and though it's quiet and a bit resentful, this time he sounds like he means it. 'It was just Saturday-night banter, you know, and, well, no one understands how hard it is for me.' He's relaxing now as he explains things. Unfolds his arms and angles his body towards me. Mark looks much better than I do for staying up all night, though I can smell the stale alcohol fumes rolling off his skin and wafting towards me on the breeze carried by the river.

'OK. How hard is it for you, then?' I put my legs up on the bench, so I'm resting my chin on my knees.

'Well, the thing is that I live in, like, two different worlds now. My Chelsea world and my North London world and I don't . . . I've never told anyone this before . . .' Mark covers my hand like now he's got permission to touch me, even though I don't remember giving it. 'But I don't feel like I fit into either world now . . . I know it was wrong what I did, but you and Tab, you were like passports to each world, so when I was with you I felt like I belonged. It sounds crazy but . . .'

'It sounds like total rubbish. You don't fit in? Cry me a river.' Mum is always saying that to me when I'm moaning about something. It's really annoying, except that when I snap it out now, it's actually deeply satisfying. 'You're telling the mixed-race girl that *you* don't fit in. You don't know shit about not fitting in. You're a white, straight, fit dude. You're always going to fit in, Mark, no matter that your parents split up or your dad lost all his money so, like, just . . . just . . . check your privilege.'

There's no comeback once you've told someone to check their privilege. Especially when that someone is a white, straight, fit dude. It's game over. End of.

231

Mark doesn't say anything. I think his privilege checker is still loading.

I open my bag and hold out his other phone and immediately he's all grabby hands. 'Give me it!'

'Not so fast.' I hold it just out of reach. 'I'm not finished yet.'

Mark screws his face up into something ugly. 'What else is there to say?'

'Plenty. You need to think about how you treat people. How you talk about them when they're not there. Like, I met your Chelsea friends last night, the two Gileses and the rest of them, and they weren't arseholes at all. They were all right and . . .'

'You did what?' I really think Mark might cry.

'Oh, don't worry. They didn't know I was the infamous Sunny, your "stalker".' I make air quotes and Mark's face is red. So very, very red. Redder than post boxes and Beefeater uniforms and the Central line.

'Look, about that, I only said that . . .'

'Stop lying! Just. Stop. It.' I'm sick of talking to Mark. Of trying to get through to him. To make him see the error of his ways. Of even trying to devastate him. He's not worth the effort that would take. 'I could destroy you at school, you know. Make your last year a living hell just by telling everyone what you've been doing.'

'You're behaving like a total psycho,' Mark snaps, but he doesn't snap it that hard because suddenly I'm dangerous.

I've never been dangerous before. It feels like a badge of honour. Mark's had to admit that I'm unpredictable, an unknown quantity, that I've got him on the ropes. Not a pushover any longer. 'Whatever.' I say it slowly so that Mark knows that even though I'm wearing shades, I'm rolling my eyes. 'I'm not giving you a pass because your dad lost his job and your parents got divorced and your world got turned upside down. Not when you picked on two girls who didn't have much self-confidence and played them without even thinking about their feelings. God, I almost had sex with you! You know how big of a deal that was to me, how much trust that took. And all the time, everything you said was bullshit!'

'Not everything. I did . . . I do really care about you, Sun,' Mark says. He tilts his head. 'I know I've acted like a twat tonight but I did have a lot to drink and . . .'

'You've been acting like a twat for months, I just didn't realise it.' There's no point in listing all the ways that Mark has been a twat. He's probably been a twat in ways that I haven't even begun to figure out yet. 'Anyway, I'm not going to destroy you because, unlike you, I'm not a twat, but then I can't speak for Emmeline. She doesn't try so hard to be good.'

Mark puts his head in his hands, then gives me that old imploring, sideways look, like he hasn't heard a single word I've said. 'Hey, Sunny, can't you talk to her?'

'I could but I'm not going to. Anyway, here's your phone. You're lucky I don't chuck it in the river.'

Mark stands up. For so long, he took top spot in my thoughts but now I just want him gone, want this to be over. I hand him the phone, careful that we don't touch each other during the exchange. He's more worried about scanning for scratches or noxious fluids, then stuffs it into his shirt pocket. He shakes his head. Looks sad. 'It's like I don't even know who you are any more, Sunny,' he says. 'Come on, we can move past this.'

'Oh my God, are you joking?' He's not. He looks deadly serious. 'I don't want to move past this. In fact, let's never do this again.'

'I'm not a bad person, Sunny. Well, OK, I admit I've done some bad things, but I do love you.'

I look up at Mark. Really look at him. At his hair, his deep blue eyes, his mouth, which I used to think was made just for my kisses; all the parts that added up to the boy I loved. There are thousands, tens of thousands, hundreds of thousands of boys in London, and now Mark's just another one of them. He isn't all that. I just let him think he was.

'You know what? I can do so much better than *you*.' I make a flapping motion with my hands. 'Go on, boi, walk away.'

Mark isn't expecting that. He doesn't walk away but stands there opening and shutting his mouth so he looks completely gormless, and then he shakes his head and starts to walk away. I sit there and watch him go. I'm pretty sure his last words are a muttered, 'Stupid bitch!' but I still don't care.

Bitch is just a word that boys say when they don't have the power to hurt you any more.

If this were a film, there'd be a panoramic shot of the Thames, sun already sparkling on the water, the London skyline magnificent in the background. A muted, melodic lo-fi track would play softly as I'd say, 'But I'm not a bitch. I'm a strong, independent woman.' The camera would stay on my face for a significant moment as I pondered the emotional journey I'd been on.

But that stuff was for Richard Curtis movies. Being a strong, independent woman is all well and good but it sounds like the tagline for an anti-perspirant. I'd rather just be Sunny,

234

who can be quite the badass when she needs to.

Now I lace my fingers together, crack my knuckles, then wait for the guilt and regret to creep in.

Except it doesn't. I feel fine. Good, even. I stood up for myself. I triumphed over evil. I feel good. I've been the angry black girl, and look! The world didn't end because of it.

But then I think of the massive to-do list on my phone and how my world really will end if I don't get through it before Mum and Terry get back, and then I feel totally not good.

Instead of gloating I should be getting up, getting on, but I just sit there, adrenalin all gone now, and it seems like a good idea to cosy up in Vivvy's outsized khaki hoodie and sleep.

It's very quiet. Someone's walking a tiny fluffy dog. A man and a woman in matching fluoro green lycra jog past – there's nothing more smug than a Sunday-morning runner. I watch a boat pootle past and a man in a hi-vis vest standing on the deck or the stern or whatever waves at me. Lifting my arm to wave back requires superhuman effort.

But while I still have some superhuman effort left, I text Emmeline. Even though it's before seven on a Sunday morning, which violates just about every unspoken rule of our friendship.

Sorry for being a bitch. Hope U got home alrite. I hate when we argue. Met Mark & totally dumped his arse. Still in town but heading back to Crouchy for big clean-up. Call u l8r. Sunny xxxxxxxxxxxxx

As soon as I tuck my phone away, it immediately starts to ring.

There's an unknown but kind of familiar number flashing up on the screen and after everything that's happened tonight, I'm wary of unknown numbers. I still answer it, though.

I mean, it's a ringing phone. I can't not.

'Hello?'

'Sunny? *Mon dieu! C'est la catastrophe!*'

It can only be Jean-Luc unleashing a flood of French in my ear. He sounds anguished and tired and at the very, very edge of the last of his nerves.

'What's wrong? In English! Try to tell me in English.'

'I got the wrong bus. I fell asleep. I ended up in a dreadful place called Surbiton. Then I got on another bus. *Et maintenant,* I'm on another. *C'est un cauchemar!*'

I don't know what a *cauchemar* is but what a nightmare. 'Where are you now?'

He gives a little hiccup, like maybe he's biting back a sob. 'I don't know.'

Think, Sunny, think. Make your sludge-like brain work. 'Isn't there an electronic board on the bus that tells you what the next stop is?'

'Hmmm, I have a look.'

How could Jean-Luc miss it? It should be there right in front of him.

'Are you wearing sunglasses?'

'I have to, Sunny. The light is too bright. My eyes . . .' he tails off weakly.

I hear a disembodied voice in the background. 'The next stop will be Waterloo station.'

'GET OFF THE BUS! GET OFF AT THE NEXT STOP!'

236

'Don't shout, I beg of you.'

'Get off the bus at Waterloo Station. I'm just round the corner. I'm sitting outside the Royal Festival Hall.'

'*Quoi? Qu'est-ce que tu dis?* My battery's going . . .'

'Get off the bus, Jean-Luc. Follow the signs to the Royal Festival Hall. The South Bank. I'll be waiting for you.'

The call cuts out. Static. Then silence.

It's impossible to know how much Jean-Luc heard or how much he understood when he'd forgotten most of his English.

I think about going to look for him but there are a multitude of bus stops around Waterloo and I'd be bound to go to the wrong one. Or Jean-Luc might be on the upper level of the Royal Festival Hall while I'm on the ground level. He could be heading in entirely the wrong direction towards Westminster. Or . . .

The best thing is to just stay put, but it feels a lot like doing nothing while a distressed Frenchman wanders around SE1 getting more and more disorientated.

I try to call Jean-Luc just in case there's like a quarter of a percent of his battery left but I get a message that says his phone is out of service.

Then I look up bus stops around Waterloo station to see where a bus coming from Surbiton might stop at – I'm kind of impressed that I can think so clearly, though it takes me three tries to spell Surbiton.

By now ten minutes have passed and there's no sign of Jean-Luc as I sit on my bench and look left, look right, look behind me.

I stand up. There's still no tufty-haired boy in a tight suit on any of my immediate horizons. I begin to take one uncertain step after another until I'm standing at the top of the steps that lead to the pedestrianised street along the side of the RFH. It's thronged with restaurants, coffee shops, sushi bars – none of them open, so it's not as if Jean-Luc has gone into one of them to ask them to make an espresso in the largest cup they have.

My shoulders sink. My legs aren't doing a very good job of holding me up either. I think about sitting on the steps. Then I think about going back to the bench. Then I think about whether I might ever be able to go home again and then I see a tiny figure coming towards me.

It's like a matchstick man from a Lowry painting come to life. Apart from the hair and the sunglasses and that he's holding a broom. A grey broom with blue bristles.

On wobbly legs I stumble down the steps and he's picking up speed too and so we're actually running towards each other like we really are in that cheesy rom-com.

'Sunny!'

'Jean-Luc!'

We're in each other's arms and I don't think anyone's ever held me so tightly. The broom is digging in between my shoulder blades and I don't even care.

'Thank God, I found you!' Jean-Luc exclaims fervently. 'I've had such torment that you might be raped and murdered and *la belle Hélène, elle vatomber folle de douleur!*'

'I'm so sorry I let you storm off like that. I shouldn't have done that. I know that I've been so annoying tonight but generally I'm not like that. And you've got my broom! I didn't even know I'd lost it.'

'You shoved it into my hands outside The Ritz,' Jean-Luc informs me and we're still clutching each other and in the same split second we both realise that we're locked together like I'm welcoming Jean-Luc back from the war.

Our arms drop and we both take a step back but then Jean-Luc smiles at me; a crooked, tired smile and it doesn't feel awkward any more. He looks rough. Crumpled and weary, his face sallow, and when my face was buried against his neck, he'd smelled slightly sour and musty.

'Shall we go home?' I ask.

Jean-Luc nods. 'God, yes!'

'Where do you live anyway?'

'Highgate.' He looks around helplessly as if he expects some kind of instant transportation device to suddenly materialise. 'How do I get to Highgate?'

'It's easy. Northern line all the way, if it's working today.' Highgate is kind of near Crouch End. I just have to walk down Shepherd's Hill all the way to the bottom, along Park Road and then cut through behind the Broadway. It's a twenty-minute walk. The thought of it makes me want to cry. But I abandoned Jean-Luc in his hour of need and the least I can do is see him to his front door, especially as he seems to have lost most of his mental faculties. 'Come on, let's go.'

Waterloo is nearer but I'm all turned around and we start walking in the other direction. We stagger up the steps to Hungerford Bridge so we can cross the river to Embankment station.

On the other side of the walkway are the train tracks. Jean-Luc says something to me just as a train thunders past.

'What's that?'

'I said that Highgate is not home,' Jean-Luc informs me mournfully.

'It isn't? But you said . . .'

'Paris is home.' He hunches his shoulders. 'I thought for one moment at Waterloo that I go to St Pancras and catch the Eurostar and go home, but pfftttt! It's not the answer.'

'If it's not the answer then what's the question?'

'I wasn't happy in Paris. My stepfather. *Ce n'est pas un homme gentil.* You have stepfather, *non?*'

'Yeah, Terry, but I don't think of him as a stepfather. And I already have a dad. He's just, y'know, Terry.' It's hard to put into words what Terry is to me. He's been with my mum, with me, since I was four. A big, jolly, sideburned constant in my life.

'But do you like him?' Jean-Luc persists.

'I *love* him.' Oh God, now I'm getting all teary thinking about Terry, though if I don't get home soon to clear away all evidence of my crimes, Terry isn't going to be quite so jolly. Not when he sees what I've done to his beloved shed. 'I love my dad too, but he's not around so much. And even when he is, he's kind of still not there. So, do you see your real dad much?'

'No. He lives in Perpignan now.' I don't know where that is but I'm guessing it's not near Paris. Or Highgate, for that matter.

'OK, you weren't happy in Paris but you're happy in London, right?' It's very hard to get a read on Jean-Luc now he's wearing his shades again. Also, I'm stupid from lack of sleep, because he's shaking his head. Which makes no sense, because how could anyone be unhappy in . . .

'London! Pah! I hate London!'

240

I stop and grab hold of Jean-Luc's arm to stop him too. 'That's a terrible thing to say!' I gasp. 'Take it back!'

'*C'est rien!* Don't take it personally,' he says like it's no big deal, then he tries to shake free of my grip.

I hold on tighter. 'How can you hate that?' I say and I gesture with the hand that hasn't got his sleeve in a vice-like grip.

We're standing in the centre of the bridge. The sky has never looked bluer. The Thames has also never looked bluer, which is saying something, because usually it looks the colour of dirty dishwater. There are more boats bobbing along now and in the distance is Waterloo Bridge with red buses and black taxis barrelling along it. St Paul's is to our left, majestic and unchanged for hundreds of years, and beyond that the glass towers of the City of London.

London is wearing its Sunday best. It's postcard perfect. The fairest of all fair cities. 'God, you must have rocks in your head, if you can't see how beautiful London is,' I say to Jean-Luc and I let go of him and I start walking.

I'm not angry. Not really. More disappointed. I like Jean-Luc. Compared to some boys I know, he is solid. A prince among men. Tufty head-and-shoulders above the lot of them. He'd also taken unwilling custody of my broom and kept it safe even while he was completely lost.

And after everything we'd been through tonight, I couldn't imagine that we were just going to say goodbye on his doorstep and never see each other again.

We are more than that. Better than that. Not friends in the way I'm friends with Martha or Archie or Alex. And not best friends because no one could ever take the place of Emmeline.

241

Jean-Luc and I are a different shape to friendship and I haven't figured out what that shape might be but that doesn't mean he can diss London, *my* London, and think that I'll be cool with it.

'You're mad,' he says when he catches up with me because I'm speedwalking by now. 'Don't be mad at me.'

'You can't say that you hate London. London's great.'

'Whatever.' He tugs at my hoodie. 'Did you join the army since I last saw you?'

'Don't change the subject.'

'I have to change the subject. I have no money left on my Oyster card. *Alors!* I have no money left at all. Can you lend me some?'

We're at Embankment station now. I still have the twenty-pound note that Vic lent me and I put a tenner each on our Oyster cards. We're just about to go through the barriers and Jean-Luc is *still* trying to convince me that London sucks because 'it's so dirty. People spit in the street like savages . . .' when Emmeline rings.

'Shall we not do a whole big speech because it's really bloody early on a Sunday morning but just agree that we both acted like dicks and we're both sorry and we're still BFF, right?' she says before I can even say hello.

'That's absolutely fine with me. I'm sorry if my text woke you up.'

'I had to get up for a wee anyway,' Emmeline sniffs. 'Are you back home yet?'

'I wish! I'm at Embankment.'

Even though I'm on the phone, Jean-Luc has really warmed to his theme and is now going on about how 'confusing London is. All those different zones. I don't understand the zones. Or the tube map. The Circle line – it's not even a circle.'

He's starting to do my head in.

'But you're heading home now right, 'cause I was going to come over and help you clean up on account of the fact that we're best friends and I love you so much I'm prepared to get by on about three hours sleep,' Emmeline says. 'What time do you think you'll be home?'

'*Mais oui*, Sunny, you like London because you live here, but why do they call it a Circle line? *Pourquoi? C'est ridicule!*'

If Jean-Luc and I were going to be something that was a different shape to being friends then we were going to have to get a few things straight.

'Actually, change of plan,' I tell Emmeline. 'I'm not going straight home. I have to make a detour.'

'But Sunny, have you even had any sleep?'

'Not a bean. I actually feel like I might puke but I'm taking Jean-Luc to my favourite place in all the world because he's being an absolute pain in the arse and it's the only way to shut him up.'

Jean-Luc lifts up his shades so he can give me shade. '*Moi?*'

'*Oui. Vous.*'

'*Non, tu.*' He looks even more hurt now. 'We're friends. Friends say *tu* not *vous*.'

'Jesus! Get a room, why don't you,' says Emmeline. 'What's going on with you and him? What went down with Mark? And, hey, Sun, when we left your house yesterday evening it looked like someone had dropped a dirty bomb on it. I really think you should go straight home. Like, now, so there's an outside chance you can make things right before your mum . . .'

When I think of collecting up all those encrusted plates and, ugh, varnishing the shed, I can't face going home ever again. 'I can't even be bothered,' I tell Emmeline wearily. 'It's a tip. I'll never get it straight in time, even if I went home now. Mum and Terry will just have to do their worst. Ground me or something.'

'But you might not be able to go to Notting Hill Carnival tomorrow. We always go to the Carnival on Bank Holiday Monday.'

'Maybe they'll give me a stay of execution until after tomorrow,' I say, but I'm not counting on it. 'Look, I'll call you later. Let you know what the grounding situation is and describe the look on Mark's face when I told him to check his privilege.'

'You didn't?' Emmeline gives a throaty plughole gurgle of a laugh. 'I'm really liking this new, improved Sunny.'

'Yeah! Me too. Laters, right?'

'For sure.'

I finish the call. Jean-Luc looks at me expectantly. 'We're friends? *Tu* not *vous*, yes? And we go home now?'

'Yes, yes and kind of.'

'What do you mean "kind of"?' He follows me through the ticket barrier. 'We're not going home?'

'Yeah, we are but we have to make a detour first.'

We turn left, down the steps, down the escalator, more steps and onto the northbound Northern line platform. The Edgware train is coming first, but that doesn't matter – we don't need the High Barnet branch if we're not going to Highgate.

'I have to go home now.' Jean-Luc is whining, maybe even whimpering. 'Vic, he stays out all night but I never do. *Ma tante Elise*, she'll be so worried about me.'

That gets my full attention. 'You live with your aunt?'

'*Oui. Et mon oncle.*'

'Vic lives with his parents? Despite his whole ladykiller routine?'

The indicator board warns us sternly to STAND BACK, TRAIN APPROACHING, but I can already see the ghostly glow of the train lighting up the tunnel, then it's hurtling towards us, the mice on the tracks scurrying for the safety of their little hidey holes.

Jean-Luc grins like he's suddenly forgotten how tired he is. 'Of course, Vic lives with his *maman* and his *papa*,' he tells me as the doors open and we step into the carriage. 'Why else would he have to sleep over with his young ladies?'

We sit down, empty seats on either side of us. 'He can't take them home? Aunt Elise wouldn't approve?'

He doesn't laugh so much as giggle and it makes me giggle too. 'Aunt Elise, she's very, er, liberal, but the young ladies might not approve of Vic's single bed and the duvet cover with the racecars on it. *Non?*'

'*Très non!*'

He giggles again. 'Please don't try to speak French, Sunny. Haven't we talked about this?'

We had, but while we were talking about Vic . . . 'So, is Vic the reason you hate London? Like, I think he's great but he really let me down earlier. He said that he had my back but then he went and hooked up with some random girl and deserted me. Does he do that to you? When he's not taking the piss out of you or pretending to be you when he's hooking up with random girls?'

Jean-Luc rocks back in his seat. 'I love Vic. He's my cousin. *Mon frère, mon meilleur ami, mon camarade.*' He shakes his head. 'Not Vic. It's just . . . in London, it rains all the time.'

'It's hardly rained at all this summer. Try again,' I tell him.

THE STATE OF ME

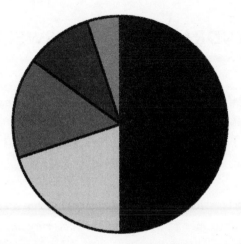

 50% **Being so tired that everything hurts and any sudden movements are going to make me vomit**

 20% **Summoning up enough energy to hit Jean-Luc if he keeps slagging off London**

 15% **Feeling a sense of smug satisfaction at ridding myself of my no-good, cheating boyfriend**

 10% **Heart stirred by the view of London, my London, from Hungerford Bridge**

5% **Being so over carrying this bloody broom around**

8.00 a.m.

ALEXANDRA PALACE, MUSWELL HILL

Known locally and fondly as Ally Pally, Alexandra Palace opened on 24th May 1873. Named after Princess Alexandra of Denmark, who'd just married Prince Edward, the Prince of Wales, it was designated as the People's Palace.

Hurrah! Except, not hurrah but disaster! Sixteen days later, the Palace was destroyed in a fire. But the Victorians were not ones to mope. Oh no. They got straight on to rebuilding it and on 1st May 1875, Ally Pally reopened.

Its extensive grounds housed a Japanese village, a racecourse (there's still a pub at the bottom of Muswell Hill called The Victoria Stakes) and a cricket pitch, boating lake and pitch-and-put golf course, which are still there to this day.

Ally Pally is most famous as the site of the world's first television broadcast in 1936 by John Logie Baird. During the Second

World War the TV transmitter was put to good use in jamming German bombers' navigational systems.

In 1980, Ally Pally was again struck by fire and was closed while extensive repairs were carried out. It opened again in 1991 and long may it reign over North London.

Jean-Luc is so caught up in banging on about his non-love for London that when we get to Euston, it's easy to take his hand and tug him out of his seat so we can change onto the Victoria line.

We're still holding hands as we walk down the long tunnel at Finsbury Park and emerge, blinking into the sunshine.

'You took us on the detour,' Jean-Luc says accusingly, but he still doesn't let go of my hand, even though it's very sweaty, sticky hand-holding. 'The other thing I detest about London: sneaky detours.'

'It wasn't sneaky, I gave you fair warning.'

I could let go of Jean-Luc's hand, I don't want to give him the wrong idea, but there's every chance that he might bolt instead of walking to the W3 bus stop. There's also a much greater chance that without Jean-Luc holding onto me and hoisting me onto the bus when it arrives, I may just collapse in a heap.

'Where are you taking me, Sunny?' Jean-Luc asks as we sit on the seats reserved for the elderly or people with children, neither of whom take buses this early on a Sunday morning.

'My favourite place in London.' I think about it. 'Actually, my favourite place in the world. And if you still hate London after I've shared it with you, well, then you're a lost cause.'

It doesn't take long to get there. We pass through Crouch End and I think I've probably gone quite mad because the bus stops at the top of my road and it would be so easy to get up, get out, stagger the last few steps, open the front door, then collapse face-down in the hall, not even bothering to make it the few centimetres to our door so Max from upstairs will have to step over me when he takes Keith, his Staffie, out for a walk.

But I don't move. I just stare down at Jean-Luc's fingers tangled in mine. Then his fingers twitch, like an electric current passing between us, and when I glance across at him, he's staring down at our hands too.

It's far, far, *far* too soon to be holding hands with a boy. I started off holding hands with Mark, before we'd even kissed, and look how that turned out.

I snatch my hand out of Jean-Luc's grasp, but it's more of a clammy fumble. He scratches his head, mutters something in French and I gaze out of the window and practise taking deep, even breaths until we take a sharp left and the bus starts climbing up the hill.

'Next stop,' I squeak and press the bell.

We get off at the stop right in front of the palace and dart across the road.

'What is the place?' Jean-Luc asks. He glances back at the magnificent palace, the sun glinting off the glass domes of its roof. 'It looks like a cathedral.'

'It's Alexandra Palace. Ally Pally. But it's not a palace. They put on gigs and exhibitions and stuff. They have a huge antiques market there a few times a year and, oh, all sorts of things, but forget about the palace.'

'C'*est difficile*. It's so big.'

Another time, if there's another time, I'll take Jean-Luc up the steps so we can walk alongside the palace, into the covered walkways that I've ducked into to shelter from the rain. I'll show him the plaque to the German civilians that died here in an internment camp during the First World War. The BBC office that leads up to the TV transmitter. We'll walk past the ice rink and around the boating lake, maybe feed the ducks. Watch the boys in the skate park. Have a go on the swings. But not today.

Instead I guide him along the path that curves around and around. We smile and say hello to a woman walking a dog with a tennis ball wedged in its mouth, but she skirts around us with a wary look. By now, we must look like survivors from some kind of dystopian disaster.

Then the path levels out and comes to a crossroads, but I keep walking, Jean-Luc still muttering at my side. We're on a wider path now, flowerbeds and benches line one side, and on the other is the sloping green of the South Lawn.

When we get to the middle bench with the angel that sits on the top of Ally Pally directly behind us, I sit and pull Jean-Luc down beside me. 'Look at that,' I say. 'Look at that view and tell me that you still hate London.'

On a clear, sunny day like today, you can see all of London sprawled out like a feast. Terry reckons you can even see the TV mast at Crystal Palace. God, it's hard to think that only twelve hours ago, I was at Crystal Palace, a city apart from where I am now. There'd been a different view, another way of looking at the place that I've always called home.

251

I can't see the Crystal Palace TV mast. But I can see the tower of Canary Wharf, the tiny light on top of it flashing at second intervals. I can see the Gherkin, *again*. Far over to the right is the Post Office tower, Euston Tower, Centre Point and in the middle is the Olympic stadium, which had been lit up every night when the Olympics were on. And in between and dotted about are the church steeples and the high-rise flats, old buildings, new buildings. London. My London.

'The view is incredible,' Jean-Luc admits rather grudgingly. 'But . . . it's a view of a city I'm not . . . I don't belong here. It doesn't mean as much to me as it does to you. It's your favourite place, *oui*?'

'Absolute favourite place,' I say, but it's not really that much to do with the view, even though every time I see it, it makes me feel proud. Makes me feel like I do belong.

Jean-Luc has told me why he hates London and now I tell him why I love London. Not even London. I narrow it down to this park, this path, this bench.

I tell him about the fireworks display and how Terry makes us get here hours early so we can camp out in our favourite spot just where we're sitting now, so that when we look back at Ally Pally we can see the angel and the stained-glass rose window, which is bigger and grander than anything you'd find in a real palace. Afterwards we walk home to Crouch End and everyone comes back to ours for hot sausage rolls and mulled wine.

I tell him about borrowing Keith, Max from upstairs's Staffie, so he can career down the slope in front of us to chase the crows. Then he stands under whichever tree they're sitting in

252

and barks at them, like that's going to persuade a crow with a deathwish to swoop down to see if Keith can catch him.

I learned to ride a bike without stabilisers along this path, my dad and Terry keeping hold of the back of my saddle while Mum filmed us and I screamed, 'Don't let go! Don't let go!' When they did let go, I immediately crashed to the ground. Then I show Jean-Luc the scar under my chin from where I hit the tarmac.

I tell him about antiques fairs with my mum, the tattoo show with Emmeline, hanging out with Alex and Martha as we watch Archie fall off his skateboard again and again, getting up early on Saturday mornings to watch Dan doing the Park Run, so many picnics, so many games of football – but I always end up here on this bench. It's the perfect place to sit with the people I love in the city that I love. This place I'll always call home.

Jean-Luc listens to all of this and then he sighs. 'Maybe I don't like London because I just don't belong here.'

'You're an idiot,' I tell him kindly and I really hope once I've slept that I don't lose this Sunny who's stopped being afraid of everything and everyone and especially what everyone may or may not think about her. 'Stop being so hard on yourself and stop being so hard on London. We had a great time tonight, didn't we?'

'Well, I will always have fond memories of being chased by a gang of young hooligans after we stole their bicycles,' Jean-Luc says in a flat voice, but then the corners of his mouth lift up. 'That was exhilarating.'

'We met so many good people – Shirelle and the others in the chicken shop, and I got a free ride on a rickshaw . . .'

'. . . and nearly died in the process,' Jean-Luc reminds me. 'Though it was good to see Audrey make the mockery of Vic.'

'She totally mocked him. And we hung out with Duckie and I danced the Charleston in a convenience store. Even Jeane wasn't so bad. And apart from the Mark stuff, it's been the best night of my life. In fact, if it hadn't been for the Mark stuff, I wouldn't have had adventures and I wouldn't have met Vic . . . or you.'

'But we were at the picnic. Sooner or later, we'd have said hello,' Jean-Luc says, but I shake my head.

'I wouldn't have said hello to you,' I admit and he's back to looking wounded and sulky again. 'You looked far too cool and scary for me to say hello to. You know, with the hair and the shades and the FuckYeah!TheGodards Tumblr.'

'I hate that Tumblr. And it sounds as if you're describing the girl at the picnic with the hair and the shades. The one who looked far too cool to bother with the likes of me.'

'But I was crying! I'd had the romantic disappointment,' I point out and I'm blushing slightly because I couldn't believe that anyone, let alone Jean-Luc, could have seen me at the picnic, all sweaty and rumpled and with my stupid shorts riding up, and thought that I looked cool.

And then Jean-Luc takes my hand but he doesn't just hold it, he lifts it to his lips and presses a kiss to my knuckles.

'I know it's too soon, after the romantic disappointment, but something did happen tonight. For a while, when I was fearing for my life and trying to find a lavatory in the middle of Piccadilly, I forget that I'm miserable.'

It *is* too soon. Not just because I don't want to be one of those girls who can't function in society unless she has a boyfriend. I also don't want a boy coming between me and the new me that I've decided I'm going to be. Not even Jean-Luc. Though that didn't mean . . . 'We should hang out to start with,' I say before I can lose my nerve. 'Be friends.'

'But Vic says there's this thing. The – what does he call it? The friend zone. Is not a good place to be. He says that once you're in the friend zone with a girl you can never climb out of it.' He rests his head on my shoulder. I think it's less about trying to be romantic and more about him being so tired that everything, from toes to fingers to hair, hurts if, like me, he's feeling like death warmed up. 'Are you friend-zoning me?'

This not-losing-my-nerve thing is really hard. 'No. Because we can be friends who hold hands. Like, we'll be friends on a promise. And anyway, I really don't think you should be taking relationship advice from someone who sleeps in a single bed with race cars on his duvet cover.'

Jean-Luc shifts position so he can grin at me and I stop talking in favour of leaning heavily against him. He's far too bony and he really doesn't smell that great any more but I may never move again. Stay here on this bench for ever and ever . . .

'I told you she'd be here! Hey, Sunny! Whatever you do, don't go to sleep. Don't shut your eyes!' It's Emmeline bellowing from what sounds like a long, long way away. Am I dreaming?

I manage to raise my head and it is Emmeline running down the steps behind us at the head of a motley collection of people clutching bin bags and buckets and huge Styrofoam cups of coffee, two of which are handed to me and Jean-Luc by Charlie, who says, 'Christ, you both look awful. Get this down you.'

I take a grateful gulp. It's just how I like it: three shots of coffee, a lot of milk, no foam. 'What are you guys doing here?'

With Emmeline and Charlie are Archie, Alex, George of all people, and Martha, who sits down next to me and grabs my hand. 'How are you doing, Sunny? Are you OK, hun? You don't have to put a brave face on it. I bet you're feeling terrible because of the whole Mark situation. Never mind. I made you bacon sarnies.'

I'm not feeling terrible. Well, I am because of the no-sleep thing, but not terrible because of Mark, and anyway, the sight and the nose-twitching smell of bacon shoved between pieces of brown toast and slathered in ketchup really perks me up. 'I'm fine. Absolutely fine,' I say. 'Thanks for breakfast.'

I hand one of the sandwiches to Jean-Luc, who eyes it suspiciously, then decides that even though it's not a flaky croissant or a croque monsieur or scrambled eggs with smoked salmon or whatever it is that French people eat for breakfast, it will do and he takes a large, enthusiastic bite. 'Thank you,' he mumbles around it. 'Thank you so much.'

George plonks himself down on the ground in front of our bench. 'Did you know that you've gone viral, Sunny? You're even on the Reddit home page. There's a three-minute clip of you doing some kind of weird Ginger Rogers shit. Did you take a bunch of drugs tonight?'

Emmeline winks at me as she sits down beside Jean-Luc. 'Hello again,' she says to him. 'You're the nice one, aren't you?'

'Jean-Luc, though Vic isn't so bad when . . . he . . . er . . .' He tips his head back. '*Je suis trop fatigué pour parler Anglais.*'

I introduce Jean-Luc to everyone. Then try again. 'It's great to see you all, like, especially with coffee and bacon sandwiches, but what are you doing here? It's eight o'clock on a Sunday morning!'

'Em said you were going to be grounded until you were thirty if you hadn't managed to clear up the flat before Helen and Terry got back,' Archie says. He frowns like he's not entirely down with the whole getting up at such an ungodly hour on a Sunday. 'Apparently I'm responsible for quite a lot of the mess, even though I bought you a new broom!'

'Dude! You and Mark set fire to her shed,' Alex reminds Archie. 'And Sunny's spent all night clearing up Mark's mess. Least we could do, right?' She ruins it all by making a circle with her thumb and forefinger and poking the index finger of her other hand through it. 'You didn't, though, did you, tonight? You didn't do it with Mark?'

They all look at me, apart from Emmeline who knows that I remain unsullied by Mark's penis, and Jean-Luc who knew that I'd been in no mood to give it up to a boy who'd done me industrial amounts of wrong. I still flush though. Still roll my eyes. Still let my mouth hang open in disbelief that Alex would even ask me that and in front of the assembled company.

'Oh my God, no! A thousand times, no.'

'Anyway, Sunny is too good for the likes of Mark,' Jean-Luc says, then he turns to me. 'We go now? I lose the feeling in my fingers.' He waggles his fingers at me, though they seem in perfect working order, but I can't say the same for my legs.

'You can crash at mine, if you like? Kip on the sofa while we tidy up,' I take another gulp of coffee, though it's not really bucking me up. 'I can't believe you all turned up like this. Giving up a Sunday-morning lie-in is the nicest thing anyone's ever done for me.'

'And we're going to clean for you too. So, let's get a move on,' Emmeline says and she stands up and gives me her hand and I try to take it but I just end up feebly flapping my arm.

'In a minute, right?'

George grins. 'Did you stay up all night, Sun? Not even a little disco nap?'

I nod.

'She stayed up all night like a total boss,' Emmeline says proudly. 'Totally smashed not going to bed.'

'Respect,' George says, which is huge, because George doesn't respect anyone, especially not me. 'Though I still think you have the political conscience of a fruit-fly.'

'Whatever, George. Get over it,' I say and they all turn to look at me again. 'What? What?'

'That doesn't sound like you, Sunny,' Martha pats my arm. 'It must be the exhaustion that's making you so grouchy.'

'*Non*, she's not grouchy,' Jean-Luc says. He's so slumped now that he's practically horizontal. 'She's formidable. Not to be trifled with.'

They're still all staring in disbelief because the Sunny they know is always trifled with.

'Are you too formidable to get the bus home and start clearing up?' Emmeline asks.

The bus stop is just behind us. All I need to do is stagger up the steps and wait for a bus that will drop me mere moments away from home. I could be home in ten minutes.

I get up. Except, I don't. My legs are refusing to obey me. I try again. Maybe I need more coffee. 'Can we just take a moment? My legs don't seem to want to work.'

258

'Five minutes, that's all you're getting,' Emmeline says sternly. 'We don't want to get to yours at the same time as your mum gets back.'

'Oh, but the view is pretty amazing,' Charlie pipes up. 'I've never seen it from the north, only the south. Look! There's the Gherkin. What's that big yellow block to the left?'

'It's only some flats,' George says and then we're all looking at our city and I sit between Jean-Luc who looks so cool but is so unhappy, and Emmeline who's so tough but can't tell a girl that she likes her.

Everyone hides. Everyone puts on a front. Everyone has those moments when they're lonely or scared or not the best versions of themselves.

Then I think of all the other people who have sat on this spot over the years. Women in funny, old-fashioned dresses – crinolines and bustles and hobble skirts. Men in suits and trilby hats.

All those people, all those glorious lives long gone. Only the view remains; the buildings might get bombed, condemned or demolished, but new buildings spring up in their place, each taller and more fantastic than the last. London is always changing but it will always be a place where you can have adventures, make new friends, change your story, change your life.

Can one night change your life? I think it can. Or, at least, it can change the direction that your life was going in. I need time to figure that out. To get used to living my life like every day is Saturday night.

But some things will always stay the same.

London, I love you.

Twelve hours

Two Godards

Two hundred and fifty seven text messages

Twenty-three phone calls

Four cups of coffee

Three bottles of water

Two bottles of lager

One cup of 7UP larger than a person's face

One carton of juice

Eight hot wings (extra-hot sauce)

One bag of chips

Two tartlets

Three mini quiches

One apple

One bacon sarnie

Two outfit changes

One taxi, one rickshaw, one stolen bicycle, two overground trains, five tube journeys. Three nightbuses, one day bus. One knackered Oyster card.

Four drag queens

Eight Duckie songs

One Charleston danced

One heart broken. One heart mended.

Acknowledgements

Thank you to Karolina Sutton, Becky Ritchie, Lucy Morris and all at Curtis Brown. Naomi Colthurst, Jenny Jacoby and the amazing team at Hot Key Books. I'd also like to thank Roni Weir and Natasha Farrant for invaluable editorial help.

Virginia Woolf quote reprinted by kind permission of The Society Of Authors.

Sarra Manning

Sarra Manning has been an author and journalist for over twenty years. She has written for the *Guardian*, *ELLE*, *Grazia*, *Stylist*, *Fabulous*, *Stella*, *You Magazine*, and *InStyle*. She's currently the Books Editor of *Red* magazine.

Her first adult novel, *Unsticky*, was published in 2009, followed by three others including *It Started With a Kiss* and the best-selling *You Don't Have To Say You Love Me*. Sarra has also written over fifteen Young Adult novels including *Adorkable*, *Guitar Girl*, *Let's Get Lost*, *The Worst Girlfriend In The World* and the iconic *Diary Of A Crush* trilogy. Sarra lives in London with her beloved Staffordshire Bull Terrier, Miss Betsy. You can follow her at www.sarramanning.co.uk or on Twitter: @sarramanning

Thank you for choosing a Hot Key book.

If you want to know more about our authors and what we publish, you can find us online.

You can start at our website

www.hotkeybooks.com

And you can also find us on:

We hope to see you soon!